Saber's Honor offers an introspective and positive contribution to Italian culture. It examines this crucial period and shows how one man's spirit and determination could ignite others and change the course of history.

-The Italian Tribune

SABER'S HONOR

JOS. C. DONATO

Ekstasis Multimedia: www.booksandbrush.net

Saber's Honor/Jos. C. Donato
Blairstown, New Jersey: Ekstasis Multimedia, LLC, 2013
ISBN-13: 978-0615766591
ISBN-10: 0615766595

Book design: Marlaina Donato
Author photo: Marlaina Donato

For my father Dominick V. Donato, whose love of family and relentless pursuit of our family history resulted in a treasure house of information which became my main source of reference for this book. His zeal was infectious and inspired my own quest. Thanks, Dad- without you, I would have never been able to write all of this down. God bless you.

And for my beloved wife, Marlaina Donato, for your inexhaustible patience and literary prowess. Because of you, I brushed off years of dust from an unfinished manuscript written decades before. Your consistent encouragement reignited inspiration that I thought had been smothered forever. Your extraordinary talent and abilities were my source of strength; without you, this work would have never come to fruition.

ACKNOWLEDGMENTS

Many thanks to...

—Carolina Lochetto Donato, paternal grandmother for passing down the stories of her adventurous father, Antonio Lochetto.

—Carolyn Masiello for typing the first drafts of the manuscript.

—Margaret Donato for always encouraging me to continue and complete the work.

—Ann Leal for typing the second draft.

—Mike Masiello for typing and editing the third draft.

—Marlaina Donato—for her editing, expertise, and reworking the final manuscript.

Sanza
Sant'Arcangelo
Policoro
Lagonegro
Chiaromonte
Rotondella
Golfo di
Camerota
Latronico
Sapri
Lauria
Taranto
Golfo di Policastro
Maratea
Capo Spulico
Praia a Mare
Mormanno
POLLINO
2267
Amendolara
Trebisacce
1810
Scalea
Castrovillari
Cassano allo Ionio
Gulf of Taranto
1987
C.a.l. Sibari
Diamante
Altomonte
Corigliano Calabro
Belvedere Marittimo
Spezzano Albanese
Capo Trionto
Passo dello Scalone
Capo Bonifati
Rossano
Acri
SILA GRECA
Cariati
Cetraro
CATENA COSTIERA
Montalto Uffugo
1480
Longobucco
Paola
Rende
SILA GRANDE
1708
Punta Alice
Cirò
Cirò Marina
San Lucido
Cosenza
1928
San Giovanni in Fiore
Strongoli
1512
224
Botte Donato
Cocuzzo
Calabria
Amantea
1765
SILA PICCOLA
Petilia Policastro
Crotone
Capo Colonne
Cutro
Lamezia Terme
343
Isola di Capo Rizzuto
L. T.-Sant'Eufemia
Catanzaro
Capo Rizzuto
Golfo di Sant'Eufemia
Lamezia
Borgia
C. Marina di Catanzaro
Filadelfia
Golfo di
Pizzo
Squillace
1023
Squillace
Vibo Valentia
Soverato
Tropea
Capo Vaticano
710
1700
Nicotera
Serra San Bruno
Golfo di Gioia
1423
Rosarno
Stilo
Polistena
Punta Stilo
Gioia Tauro
Caulonia
Palmi
Cittanova
Taurianova
Marina di Gioiosa Ionica
Siderno
I O
ESSINA
Bagnara Calabra
Locri
Scilla
S. Giovanni
1955
Bovalino
ASPROMONTE
Bianco
Reggio di Calabria
1760
ION
Capo
Bova Marina

THE EVER-PRESENT NOW

IS THE MOST VALUABLE COMMODITY.

J.C.D.

I
THE EARLY YEARS

Antonio Lochetto props himself up against the wall near a half-open shutter; the moon filters in through the window of the formidable stone cottage at the edge of town. The atmosphere is permeated with desperation as the man's large silhouette peers out into the night.

Twenty yards beyond the window, darting from one tree to another, shadowy figures lurk in the darkness. The pursuers whisper to each other in low voices as they tighten their circle. Inside the house, the ragged, full-bearded man awaits his fate with his left hand in a make-shift sling and a breech-loading carbine in the other. In deep pain, he ponders his options—few—if any. *How did I end up in this position, a fugitive of the law?*

He struggles to maintain consciousness. Exhausted, he

slumps into a hard wooden chair to rest. Falling in and out of reality, he battles to stay awake but surrenders to the inevitable. He drifts into delirium, recalling his days as a youth. *How ironic, in my father's home, it all began right here…*

"Papa, how was my work today?" Antonio asked during the evening meal.

"You did very well. You do have generations of stone masons in your blood," his father reminded him. "Our ancestors built churches and cathedrals throughout Italy and Europe."

"Am I doing my share of the work? I hope I do not slow down Uncle Frederico and Uncle Vincenzo too much," the sixteen-year-old questioned.

"My son, there are times when you try too hard to please," his father reassured him, "but if you spent as much time with the trowel and the chisel as you do with your gun and your horse in the mountains, you'd be the most expert stone mason in all of Calabria."

"I know, Papa. I do spend a lot of time in the mountains, but it feels natural to be there. I feel so at home that I cannot wait until I return."

"If my name was not Fortunato Lochetto, I wouldn't believe this is my son talking. Angelina, he must get it from your side of the family," Fortunato said to his wife as he shook his head. "There are no relations of mine who act in this way."

"Why is it that every time Antonio does something crazy you blame my side of the family?" Angelina fired back and stiffened.

"Cara Mia, can't you take a joke? I was teasing you. However, I do wonder where he gets his odd notions." Sighing a little, Don Fortunato reached for his vest pocket and his watch and then motioned to his son. "You'd better turn in now if you want to get up at dawn. Rosa, Tomaso, and Carlo have already been asleep for an hour."

"Okay, Papa," Antonio said, rising from the table. "You are right. I need my rest if I am to do a good day's work." Antonio kissed his mother and then retired.

Don Fortunato glanced gently toward his wife and commented, "He is going to be a fine man someday."

"I think he already is. He will be seventeen on his next birthday, no?" Angelina remarked.

"That is what scares me so. The time is fleeing so fast. He is almost a man. I read that Mazzini is advocating that Italy should be unified as a single state by throwing out the Austrians in the North along with the Spanish Bourbons in the South. Mazzini is correct. Italy should control its own destiny, not foreigners." He paused pensively and then sighed. "Enough of these serious thoughts. Cara Mia, let's go to sleep. It's getting late. Tomorrow will come all too soon."

Upstairs, Antonio listened to his parents' conversation fade as he opened the shutter to let in the cool, invigorating night air. The nearby mountains seemed only an arm's length away as did the scores of stars dotting the night sky. Lying back on his bed, with his hands clasped behind his head, he pondered the day's events and thought of the following morning which was Saturday, the last day of the work week. Of course, on Sunday after Mass, he could do whatever he pleased. This meant he could trek through the beckoning forest he knew so well, perhaps a ride on some unexplored trail or time fishing in one of the crystalline mountain lakes. Perhaps he would investigate a cave dating to prehistoric times. He still dreamed of finding an artifact or two, like fortunate adventurers he had heard about.

Barely able to keep his eyes open, Antonio began reciting his nightly devotions, but sleep enveloped him before he was halfway through his prayers.

The night relinquished its hold, and the early sun streaked through the louvered shutters. Angelina, taking advantage of the cool morning hours, prepared breakfast and made bread in the kitchen. Upstairs, Antonio listened to the sounds of his mother's cooking. Before long, the house was filled with many hearty aromas. Antonio, though reluctant to rise, surrendered to the temptation. By the time he arrived at the breakfast table, his parents were already on their second cup of tea. Even his sister Rosa had gotten to the table before him.

After a robust, albeit hurried breakfast, Antonio harnessed a pair of large chestnut horses. Every part of the massive oak wagon—axles, frame, wheels, and even the spokes—were reinforced with triple thickness to accommodate the large blocks of stone to be transported. Added to the load was the weight of ten and twenty-pound sledge hammers along with scores of heavy odd-size chisels.

Like the equipment they used, stone masons—Antonio included—were large and strapping men, but unlike his uncles and father, he was already three inches beyond six feet with shoulders and arms of imposing strength. Wearing a knee-length leather apron, Antonio had the appearance of an ancient pyramid builder. His shoulder-length red hair was tied with a thong at the nape of the neck. His steel blue eyes added to his uncommon appearance.

By the time Don Fortunato had said goodbye to Angelina and Rosa, Antonio had secured the horses to the wagon and was waiting with the reins in his hands. As his father climbed aboard, he implored his son, "Please, figlio mio, when we stop to pick up your uncles, come to a complete halt. I am tired of hearing your Uncle Vincenzo wheezing and cursing because he had to run to get aboard."

"Si, Papa. This morning will be different. I promise to come to a complete halt," Antonio assured his father as he covered his smile with his hand.

"This younger generation is always in a hurry, so today, please, *slow!"*

Antonio and his father made their way along the road with their heavy wagon as leathery, tanned peasants worked meticulously in the amber fields. Accompanied by mule and oxen, they tended their crops and found time for a few kind words for the passersby.

Just after rounding a bend in the road, Antonio and Don Fortunato came upon a mustached, barrel-chested man standing on the side of the road. Uncle Vincenzo waited nervously, holding a goat skin of wine under one arm and a leather tool bag under the other. Antonio brought the horses to a smooth halt. Don Fortunato greeted his younger brother. "Buon giorno, Vincenzo. We are a little late this morning."

"Don't apologize, my brother. I have just arrived myself," Vincenzo explained, glancing at Antonio with bewilderment. "My dear nephew, you don't know how I appreciate not sprinting after the wagon this morning like I normally do." Antonio burst into laughter and nudged his father with his elbow.

The threesome arrived some forty-five minutes later at the nearby town of Borgio, seven miles east of their home in Maida. Their work site, a partially-constructed church, stood off the piazza. A half dozen stone masons, already busy at work, stood on the wooden scaffolds that surrounded the perimeter. One of the bare-chested, leather-aproned workers smiled and waved with trowel in hand. Frederico, Don Fortunato's youngest brother, had presumably hitched a ride with a local farmer who had been en route to the local market.

Antonio pulled the wagon to a halt, and the three men quickly unloaded their tools. Every minute they wasted meant that much longer they would need to toil in the scorching midday sun. The gang of stone masons worked diligently, each knowing the man alongside was capable of executing his craft with skill and speed, each dependent on the ability of the other for the ultimate completion of the work.

They worked relentlessly until the sun was directly overhead, then one by one, each worker began to lay his tools aside and break for the midday meal. All found shaded places beneath the trees to eat and rest. Uncle Vincenzo brought out the bota of cool wine to quench their parched throats. Others uncovered loaves of bread and sections of sharp cheese and cured sausage from burlap bags and pouches. All shared in the food as each contributed.

After eating, the men stretched out comfortably as possible to wait out the hottest part of the day. Soon, in the comfort of the shade, as most others in Calabria, the men were napping. The surrounding shops and stores were closed for a few hours, loyal to the age-old Mediterranean way of life.

Only when the heat diminished, around 3:30, did the workers return to their scaffolds. Whether they hoisted massive stone blocks into precise position or applied mortar between them, the crew worked very well together. As the day wore on, the amount of progress was obvious. Within a few hours, it was time to quit for the day.

In a quarter of an hour, the wagon was loaded again

with tools and other equipment for the journey home. The trip was uneventful, as both Uncle Frederico and Vincenzo were dropped off at their respective homes. Finally, father and son came in sight of their stone cottage and were soon greeted by Angelina.

The evening meal made the day's labor worthwhile as Antonio and the rest of his family gathered around the table and enjoyed each other's small talk.

That evening, both father and son retired to bed earlier than usual, for they were both quite tired from the work week.

Save for Antonio, Sunday found the Lochetto family asleep another hour or so longer before rising and leaving for Mass. Antonio awakened early, anticipating well-deserved free time. In lieu of the very coarse work clothing, he chose to wear his finest shirt and trousers.

Sunday breakfast was something special, and Angelina had surpassed herself in its preparation. Not only was there fried ham and cheese omelets but also some sweet pastries made by Aunt Maria the previous day. They devoured the hearty breakfast in record time.

While his parents and siblings were finishing their meal, Antonio went out to the barn to hitch up their favorite horses to the carriage. Once everyone was finally aboard, Antonio slackened the reins, and the horses took off in a quick trot to the center of town. Upon arriving at the church, the Lochetto family were greeted warmly by close friends and relatives. Sundays offered the only opportunity for these friendly people to congregate and discuss local events, but before much was said, the church bell signaled the beginning of the next Mass. The small crowd filed inside.

Father Umberto, quite on in years, officiated the service. He was known to make a rather lengthy saga of the Mass, and this one was no exception. As a result of his monotone speaking voice, some of the older parishioners sitting on the rough-hewn benches quickly fell asleep while the younger generation became impatient and restless. Father Umberto made an epic reading of the Gospel. Antonio was also anxious for the completion of the morning's Mass and was looking forward to getting on with the rest of his day.

Finally, the Blessed Sacrament was offered to the people, and the concluding prayers were said. The faithful townspeople made their way back down the church steps past the watchful eye of Father Umberto.

Though, the Lochettos lived only a mile from the church, Antonio pushed the horses to a full gallop. To the dismay of his nervous passengers, it seemed only a few seconds later that they miraculously arrived home in one piece. As Don Fortunato stepped down from the carriage, he had a few choice words for his son, "I know today's youth has little respect for their elders, but to show disrespect to the church by putting me in such a state of mind immediately after Mass is unforgivable."

"Papa, believe me, that was not my intention. My

hands slipped on the reins," his son apologized.

"Basta! Enough words. There are no excuses. Now unharness the horses and get into the house."

Angelina's midday meal, in spite of a somewhat chilled atmosphere, was still a success. She had roasted a small lamb which was given to them by a close friend in return for a favor. Within a short time, all of the family's petty grievances had been forgotten. The main objective at the moment was to enjoy the feast before them.

After gorging himself with multiple helpings of his mother's succulent food, Antonio excused himself from the table. Swiftly, he made his way to the stable, picked out one of the younger stallions, and saddled up his mount. In no time at all, Antonio was riding toward the mountains. Meanwhile, Don Fortunato stepped outside to rid the ashes from his pipe when he saw the diminishing figure of his son riding away. He half smiled and shook his head.

As Antonio approached the lower slopes leading to the mountains, he began to feel the temperature change. A crisp current of air emanating from the higher elevations was a very welcome change from the hot, humid air of town. He followed a cold rushing stream upward as it twisted its way down the mountain. A quick dismount and he was dipping his cupped hands into the cool, swiftly-moving stream for a refreshing drink for himself and his horse. He couldn't help but marvel at the beauty of the land surrounding him. The clear sky, bright sun, and wispy clouds all contributed to what seemed a painting before him. He looked back over his shoulder toward town and viewed the sloping mountainside giving way to the lush plains below.

Within a few moments, Antonio was astride his stallion again and ascending higher into the mountains. His pace was much slower, as he allowed the horse to walk at his own gait. Numerous small animals scurried from the path of the oncoming intruders, while from a distance, an occasional deer stared inquisitively. The higher Antonio climbed, the more sparsely the pine and oak became. It was the perfect refuge for both animal and man. An abundant source of water and a plentiful supply of game blessed the land.

Following a narrow trail used by wild goat and deer, Antonio found himself on a ridge overlooking a deep ravine; the vertical drop was well over fifteen hundred feet. He maneuvered his horse along the precipitous ledge gently and carefully. After a few heart-stopping strides, he was, at last, beyond danger and continued his journey to the top. Upon reaching the summit, he was amazed to see the evenness of the terrain; from that particular vantage point, looking due west, a spectacular view enfolded. Before him was a rectangular plateau hundreds of feet wide with a few scattered pines, directly in the center of which was a small abandoned stone cabin that had been home for some shepherd or recluse many years before. Below the plateau, surrounded by well-tended fields and farms, lay Antonio's hometown of Maida. Beyond, ten to fifteen miles to the horizon and easily visible, was the beautiful Gulf of Euphemia, an ideal place for a painter or poet. Without question, he decided this new discovery would be his own private refuge.

Hours fled; the sun was setting, and Antonio knew he must soon begin his descent if he was to return home before dark. He stole one last glimpse at the inspiring view, then grasping the reins reluctantly, swung up onto the saddle and started back down the mountain. Within seconds, both rider and horse were once again gingerly descending the precarious ridge. Rocks kicked aside by the horse tumbled a thousand feet into the canyon below. Antonio and his animal companion anticipated each other's next move as they descended the treacherous mountain trail. He desperately tried to avoid turning the horse's leg on the rock-strewn path. A mishap could result in tragic consequences for both.

Once on level ground, they quickly advanced. Dusk fell when they were still some seven miles from home on a remote, untraveled area. From that point, the remaining four miles of the journey were relatively easy. Farmers paused as they ended their day's work in the fields to wave at Antonio as he raced by.

No more than a mile from his home, he was able to see the smoke rising from the chimney of their house. He rode in the dim light and arrived just before darkness fell as his mother was preparing the evening meal. He gave a sigh of relief that he had made it home safely and had not been caught up in the mountains overnight.

After supper that night, to escape the day's heat, the Lochetto family relaxed in chairs set up on a flat portion of their roof. Twenty to twenty-five feet above the ground, high enough to catch the cool sea breeze, the roof was level enough to serve as a balcony and faced the west toward the Mediterranean. The night was clear enough to see the natural fireworks of Stromboli, the island volcano many miles out to sea. It was like many other nights when the family viewed in awe the spectacular display of nature's power. They talked about things past and present over sweet cantaloupe and juicy peaches. The kind of atmosphere was one of soft-spoken people relaxing and enjoying the moment. Stromboli's rocketing white-hot cinders and belching red flames lightened the night sky, a sort of natural epilogue culminating another day.

This was the way of life in southern Italy in the mid-nineteenth century, lived to the fullest, one day at a time, the ever-present now the all-important commodity. And perhaps this very kind of philosophy and short-sightedness of the Italians made them able to survive the exploitations of the Austrians, French, and Spanish domination.

II
INDUCTION

Two years had passed since seventeen-year-old Antonio rode through the surrounding fields and pastures returning from his mountain refuge. He had grown three full inches taller and added twenty pounds to his already-robust frame. Taller now than his father, who was considered a large man in his own right, Antonio was six foot six with shoulders to match.

The amount of responsibility placed on him had increased considerably, thereby relieving his father of the tasks that before, were solely his to bear. Antonio's two younger brothers, Tomaso and Carlo, respectively fourteen and thirteen years old, helped their father as much as could be expected for their age.

Antonio was an ideal son, hard-working, loyal, and disdainful of anyone or anything that might endanger his family's harmony. He knew that someday there would come a time when he must leave his family and make his own life. He knew he could not make a life as a stone mason and be satisfied as his father and uncles had done. He hungered for another vocation but was not sure of the direction; he did not know this decision would be made for him.

The Bourbons of Spain were holding a tight grip on the southern part of Italy as well as the entire island of Sicily. Traditionally, the oldest son of the family was automatically drafted into the army; in some cases, the families of these young men were threatened with reprisals if they resisted compliance to the king's law. On many occasions, Antonio passed the army barracks while going through town. The troops consisted of both Spanish and drafted Italian soldiers from the entire province of Catanzaro.

One summer's morning, while Antonio and his father were loading their tools onto the wagon preparing for work, their attention was diverted abruptly when the pounding hooves of five horsemen sped toward them. Antonio looked up at the advancing riders and then glanced at his father with an ominous expression. As the men approached, it became evident that they were soldiers from the local garrison. When they came to a halt, one of them dismounted with precision and introduced himself, "Buenos dias, senores, on this fine morning. I am Sergeant Haime Miquel Mendoza of His Majesty's Cavalry.

I would like to have a few words with both of you, if I may."

"And what kind of business would a Spanish cavalry officer have with us Italians?" Don Fortunato answered.

"I will come to the point, senor. I would like to speak to you about a career for your son in His Majesty's service," the Spaniard quickly replied.

"I think such a decision should be made solely by my son without any outside influence." Anger flashed over Don Fortunato's face.

"But Papa," Antonio interrupted, "I have made a decision already. I will never serve in a foreign army occupying our land."

"Senores, you do not understand. When King Fernando II asks, it is not your prerogative to refuse," the sergeant rebuked, "for if you do not abide by the king's law, things could become ugly for you and other members of your family." The sergeant had barely completed his words when Antonio reached around Don Fortunato and grabbed the Spaniard by the collar. Don Fortunato grasped his son's arms from behind and pleaded with him.

"Antonio, don't! Let us not use the same barbarian tactics that the Bourbons use on our people." Antonio finally released his hold on the sergeant.

"That was a very foolish move, young man. If I wanted to, I could take very drastic measures against you immediately," the indignant Spaniard hissed as he straightened his collar. "But for the welfare of your father, though you do not deserve it, I will give you another chance to reconsider. I will return in two days' time for your affirmative decision. Think it over carefully, or your freedom could be compromised. There could be severe consequences." The sergeant remounted his horse. "I bid you good day, senores." He briskly spurred his horse and in a few strides, the group of soldiers galloped away and disappeared from sight.

Don Fortunato turned to his son and said, "We must talk and consider all the aspects and not make a hasty decision that we might regret for years to come." Antonio looked into his father's eyes.

"You are right, Papa, but for some time now, I have seen this coming and pondered a military career."

"Unfortunately, the Spanish rule in Calabria gives the oldest son no choice. If you refuse, a sentence in prison will follow, along with reprisals and harassment against the family. Because of this sad situation, there are thousands of Italians in the service of the Spanish army. What a vile dilemma." Don Fortunato exhaled with frustration. "Spanish tyranny is squeezing Italy dry of its youth." He paused and continued half-heartedly, "My son, let's hurry. The day is getting on, and we have a long ride to work. We will discuss this matter at length when we return home."

"Si, Papa. We will talk later."

All during that day, Antonio was unusually quiet and avoided unnecessary conversation; God help anyone who attempted otherwise. He went about his labor diligently, putting all of his concerns into his work load, completing a third of the east wall almost single-handedly. Earlier that day, the other workers were made aware of the situation by Don Fortunato. The men respected Antonio's wishes and left him to his work and thoughts.

The ride home that evening was rather somber; both father and son spoke only sparingly. The same atmosphere prevailed at the supper table that night until Antonio finally spoke up, "Basta! Enough thinking has been done for one day. I have made my decision. Papa, you will abide by my choice."

"But of course. You are a man now. You should make your own destiny," his father replied gently.

"Very well. I have weighed the pros and cons and have decided to go with the Bourbon cavalry. This will insure our family's well-being. Now there will be no reprisals or harassment of the people I love most. Besides, I won't be the only Italian in service of the Bourbons."

"I respect your decision because of the circumstances. I will abide by the choice you have made," his father said, after much hesitation. Angelina touched her son's hand, her eyes filling with anguish despite her acceptance.

"For some illogical reason, I feel as though a millstone has been removed from my shoulders. I will proceed and follow up my decision," Antonio said with certainty.

The remainder of the evening was somewhat subdued but less apprehensive. Antonio had cleared the air to some extent, and the other members of his family were almost back to their normal selves.

Antonio rose a little earlier the next morning. He paused in front of the window to admire the crimson dawn. A half hour later, after putting his mind in order, he descended the narrow steps to the kitchen for breakfast.

When Antonio arrived at the table, his mother was frying thin slices of ham in a large skillet. The aroma of just-baked bread filled the room. A dozen or so fresh rolls lay on a linen cloth waiting to be savored. Antonio kissed his mother on the forehead and said, "Mamma, I think this morning I could eat everyone's portion." He smiled with affection. Angelina looked up at her son, knowing his eagerness too well.

"Well, my son, sit down and try to satisfy your hunger with what I've already prepared."

Within ten minutes, Antonio devoured half the rolls, and three quarters of the ham had disappeared along with five eggs. He washed it all down with three mugs of steaming tea. Don Fortunato arrived at the table and was pleased to find his oldest son in better spirits and his normal appetite returned.

After Antonio finished his breakfast, he informed his parents of his plans for that day. "Papa, this morning I will not be going to work with you as usual. Instead, I am going to the garrison in town to speak with the sergeant about accepting his proposal."

"Go ahead, if this is what you think you must do," his

father said. Angelina nodded, but the sad look in her eyes gave her away.

In a short while, Antonio was saddling his horse for the ride into town. He grasped the pommel, mounted, and spurred his horse. It was a short ride from his home to the barracks on the opposite side of town.

As he came upon the low row of buildings, he could see small groups of soldiers gathered here and there. More than one trooper turned to look when he dismounted in front of headquarters. They were in awe of his stature, for he stood a full head taller than anyone present. His simple attire—a billowing shirt worn with rough, tightly-sewn britches and high leather riding boots—was typical of the region. Antonio politely asked a nearby soldier for directions to Sergeant Mendoza's office.

Once inside headquarters, Antonio observed military personnel milling about. He spied a door with the sergeant's name and then knocked. A deep and commanding voice signaled for Antonio to enter. He cautiously opened the office door to see a surprised Sergeant Mendoza. The Sergeant walked quickly around his desk with his hand extended in a gesture of welcome. The smiling Spaniard said, "I am glad you had a change of heart, young man. Both you and King Fernando II, whom you will serve, will both benefit greatly from this union."

"Actually, Sergeant, it was not a change of heart, rather, the lesser of two evils," Antonio remarked, offering his hand reluctantly.

"Regardless of your reasons, you will be handsomely

rewarded for your service in His Majesty's army." Evidently Sergeant Mendoza overlooked Antonio's comment.

"That remains to be seen," Antonio countered, "Since I have made my decision to join, I would like to go into the cavalry rather than the infantry, for the reason that I am a fairly good rider and can handle horses well."

"Excellent, my young man," explained the sergeant, "Spain needs well-trained dragoons to protect its territories. You will find that you are not the only Italian in the Bourbon cavalry. Many of your countrymen are in our service here in Calabria."

"Well, I guess this is some kind of consolation to know that I will be fighting alongside my own people."

"Bueno, then it is settled." Sergeant Mendoza shuffled some papers and handed him a document to sign. "Sign your name after you read this."

The future recruit read the information that consisted mostly of the rules of conduct expected of a soldier. Any kind of insubordination would be met with severe and quick punishment by the military.

Antonio finished reading, signed the enlistment papers, and then handed them to the sergeant. "Bueno. I am sure you will never regret, for one minute, the years of service in the King's cavalry. It can be a rewarding and satisfying career if you make it so. It can also be a miserable number of years if you act irrationally and contrary to laws of the military. Therefore, in one week's time you will report back to me and then embark on a trip to Sicily for military training." Antonio agreed and respectfully shook hands with the sergeant.

As he left, Antonio sighed with relief and then headed home. He thought perhaps, things would turn out for the best, despite the circumstances. The future seemed a little brighter than before; after all, he was an excellent horseman and marksman. Being an excellent shot was a result from necessity, for there were times when he had gone into the mountains with only a handful of cartridges to hunt game. Cartridges were very expensive, and it was imperative that each bullet find its mark.

Antonio rode further as the feeling of despair was replaced by one of optimism. Whether or not it was rationalization on his part, an atmosphere of hope seemed to prevail.

When he arrived home, both of his parents were obviously in a somber mood, evident by the expressions on their faces. Their attitude soon changed when they saw their son's enthusiasm as he spoke about his future in the military.

The following week before Antonio's induction, time seemed to go by quite normally considering the inevitable; he worked and lived as he had done in years past. His family, surprisingly enough, reacted almost calmly to his impending absence. They went about performing their work and other activities that made up their daily routine.

The remaining days passed swiftly, and before one realized, it was the morning of his departure. Rising early,

Antonio entered his mother's kitchen with a large, coarse sack filled with clothing and necessities. He caught his mother's sad eyes as he gently swung the bag to the floor. He walked toward her and embraced her, trying to reassure her. "Mamma, please do not be so sad. Before long, I will be home on leave eating your delicious roasted lamb. Actually, I will not be that far away, only a few miles across the strait from Reggio. I bet on a clear day, if the wind is right, I will smell the aromas of your kitchen." His mother sobbed and then wiped her tears.

"Look at me," she said, "I'm the baby. I should be the strong one. Excuse me, my son, you are right. Before long, you will be home again making a pest of yourself in my kitchen." She recovered quickly and continued to make breakfast.

Antonio sat down and poured himself a cup of tea and was sipping it when his father walked in. Don Fortunato made an attempt at being cheerful and commented on the beautiful morning, but it was obvious that his words were coming from a sad heart. Antonio agreed that the day was much cooler than the one before. Angelina placed Fortunato's breakfast before him and also another biscuit into her son's outstretched hand. The rest of the family, his two brothers and sister, would not be awake for another hour. Antonio preferred it this way.

In a short while, both men of the family finished eating, and an uncomfortable period of silence followed. Antonio finally broke the lull and said, "It's getting late. I must go now to arrive at the barracks in time." Trying desperately to avoid looking into his parents' eyes, he lifted his gear to his shoulder. He reached out his arms and embraced each of them and then walked out into the dawn.

III

MARCH TO SICILY AND CAMP LIFE

On his way to the barracks, Antonio could still see the diminishing image of his loving parents in his mind's eye. He rode to the site and noticed a considerable number of riders already assembled. A closer look revealed that these men were also new recruits. Their uniquely-made clothes differentiated the area from which they originated. He was quite pleased to recognize two acquaintances from nearby towns. The sight of one in particular, a smiling-faced young man from Pizzo, was an unexpected joy. Still on his horse—Giacomo, waving and shouting—fought a path through the other riders to his friend's side. Antonio was overjoyed to see Giacomo again for it had been a few years since he and his family had vacationed in Pizzo, a coastal resort town on Calabria's western shore.

Before the youths could get reacquainted, the Spanish sergeant emerged from the barracks. His presence was enough to command respect as he stood on the steps overlooking the new group of recruits. The forty young men before him quieted immediately. The slim Sergeant Mendoza addressed them, "Gentlemen, I am very glad that you could all make this reunion. Briefly, I will try to inform you of the activities in store for you before your arrival in Sicily within the next two or three days. Soon you will ride south and hopefully arrive in the town of Rosarno by nightfall. Anyone who lingers behind or who intentionally slows the rest down will be reprimanded on the spot, in front of all. I do not know how to impress upon you the importance of following orders. Nothing less will be tolerated." He curled his dark mustache between his index finger and thumb and took a few paces. "By the second night, you should arrive in Reggio, and the following morning, a ferry will carry you across to Sicily to Messina. Blankets and mess kits will be distributed among you. Oh, yes, and one more note, in case you were not informed—you will be sleeping under the stars for the next few nights. Gentlemen, I wish you the best of luck in the service of His Majesty King Fernando II. Thank you and good day," he said before pivoting and smartly reentering the barracks.

A corporal, who was standing by, motioned to the two squads of cavalry. One squad slowly moved to the front of the recruits, and the other moved to the rear. Then in a column, two by two, the corporal led the recruits out of the military post to the road south.

The fifty men kicked up quite a cloud of dust as other highway travelers gave the right of way to the impressive group of riders. The scene was a rare sight to the local people of the area; at first glance, the legion of multi-attired horsemen appeared as a group of civilian prisoners being escorted by Spanish troopers.

The men passed tiny, mountainous villages as they rode southward, through steep chasms across clear rivers rushing their way toward the sea. The rugged territory, though harsh, was as beautiful as it was demanding. It took a hardy breed of people to eke out a living in such a challenging place; it was an accomplishment to be a farmer or shepherd.

After six non-stop, hot, and dusty hours of riding, the multi-clad legion was finally ordered to a halt. A short break for food and drink was allowed alongside the road's edge. Canned rations were distributed through the ranks for those who desired them, but most of the recruits had anticipated a long ride and brought food provisions with them. More than likely, this was the last meal before they relinquished their stomachs to the military. To the surprise of many, some young men chose to not eat at all and slept during this time instead.

Small groups had begun to form among the recruits according to region of origin—those from Saracenna in one group, those from Cosenza in another, and those from

Catanzaro in the third group. But all had one common denominator; they were all from Calabria.

The regular Bourbon troopers also gathered and ate together. They, too, welcomed the cool shade along the tree-lined road. It was a temporary refuge from the dusty, hot march. As so often happens, the time flew by, and the word was passed on to break up camp and continue the ride. Both men and their mounts were weary and very reluctant to give up their places of rest, but within minutes, all were ready to move on.

The hours passed by as Antonio began to comprehend what army life was truly based on. The execution of an order and its entire function depended upon discipline and obedience to the superiors. It was completely distasteful to his innate independent spirit. To be told when to rise in the morning, what time to eat, and when to wash was entirely alien to his nature. However, he knew that without such orders, an army could not operate effectively; there would be utter chaos if each individual did as he wished. The regimentation was a necessary evil, no matter how repulsive.

Mile after mile of endless and seemingly pointless riding was beginning to wear on the recruits. The veteran troopers possessed immunity to fatigue and appeared to accept their fate without question. They weathered the long trek much better and maintained a surprising air of vigor. On the other hand, the new recruits were almost on the verge of collapse. At times, along the ranks of the column, the seasoned veterans would belittle and taunt the new men. If they could not endure this short jaunt to the hills, how could they survive a forced march upon which their lives depended? The recruits countered this treatment with resentment and anger. Before long, words were being tossed back to the veterans, and a hot rivalry was underway.

Fortunately, to the relief of all, the town of Rosarno finally lay only a kilometer away. There, on the outskirts of town, the men were to bivouac for the night. Both new and seasoned soldiers alike were anxious to make camp.

Campfires soon appeared here and there. Small two-man tents were set up as darkness engulfed the weary riders. In contrast to the midday meal, the night's fare was eaten in a subdued atmosphere. Exhaustion was more prevalent than hunger. While a few lingered over their food, others chose to curl up in their woolen blankets to sleep. It was not long until the majority of the recruits were all slumbering. Some of the veterans took their cue from the younger men and also turned in for the night. Countless stars flickered in the black sky, their light a blessing upon the encampment of tired men.

Sunrise prodded the men into another day. Remorsefully, the small legion gave up their rest, broke camp, and continued. An early start was imperative; to travel during the day's hottest hours could prove to be even more challenging.

Within an hour, the small army was riding at a brisk gallop as mile after mile of dusty road was consumed. Surprisingly, the new recruits were amazed at the distance they traveled without getting fatigued. Hours passed as they moved south along the coastal road. The picturesque scenery mesmerized the silent horsemen. The winding road hugged the edge of the ocean cliffs, tenacious mountains giving way to the calm, indigo sea below. Every bend in the road afforded the traveler a majestic view of the Strait of Messina. Small coves and inlets emerged from the precipitous coast, harmonizing with one unparalleled view after another.

In such an atmosphere, time passed swiftly. Again, the small army halted to eat and drink cool water. The interlude was much appreciated by all and a welcome pause after the hot morning ride.

They returned to the road and moved southward toward Reggio. The rhythm of the march swallowed up the miles. They traveled through small towns situated along the strait facing Sicily and continued their journey as darkness enveloped them. The men halted, the town of Reggio spreading out before them. In the background, lights from the opposite shore dotted the dark outline of Sicily. There the horsemen would spend the last night before crossing over to Messina.

After the routine of making camp and preparing something to satisfy their hunger, the men crawled into their blankets to sleep.

The sky was exceptionally clear the next morning, and the sun's heat wasted little time in making itself known. Gazing from the elevated camp sight, Antonio and his companions could easily distinguish the ships being piloted through the unpredictable waters below. Cargos destined for Mediterranean ports sailed through the strait.

Word was passed through the ranks that a ferry was waiting in the harbor to transport the men across to Sicily. The army of recruits wound their way down the mountainside to Reggio. At the edge of town, two mounted Spanish cavalrymen were waiting to escort the men through the busy streets to the moored ferry. The sound of steel-hooved horses resounded between the buildings lining the cobblestone streets. More than one passerby looked over his shoulder at the unusual army before noisily making his way through the shop-lined avenues. For just a moment, the fast-paced town had been interrupted by a small band of intruders.

The riders approached the harbor side of Reggio where a fairly large ferry, secured to the dock with massive hemp ropes, was visible. The troopers neared the water's edge as spirals of black smoke billowed into the sky. Two gangplanks led down from the boat, bustling with hurried passengers and cargo being loaded aboard.

The soldiers, single-file, dismounted and guided their horses up and onto the waiting ferry. Once aboard, each man secured his animal in the boat's horse stall area. Moments later, the vessel disembarked and left the harbor. At first, the sound of the boat's engines alarmed the high-spirited horses, but once underway, they were soon calmed by their reassuring soldiers, and the animals began to settle down.

In a short while, before anyone realized it, the ferry had reached the midway point between Reggio and Messina. For many of the young men, it was their first trip across the strait and a pleasant one, as they were accustomed to only seeing mountains and farmlands.

The ferry reached the opposite coast as brightly colored dwellings of fishermen were discernible to the passengers aboard. White-faced buildings with red, yellow, and orange shutters and doors overlooked the oncoming vessel, some perched so precariously on the side of the steep ledges that the passengers aboard feared that something could come towering down upon them. They neared the shoreline, and men scurried about as they prepared the rope moorings for the incoming ferry. The sound of the noisy steam engine stopped when the boat cut its engines. Then they drifted and headed straight between the narrow, funnel-like pier. The people as well as the animals aboard felt the dull thud as the ferry bounced off the sides of the wooden pilings. When close enough to the dock, heavy ropes were thrown aboard and made secure. The water lapped and splashed up between the sides of the ferry and the pilings. It was too much for the jittery horses, and once again they had to be calmed before any could be taken ashore. With gangplanks in place, both passengers and horses alike began to exit. The horses were led down the gangways slowly and carefully to avoid injury.

In less than fifteen minutes, all of the troopers and their mounts were safely ashore as they trotted through the stone-paved streets of Messina. Many times the advancing column of riders approached a busy intersection and was given the right of way to proceed. They traveled at a rapid pace and soon they were outside the city limits.

The sloping foothills leading up to the mountains of the interior lay before them. They made their way along the road toward the town of Milazzo on the northeastern section of Sicily then turned south and traveled to Pozzo di Gotto where their cavalry training camp was located. A difficult ride was required to traverse the formidable mountain range that extended diagonally from the eastern coast of Sicily to its northern coast.

The column quickened its pace as the horses were spurred into a faster gait. The ever-ascending dirt road curved its way upward toward the mountain summit. The company of recruits reached the crest within an hour. They saw the warm waters of the Ionian Sea to the south and the cobalt waters of the Tyrrhenian Sea stretching to the north. To enhance the scene still further, the scent of mountain laurel perfumed the mile-high scenic view.

The men moved at a steady pace along miles of lofty roads. They were midway to their destination by noon which meant they were situated well into the rugged interior. The column paused to eat and rest for a while by a clear, cascading stream.

Having refreshed themselves, the recruits returned to

the arid, winding road. The road gradually descended toward a plateau, making the remainder of the journey easier for the horses. They progressed further north not realizing the true extent of the decline. The shimmering, blue Tyrrhenian Sea and the Cape di Milazzo sprawled out far beneath them. Both man and beast were exhilarated and seemed to have absorbed vitality from the very nature of the beauty that surrounded them. On the right side, five hundred feet below, the sea slapped the jagged coastline, and further west, the Cape extended seven miles where an ancient naval battle took place two thousand years before.

Having reached the beginning of the peninsula, the column of recruits took the twisting road south to the town of Pozzo di Gotto. Their final destination was some eight miles further. It was late afternoon, and the rest of the trip took a little more than an hour to complete.

At last they arrived at the bustling military town as the sun perched very low on the western horizon. The crimson and glowing orange beams of light gave the town a dreamlike luminescence. The busy road through town led past shops and businesses as it continued south. Silhouettes of army barracks in the background were distinguishable against the burning sky. The grassy, flat terrain extended for miles, disappearing into the horizon.

Minutes later, the column was in front of what proved to be a large mess hall. The chatter of many men and the distinct clatter of dishes reverberated out of the low-slung windows into the night. A tall, lean, mustached Spanish officer walked out onto the wooden steps of the building to greet the newcomers. Standing with his hands on his hips, he inspected the group of men before him. "Welcome young men of Calabria," he said, breaking the uncomfortable silence, "I am in your debt that you could find the time to visit us on this beautiful evening." Antonio reacted to the sarcasm by rolling his eyes at his friend Giacomo. "Excuse me for not introducing myself. I am Lieutenant Ramon Cordova of His Majesty's 3rd Cavalry Brigade. I will be your commander, father, and nursemaid for the next twelve weeks. I will get to know each one of you better than you even know yourselves. When you have completed the training, you will be the best prepared fighting cavalry unit in Europe. You will be dedicated, honorable, and proud men admired by all." Giacomo's horse stomped the ground impatiently, and Antonio, yawned, equally as bored. "For now, this will be all. Sergeant Sanchez will show you to your living quarters. I trust you will act wisely and follow instructions to the letter. Any insubordination will be dealt with immediately. Rest well, for tomorrow's training is the first step to being an accomplished cavalryman. Goodnight, gentlemen," the arrogant lieutenant finally concluded before returning to the lamp-lit mess hall.

Sergeant Sanchez, who had been standing by Cordova, descended the stairs and proceeded to speak quietly to the mounted Spanish veterans who had escorted the column of recruits to the camp. Within moments, an arm was waved, motioning for the column to follow. The still-mounted recruits followed behind their Spanish escorts who led them to a long single-floor structure. The barracks were quite large and could easily house a hundred men if need be. Windows lined both sides of the narrow building. It would be their home for the next three months.

The column was then ordered to dismount and unload their belongings. They entered the vacant building where oil lamps were lit; the light revealed two rows of bunks, each row against the outside wall with a wide aisle in the center. Each recruit selected his sleeping place and began to unpack his gear. Before long, the chatter of young men filled the long room. One by one, they soon slipped into their bunks and fell sound asleep.

When Sergeant Sanchez arrived, he was astonished to find that every man had already turned in for the night. He had come in to enforce the curfew, but of course, arrived too late to do so; he walked down the wide aisle between the bunks, smiled, and shook his head. Apparently the day's activities were a bit tiresome—the ferry ride from Reggio to Messina and then the long ride over the mountains to the training camp—all took its toll.

As countless nights before, the heavens put on a display of celestial beauty. The night air was sharp and clear, and thousands of stars pulsated against the sky.

In one of the bunks, Antonio gazed up through a nearby window in wonder. He was deep in thought about his family and how they were doing without his help, but he had a great deal of confidence in his father's ability. He soon fell asleep with this in mind.

Awakened from their sleep by a shrieking bugle, the men commenced another day in the life of a recruit. It was five in the morning and if the sound of the bugle did not disturb the young men, the harsh voice of Sergeant Sanchez jolted the most stubborn from their bunks.

After they washed with water from large, wooden tubs, they dressed hurriedly and put their beds and footlockers in order then stood at attention in front of their bunks while they waited for some kind of inspection. As anticipated, the lieutenant—accompanied by the sergeant—entered their quarters. "Buenos dias, senores," greeted the Spanish officer, "I trust you slept well last night, for today you will begin your basic training. The sergeant will be at your side constantly. He will get to know you as well as your mother knows you. In the course of your training, you will learn the use of the saber and how to ride and shoot. You are probably thinking that you already know how to ride and shoot, but here we will teach you the correct way. If you refuse to grasp our methods, you will not be hurting us, but you may be endangering your own life at some future time. You will get out of this training what you put into it. I will now turn you over to our capable sergeant who will inform you of today's schedule." The fiery lieutenant turned briskly and left the barracks.

The first few days of training were a sharp change in the

lifestyles of the former civilians. It was very difficult for the recruits, namely Antonio, to be told when to rise, when to eat, what to wear, and how to act with superiors. Slowly but surely, it became part of their daily routine.

The horsemanship displayed by the young Italians astonished their Spanish instructors. These recruits lacked only technique and method, which they were soon taught. Their instinctive knowledge of horses and riding would be a great advantage to them in time to come. Early in their training, these eager future soldiers unknowingly established an intense rivalry among the other cavalry companies; their competitive spirit and willingness to learn was an advantage, and this, of course, delighted their superiors, for it would be much easier to instruct them. Other companies soon challenged the Calabrian group. Riding matches were set up as the competition heated up, and each unit was vying to be the best in the camp.

Marksmanship was the next phase of training. In the cavalry, the carbine was used, for the rifle was too long and cumbersome while riding. Daily drills were held to accustom the recruits to the handling of the carbine; instruction, both mounted and dismounted, was taught. Antonio, much like his friends, was already at home with carbine in hand from his many hunting trips as a youngster in the mountains. As a result, every man in the Calabrian company qualified as an expert marksman. Both Sergeant Sanchez and Lieutenant Cordova were proud of their natural aptitude.

The next course of training was devoted to the use of

the saber. Unlike training with the familiar carbine or horsemanship, the saber was totally alien to the young men. Saber instruction was probably the most vital part of being a cavalryman. The combination of the horse and sword was used successfully against mob insurrections and opposing infantrymen. The cavalry was an integral part of an effective advancing army. Unlike the infantry or other branches of the military, the cavalry saber was the personal weapon of every trooper, his primary offensive function. The carbine was carried as a secondary defense when the sword could not feasibly be put to use.

One sunlit morning, during the last weeks of training, the lieutenant addressed the recruits while astride his black stallion. The lively Spaniard had their undivided attention when he drew his saber and began, "This, gentlemen, is your weapon, not the carbine; this is the reason you are mounted, for if you solely depended upon the rifle, you would be on foot serving in the infantry. Nevertheless, you are in the cavalry, and the use of the saber together with your horse makes you the most unique fighting unit in the military. This blade will become part of you, an extension of your arm." The lieutenant sliced the air with his weapon. "In the next few weeks, you will live, eat, and sleep with this length of cold steel until you become proficient. Using it will become second nature, without forethought. It is forty inches from tip to hilt and is the most dependable ally you will have. It is made of the finest steel in all of Spain, handmade by the most expert craftsmen of Toledo who make the best swords in the civilized world, which I am sure you are aware of." Antonio was intrigued and listened intently. "Now, I would like to teach you the basics pertaining to the saber. First of all, when it is worn by a dismounted trooper, it is habitually attached to the belt by saber slings with the sword guard to the rear. The mounted trooper, on the other hand, holds the saber scabbard in the carrier attached to the offside of the saddle. When the command '*draw saber*' is given, the trooper, on draw, reaches with his right hand over the reins and grasps the hilt and draws the saber from the scabbard. There are six other commands, which Sergeant Sanchez now will cover. They are important techniques in saber-to-saber combat. Once again, I will turn you over to the able hands of the sergeant for in-depth instruction of this marvelous weapon." Lieutenant Cordova, with the reins held loosely between the fingers of his right hand, gently turned his stallion and departed.

The stocky Sergeant Sanchez drilled the young Italian troopers with relentless energy, to their dismay, for seven long days. Numerous combat procedures were exercised repetitiously until the movements with the saber became second nature. The recruits were divided into two groups; mock charges between them realistically simulated hand-to-hand combat in the field. The daily exercises of horse and rider became effortless as they learned to move as one. Many a straw-stuffed manikin was slashed to shreds during the countless saber drills. Scores of squash, namely pumpkins supplied by the local farmers, were minced during practice runs. The recruits improved, their ability to wield the sword now with a firm yet relaxed, confident grip. The agility and accuracy demonstrated by them revealed the true effectiveness of this potent and deadly weapon.

The last day of basic training finally arrived, to the relief of all in the company. The following day would be the inter-company competition in related cavalry events. All of the different units representing the entire camp would compete with one another for the honor of being the best trained in the regiment. Individual events such as horsemanship, marksmanship, and swordsmanship would have each trooper vie for the best in each category.

On the morning of competition, all of the companies were involved in a dozen simultaneous events. The huge parade field was divided into sections according to activity; only one of the fifteen companies comprising the 3rd Bourbon Cavalry could win. An individual trooper would also be selected in each category on the basis of the most points amassed.

The hours flew by as both the heat of the day and the competition intensified. The fiery rivalry between the units spurred every trooper to put forth his best effort so that his company would be chosen to fly the first place golden banner.

By midday, halfway through the competition, the Calabrian unit was in sixth place in the field of fifteen. The enthusiasm and high spirits displayed by all satisfied their Spanish superiors beyond expectation.

At three in the afternoon, the successful Calabrians had moved to tie for first place. The other company was primarily comprised of energetic Spaniards; their first place standing resulted from the efforts of the outstanding performances by a handful of determined Castilians. They far excelled the others in horsemanship and also obtained the highest scores in the shooting category. The saber competition would be the decisive event that would break the tie between the Calabrian and Castilian units; it would come down to a contest between only two men, one from each side.

The Spanish unit was represented by a lean, well-groomed trooper; he impatiently waited on his spirited white stallion for his Italian counterpart to come forward. A tall young man astride a black stallion came forth from the Calabrian side, red hair blowing, likes of which the Castilians had not seen before. Antonio had been selected to represent his unit in the last match specifically for his adroit ability with the saber and enormous reach.

Both riders were poised side by side, each chosen to ride the parallel course. Ten large melons spaced evenly apart lined one side of the one hundred yard course that stretched before them. The object of the event was to slash through all ten melons at a full gallop.

The first to make the pass down the course was the Spaniard, riding almost side-saddle with one hand on the pummel; he approached swiftly, and to the delight of his fellow Castilians, systematically halved the first five before slicing through the remaining melons.

Upon his opponent's completion of the course, Antonio and his horse got a running start. As his opponent before him, he proceeded to halve every melon on the course in very much the same style while the Calabrian unit cheered. It was a dead heat between the two troopers, and the tie remained. Their Spanish superiors were bewildered as how to break the deadlock between the two opposing teams. Lieutenant Cordova finally leaned over and whispered into Sergeant Sanchez's ear; the sergeant agreed wholeheartedly, for a wide grin spread across his face. Sergeant Sanchez proceeded to place a melon on the right side of the course and then another on the left side in a staggered fashion. There were still ten melons to slice, but the degree of difficulty was much greater; the rider first had to hold the saber in his right hand, slice a melon then transfer the saber to his left and slice the next one. This technique would be employed through the remainder of the course.

Again, the young Spaniard was the first to try the course; he approached at full gallop and leaned to his right side, sliced the first melon, and then quickly placed the saber in his left hand to cut the melon on that side. He continued to expertly handle his horse and weapon, slicing through the first seven with surprising ease. When he approached the eighth melon, he fumbled when passing the saber from one hand to the other and galloped right past it. He recovered in time to halve the ninth and tenth.

His loyal comrades hailed him as he finished the course. Nine out of ten cut melons was an excellent achievement considering the staggered course and degree of difficulty.

Antonio was amazed at both his opponent's ability and agility. He doubted that he could equal such a feat when he took his turn. He knew he could never simultaneously maneuver his large frame on the horse and exchange the saber from one hand to the other. He approached the line and had a thought...perhaps he would not have to change hands with the saber at all. He approached the first melon to his right and sliced through it confidently; then instead of changing hands with the saber, he leaned over as far as he could to the left side of his horse and slashed the upcoming melon with the saber still in his right hand. Those watching were amazed at the gymnastics of the long-stretching and resourceful Calabrian. Antonio made full use of his large frame as he continued to conquer the remainder of the course. His fellow Italians let out a boisterous cheer when the last melon was cut. Even Lieutenant Cordova praised him, galloping up to Antonio. "Fantastic, Antonio! Congratulations on a perfect score. Even though your method was unorthodox, you managed to overcome an obstacle that could have defeated you. Again, congratulations. You have earned it. The whole company is very proud. Well done!" A jubilant Antonio smiled as he waved his saber at his supportive friends.

IV
MILITARY LIFE AND RETURNING HOME

It was the end of September by the time Antonio and his regiment of Calabrians departed from the training camp in Sicily. They were assigned to a Bourbon garrison at Catanzaro in southern Calabria. The newly-trained soldiers crossed the strait to Reggio and rode northward until they arrived three days later at the Catanzaro fort. Fortunately for Antonio, this was only fifteen miles from his hometown of Maida and only half a day's ride from his home and family.

It was dark before the weary regiment was finally assigned to their respective barracks. After three days of hard riding, the young troopers were eager to crawl into their bunks and sleep. The following day was Sunday, which would be a leisure day for them, and the only restriction would be to report back to the post by nine o'clock that evening.

Antonio rose early after a restful night's sleep and intended to take advantage of the time to visit his parents whom he hadn't seen in three and a half months.

He saddled his horse beside the barracks and left the still-sleeping garrison. He wasted no time in putting ample distance between himself and the post.

He rode westward to familiar mountains and streams he had loved so much, the wind in his face and the sweet fragrance of grass again filling his lungs. The further he rode to higher ground, the more he remembered being a youngster exploring the many hidden valleys that were so indicative of the region. The crisp air against his skin, the pungent smell of mountain pine, and the tranquil sounds of birds were all reminiscent of his carefree youth. His heart longed for lost freedom.

His horse, climbing effortlessly, also seemed to be caught up in the rapture. Before the sun reached directly overhead, Antonio began to descend to the foothills that stretched into the open plains leading to Maida. He passed meticulously cultivated acres as laborers gathered the last of the remaining crops from their fertile soil. More than one farm hand straightened to get a better look at who they thought was a galloping stranger. Antonio was quite an impressive figure in his uniform as he rode by some of his old friends. He shouted their names with enthusiasm and drew their attention by waving. At first, some of them were startled by his military appearance and hesitated to return the wave until they took a second glance and realized it was their big friend. They finally responded whole-heartedly, waving their arms to Antonio who had seemingly left as a boy and returned a man.

Moments later, Antonio was able to make out the beloved outline of his home at the edge of town. Finally, with his heart beating with expectation, he approached the back of his house and saw his two younger brothers Tomaso and Carlo grooming one of their father's mares. Spurring his horse to a run, Antonio shouted, and startled, his siblings looked up. Tomaso was the first to recognize his older brother and dropped the combing brush; he ran toward Antonio while Carlo ran to the house to inform their parents. A smiling Antonio reined to a halt, reached down and scooped Tomaso up. He placed the boy behind him on the horse's back and then hurried to the house. Carlo soon emerged with Don Fortunato and Angelina, and they all ran toward their returning soldier. Antonio sprang from his horse and engulfed his exuberant family in an embrace. With tears of happiness, both parents agreed on how well he looked in his cavalry uniform. He walked to the house with an arm around each of them while his brothers admired his saber and carbine.

Inside his mother's kitchen, the familiar aroma of herbs and his mother's cooking reminded him of his carefree days. Antonio sat down at his old place at the table, rested his elbows on the heavy-worn oak boards and shared the Sunday meal of stewed seafood, pasta, and vegetables. It was good to be in the company of the people he cared for most.

His father and brothers kept a continuous flow of questions concerning all of the aspects of army life. Having answered all of the questions as best he could, Antonio began eating with earnest and satisfied his unchanged voracious appetite. His mother was very pleased to have her eldest back, appetite and all, for only he showed such appreciation for her efforts in making a fine meal.

After eating, he and his father took a short walk. Don Fortunato was proud to hear that his son was doing so well for such a short period of time that he had been in military training; he could see by his unrestrained enthusiasm that his son had found some fulfillment in army life.

Angelina had just finished cleaning the last of the dishes when the two men returned. Antonio informed both his parents that he could not stay much longer; he wanted to stop by and see his childhood sweetheart, Teresa Riccio, whom he also had not seen in months. His parents were very understanding about his short stay and realized he had less than half a day's trip back. Antonio promised to return every Sunday while he was stationed at Catanzaro.

After saying goodbye, he mounted his patient horse and saw his mother darting from the house with a small cloth sack. In a breathless voice, she said, "My son, please don't forget this. You may get hungry on the way back to the garrison." Antonio smiled and reached for the bundle and placed it into one of his leather saddle bags.

"Mamma, I know I have a large appetite, but there is enough food in this sack for an entire regiment," Antonio said, glancing over his shoulder with a laugh. "Tell Papa I will see you all again next week. I must be off if I am to see Teresa today. Take care." He bent forward and kissed his mother on the cheek, turned his horse, and waved goodbye. He galloped away, disappearing down the dusty lane.

Antonio had not been on that section of the road since the previous spring. The twists and turns along the way were the same, yet oddly changed, much like Antonio himself; all things took on a different light.

The three mile ride to see Teresa was short, and before long, he saw the spiraling smoke rising from their farmhouse. The solitary stone structure and its two equally well-built outbuildings stood as sentinels over the hundred acres of farmland. It was one of the more prosperous farms in the area, providing both animals and crops for market. The family's good fortune was attributed to their constant efforts and strong backs rather than luck.

When Antonio rode up to the house he saw his black-haired Teresa waving excitedly to him from a second floor window. By the time he dismounted and secured his horse to the iron-ringed hitching post, the front door burst open as Teresa came dashing toward him. The obviously reserved Antonio turned around to face her and noticed that she was even more beautiful than he had remembered. She reached up and flung her arms about his neck causing much embarrassment in the young man.

Within seconds, her irate father, Signore Riccio, shouted to his rambunctious daughter, "Teresa! Is this the way a young lady acts? Please restrain yourself and invite Antonio inside."

Signore had known Antonio since he was an infant and was best of friends with Don Fortunato; he had always liked Antonio but never dropped his austere manner when in the young man's company.

Once inside the house, Teresa did what was expected of her, retreating to a less emotional state which was the preferred demeanor of her gender. Antonio and her father conversed, and they were soon joined by Signora Riccio who was carrying a tray of multicolored liquors. She set it down near a large dish piled high with assorted sweets. Antonio was not much of a drinker, but of course he did not want to insult their hospitality.

The conversation was dominated by the men, and Teresa and her mother nodded their heads in response. All too soon it was getting late in the afternoon, and Antonio had to leave. He apologized for his brief visit and promised to stay longer on his next leave home. His hosts understood his early departure but expressed their wishes for a longer visit.

With a wistful heart, he bid farewell and left Teresa and her parents standing on the steps of their front porch as the tired sun washed the Riccio home in a crimson glow.

Antonio gently turned his horse toward the mountain road, memorizing the windblown image of his sweetheart. The red sun perched on the western horizon, warming the back of the returning soldier as he headed eastward toward Catanzaro.

The dusty miles flew by as Antonio journeyed back to the post, pausing only once to grab a morsel of food that his mother had packed and eating as he rode. It was already dark when he arrived back at the garrison, but he arrived in time for curfew. Some of his friends had begun to worry about his absence and did not want to see him get reprimanded for being late on his first leave. They were relieved when they heard the sound of his horse galloping up to the barracks.

The next morning, after reville, the troopers were called to assembly for further instructions concerning their duties of the day. They made an impressive sight on their well-groomed horses with their gray cardigans, long capes flowing from their shoulders, and knee-high black leather riding boots. Their saber scabbards glimmered in the bright sunshine as did the high-gloss stocks of their carbines.

The sergeant stood before them and said, "Gentlemen, I have to complement your smart appearance, and I hope you can perform your duties as well as you look." He then proceeded to read the orders of the day which required daily patrols consisting of four troopers to each group. They were to travel the country roads in search of any signs of rebellion against the local authorities. The attitude of the people was hostile toward their Bourbon rulers in the previous months. The patrols were to be assigned to a designated area for six-day intervals, at the end of which they would exchange for another location. This continuous rotation of troops would ultimately familiarize them with the surrounding countryside.

When the sergeant completed his orientation, the cavalry units were dismissed and immediately sent out on their mission.

After the first week of residing at the fort, the men took their new routine in stride. Their frequent trips on the roads they patrolled brought them into constant contact with the people. In the beginning, Antonio and his companions established a very cordial relationship with them, but this easy rapport with the locals soon deteriorated to a feeling of mistrust. At first, the troopers thought the changing attitude was attributed to the fact that they were in an unfamiliar area, but it was evident as time went on that it was not the case. There was a certain guilt which drove Antonio and the other Calabrians to side with the peasants who had become disdainful of Bourbon authority.

On more than one occasion, Antonio and the others discussed the breach in their relationship with the townspeople. The soldiers, being honorable, and after serious consideration, chose to remain with their Bourbon comrades they had sworn to defend. Their obligation to fulfill their duty overshadowed the young Italians' instincts to support the rebellion.

As the weeks and months slipped by, it was more evident that the people were edging toward hostility that was reflected in their actions and their speech. The daily inspection patrols made by the Bourbon cavalry were vehemently resented, and the members of the new regiment were disheartened by the change of attitude toward them.

The build-up of ill feelings was finally brought to a head one winter's night. After curfew, when most of the troopers were asleep, a dozen or more peasants broke into the armory; the culprits made off with an undetermined number of rifles and thousands of rounds of ammunition before setting delayed explosives and disappearing into the night.

The ear-shattering blast jolted the troopers from their bunks. Many at the garrison thought they were under attack by some undetected enemy. Explosion after explosion emanated from what once was the arsenal. Because of the intense heat, much of the stored artillery shells were set off at multiple intervals, leading the men to believe they were being bombarded by cannons. It took some time before they were convinced that they were not under siege. In blazing orange light, scores of troopers ran about in an effort to control the fire before it reached the other buildings. A water-bucket line was hastily devised; it took four hours to finally be extinguished. The ash-covered soldiers returned to their barracks and collapsed from exhaustion onto their bunks.

Before dawn the next morning, the entire complement of the garrison was assembled for emergency instructions. The visibly outraged colonel stood before the soldiers and impatiently waited for their complete attention. He mustered up sarcasm and finally addressed them, "I am sure you are all aware that we were visited by some local terrorists. As a result of which, our armory is still smoldering. I can assure you that these villains will be apprehended and severely dealt with. It is up to all of you to scour the surrounding area and find these cowardly dogs. You will divide into your regular patrols and begin the search immediately. It is up to you to question, bribe, or coerce the people who might know the whereabouts of these rebellious swine. You know what you must do. Do not return to the post empty handed." He dismissed the troopers; they assembled into their patrols and disappeared into the breaking dawn.

Within a short time, every patrol sought out possible hiding places that might be harboring the insurgents; many of the untraveled roads leading into the mountains were methodically combed for any signs. There was not a single farm house where the inhabitants were not questioned. The hostile reception from all shocked the cavalrymen, where months before they had been welcomed. They also could not rely on the honesty of the townsfolk and capturing anyone would be solely from their own efforts.

That evening, one by one, the cavalrymen returned dejectedly to the garrison. They all found themselves empty-handed and bewildered; they had obtained no further information than what they had already known. The Bourbon colonel awaited the return of every patrol as his anger mounted when each unit reported their lack of progress. Before any of the troopers dismounted, all of the patrols were ordered to assemble for the second time that day. On the steps of the headquarters, the outraged colonel spoke out, "Gentlemen, I know you all tried your best to obtain the whereabouts of the Italian dogs who assaulted our garrison last evening. I suspect your approach is misguided. You believed these people would confide in you and direct you to the hiding places of these despicable men. This was a naïve assumption with no results. Beginning tomorrow, we will institute new measures to extract the information we need. The relaxed attitude of the past will cease, and in its place, a tougher policy will be set into motion. If this method also fails, an even more severe policy will be adopted. Therefore, tomorrow morning, any person or persons whom you may think might be holding back any details concerning the rebels should be brought to the post for further questioning. All of you know your assigned patrols for tomorrow so please carry out my orders to the letter. Do not show any favoritism toward the people, for any number of them could be accomplices to those rebel swine. Do what you must do. Good luck and be safe. That will be all. You are dismissed."

These stern words fell heavily on the ears of the Calabrian troopers whose hearts were still on the side of the peasants. This dilemma tore the young soldiers in opposite directions, their emotions reflecting deep inner turmoil.

The following morning the patrols left the post in a somber mood. Regardless of their personal feelings, the men were determined to carry out their orders as best they could. If they thought the previous day of seeking the rebels was difficult, the troopers were in for a rude awakening.

The squads fanned out into the countryside and stopped at house after house to no avail; many occupants refused to answer the pounding on their doors. It was apparent that one day of questioning was all that the people were willing to submit to. Those who did open their doors were of very little assistance and denied having any knowledge of the identity of the insurgents or of their whereabouts. By the end of the second day, the capture of the rebels seemed improbable, if not hopeless.

The commandant was in a rage for he could not believe that the people would be that close-mouthed. Fortunately for half the soldiers at the fort, it was Sunday and only half of the patrols would be sent out to continue the search. The others, which included Antonio, were given leave. He did not feel up to visiting his parents or Teresa, but it had been a few weeks since his last visit. He knew they would be worried if he was absent from home for too much longer.

He left the garrison in a subdued manner and rode home to Maida. This time the ride seemed to take forever. Even the weather seemed to reflect his unhappiness. The sun hadn't shone for two days, and it was a cloudy, damp day, typical for the winter season in southern Italy thus making the journey very dreary.

When Antonio finally arrived home, he had not been there for quarter of an hour when his parents noticed a change in his demeanor. He had always been outgoing and hopeful in attitude, but this time he projected apathy. They had never seen this side to their son. Antonio tried to shrug off the reason for his mood when he was questioned about it. He told them it was the burden of additional duties. He did not inform them of the events of the past few weeks, but his father and mother had heard about the armory being destroyed. Not to worry his parents, he attributed the incident to a faulty explosive cap that was accidentally detonated.

To his parents' disappointment, he left after the meal, much earlier than usual. They understood and respected their son's need for hasty departure but still worried about him. "I do not know when I will be back home again, since conditions at the garrison are deteriorating daily," Antonio said when he kissed and hugged them goodbye.

He left them and took the road north to Teresa's house. He quickly covered the short distance and planned to only pay his respects. When he arrived, he jumped up their front steps with two leaping strides and knocked on the door. Signore Riccio responded and smiled when he saw that it was Antonio and welcomed him in. The family had just completed their Sunday meal. Teresa's father then suggested that his wife return the food to the already cleared table. Antonio begged their pardon, for he had just finished eating and could not eat another morsel but asked for a few moments alone with Teresa before moving on. Consent was given to the young couple, and they walked hand in hand outside to talk.

Antonio explained some of the incidents that had occurred at the garrison. He then informed her that because of these events, he did not know when his next visit would be. "Maybe you should just forget about me, Teresa," he said with sadness, "Since I will be gone for an undeterminable amount of time."

"Antonio, I am very hurt by your suggestion," she whispered and paused. "And though you would be gone for some time, it does not matter to me. You matter to me. I want to continue our relationship regardless of the circumstances, for I truly care about you." Antonio touched her cheek, and even though he did not admit the depth of his feelings, he was pleased to hear her say these words.

All too soon, it was time for Antonio to leave if he was to arrive at the post before dark. He hugged his dark-eyed Teresa, bid farewell to her parents, and left hurriedly.

He nudged his horse to a faster gait and took the road leading to the mountains. The day had become even more dismal as he climbed higher. The dark, low-hanging clouds and a heavy mist swallowed up both horse and rider. They vanished into a gray abyss. Had he not been familiar with his surroundings, he would have found it impossible to maintain a sense of direction. Even with this knowledge, Antonio was forced to ride at a much slower pace. Not only was it foggy, but the days were shorter that time of year. Early darkness would soon make visibility almost impossible. He handled his horse very carefully on the treacherous, winding trails to avoid endangering the safety of his loyal animal and his own person.

After a few tense hours of riding, they began to descend out of the dense cloud cover to find clearer views. To the relief of both Antonio and his horse, conditions improved greatly as they approached Catanzaro and the garrison.

It was at this particular place and time, a few miles from the Bourbon post, Antonio was ignorant of the fact that he was being watched by a handful of desperate men. They were the very same rebels who had sabotaged the armory, and they contemplated the fate of the lone, returning trooper. One of the seedy-looking men commented to his companions, "I could easily squeeze the trigger and pick off this Bourbon vermin and there would be one less to fight against."

"No, not now, you fool," one of his accomplices interrupted, "You would only be killing one and maybe alerting the entire fort. They could hear the shot, as we are not that far away from the garrison. Even if they didn't hear it, they would come out to investigate if he did not return by a certain hour. This is not the right time to start something. Believe me, there will be better opportunities in the future."

Fate alone saved the life of Antonio on that misty, dark evening as he rode across the open fields back to the fort.

V
WORSENING CONDITIONS

During the following weeks, the townspeople let their discontent known, worsening already critical conditions. Trees were felled, blocking the roads used by the Bourbon patrol units. Rocks were hurled from ambush, spooking the horses of passing troopers, and the opportunity to verbally assault the soldiers was never overlooked. The windows of the garrison were shattered and saddles slashed during the growing surge of rebellion.

On a routine patrol, their greatest but most valid fear became reality when a shot was fired, and a trooper slumped over in his saddle. Two of the four in the unit darted in the direction of the rifle blast, but the assassins had already vanished into the hills. The troopers returned to their fallen comrade to find him motionless in the arms of his distraught comrade.

All of the men at the garrison vowed it would be the first and only fatality at the hands of the rebels. From then on, there would be no leniency or quarter given to the radicals. Orders were not necessary; the enraged cavalrymen were more than ready to use harsher methods, already demonstrating their own brand of belligerence. A camaraderie among the troopers, both Bourbon and Calabrian, was born from the turmoil, bonds that would endure for many years to come.

As a precaution, all patrols leaving the garrison were now assigned forward observers. The lone scouts rode half a mile ahead of the others, carbines in hand, in an effort to flush out any surprise attacks. Prior to the violent rebellion, the members of the patrols always rode with their carbines tucked in their leather scabbards.

During one of the daily patrols, Antonio had pulled duty with Giacomo, his boyhood friend from Pizzo. Both were glad to have the same tour, for they had not had any time together since they first arrived at the garrison months earlier. As instructed, the assigned scout rode ahead, periodically leaving the main road to head into the underbrush and cross the road diagonally in an effort to break up any impending ambush.

On that particular day, the scout had been making his way along the dusty road when he heard the noise of a swollen river that bisected the road. A sturdy bridge, seventy-five feet in length, spanned the gap with twelve-inch thick beams and three-inch floor planks. The scout approached with caution, noticing a dozen or so men trying to dislodge the planks with heavy crowbars to make the bridge impassable. Surely they knew that wagons bound for the garrison with vital supplies would have no other route connecting Catanzaro to the seacoast and its military supply ships.

The scout turned his horse and then pushed into a full run back to the other troopers only when he thought he was out of range, but he failed to realize that a rebel lookout, positioned in a treetop, had spotted him and the others on the bridge below. Antonio, Giacomo, and the rest of the unit were leisurely making their way along the road when they heard the sound of hooves coming their way. They dismounted immediately and hid behind the dense brush. Within seconds, the hasty rider rounded the curve right past the hidden troopers. Realizing that the rider was their own scout, Antonio shouted after him and only then did he come to an abrupt halt. Out of breath, he informed the troopers of what he had seen on the bridge ahead.

They planned a surprise charge, but when they neared the half-dismantled bridge they realized the villains were nowhere to be seen. The troopers dismounted to inspect the damage. A shot rang out as soon as they stepped foot onto the bridge. Giacomo fell to the wooden planking and held his leg in pain. A series of shots followed from the opposite side of the river, splintering the planks beneath the troopers as they ducked for cover. Still more bullets came and raked the floor of the bridge and another soldier fell; the young man gripped his injured shoulder. Blood seeped out of the wound and soaked his cardigan.

Antonio was enraged at the sight of his wounded companions, especially Giacomo, whose injury was clearly agonizing. Antonio quickly motioned to the scout to follow him. They sprang onto their horses and sped across the remaining planks to the other side of the bridge as bullets flew, some slamming into the wood.

Once they reached solid ground, Antonio put the leather reins into his mouth and clenched them between his teeth, held his carbine in his left hand and drew his saber with the other. He spurred his horse and charged the cluster of trees harboring the rebels. The scout followed close behind Antonio's heels, and with sabers drawn, the two made a frontal assault upon the hidden snipers, disappearing into the low-hanging foliage. Within seconds, screams and shots rose above the raging river as troopers on the bridge listened in pained suspense. Then silence, minutes later.

Antonio and the scout finally emerged from the thick foliage and paused to wipe blood from their sabers with handfuls of oak leaves. They calmly proceeded to wave to the men on the bridge, a signal that they were all right.

"My big friend, did you teach them a lesson?" Giacomo managed to ask Antonio when he and the scout returned to the bridge.

"Did we?" Antonio smirked. "There are four rebels who will never see tomorrow, and the rest of them must still be running for their lives."

"Buono," Giacomo replied, "They were asking for this for some time now."

The weary patrol gathered up their wounded and reached the safety of the garrison. The doctor and the commandant were summoned immediately, and the injured men were carried to the hospital ward for treatment. The colonel asked a half dozen questions, among them the number of rebels involved, the kind of weapons, and the method of attack while the remaining members of the patrol provided answers.

The patrol was allowed to return to their quarters after a half hour, but Antonio opted to visit Giacomo at the hospital. The wounded but surprisingly cheerful man was glad to see his friend. Antonio was relieved to hear that the bullet had gone through the flesh cleanly and would not impede the use of Giacomo's leg in any way.

The other soldier who had taken a bullet in the shoulder was not as fortunate. The bones were shattered, making future use of the arm impossible.

During the following days, patrols were doubled and more cautious methods were adopted. Everyone at the garrison anticipated reprisal actions to be launched against them; but expectations were to no avail, and six days passed without incident. The rebel retaliation never materialized to the surprise of the grateful Bourbons.

The damaged bridge had been repaired, and the supply wagons resumed their twice-weekly trips to the garrison.

In anticipation of an ambush along the route, escort guards were increased to fend off any future surprise attacks.

To everyone's amazement, there were no further attacks upon any of the patrols or the garrison itself. The uneventful days turned into weeks, and still, no rebel retaliation.

Two months without insurrection, and the extra guards were removed from the supply wagons. Normally-manned patrols resumed their daily surveillance of the roads and countryside as before. Even the attitude of the people began to revert to polite and amiable ways as they knew there was nothing to be gained by butting heads with the Bourbon rule. The bloody events of prior months seemed like a nightmare that had no place in reality. Those in the garrison could not understand this complete change in attitude, but assumed that the few rebels who had taken part in the uprising had tested the Bourbon military to see how far they could be provoked before taking serious action and received more than they had anticipated.

The return of calmer times was a welcome reprieve for the troopers, and their schedules resumed to normal duties. After months of double work shifts and little time off, more leisure time inspired the men to be more relaxed and easy in their ways. Days off were restored, and Antonio looked forward to visiting his parents the following Sunday.

Before the first beams of sun penetrated the morning's low-lying clouds, Antonio dressed while the others slept. Carrying his boots to avoid making a sound, he walked between two rows of bunks and quietly opened the barrack door. Once outside, he slipped his boots on and made his way to the stable while he buttoned his cardigan in haste. He saddled his horse and walked the even-tempered stallion far enough away from the barracks before he mounted and bounded away for fear of some angry Bourbon sergeant finding some nonsensical job that would waste half the hours of his day.

The gray spring morning shaped up to be fresh and clear as Antonio took to the mountain road, leaving the garrison miles behind both physically and emotionally. He leaned forward in the saddle, making it easier for his horse to climb. The loyal animal extended his powerful forelegs, trying to conquer the steep mountain grade. Climbing higher into even steeper elevation, for the first time in months, Antonio began to feel like his old self. The welcome warmth of sun on his face and sharp mountain air in his lungs stirred magical, nostalgic feelings that had been buried. The almost-palpable fragrance of spring gave both man and beast a sense of promise and hope for better times ahead. Antonio memorized all of it as he and his horse traveled lightly upon the face of the mountain. He wanted to freeze the sense of bliss in order to call upon it during some future time of need.

After fording swollen, platinum streams and traversing gorges, Antonio neared the end of his journey. He rode through the next pine-studded valley into open plains which led directly to his family home. He crossed familiar fields of overturned fertile soil waiting for the planting season and then his beloved hometown of Maida came into full view.

As he approached the edge of town, Antonio thought he recognized a horse-drawn carriage a quarter of a mile ahead. He drew closer, and to his surprise, found that the carriage belonged to his father. Antonio nudged his horse to quicken the pace until he was riding alongside his startled and overjoyed family who were just returning from Sunday Mass at La Chiesa, Santa Maria Cattolica, largest of three Roman Catholic churches in town.

Antonio reached in with one hand and tousled the hair of his two excited younger brothers and his sister Rosa seated just behind their parents and then moved to the front of the carriage. Don Fortunato, laughing with surprise, held the reins with one hand and extended the other to his son. His mother reached over and quickly squeezed his hand, smiling at her strong, flame-haired boy who had grown into a man to be proud of.

Antonio escorted his family the rest of the way home, riding with joy and conversing with the people he loved so dearly.

His parents were pleased to see that their son had returned to his usual more care-free personality; there was not a trace of the sullen seriousness in his demeanor they had seen during his previous visit home. Their high spirits coincided with the warm, fragrant spring afternoon.

Antonio left his parents' house and headed toward Teresa's three miles away. He was greeted with delight, the entire Riccio family glad to see his old caring ways and easy smile. Their rapport was obvious, and despite the fact that Antonio had not formally asked for Teresa's hand in marriage, it was an understood fact that someday they would marry. They had grown to love and care for each other through the years, and her family treated him as they would their own son. His relationship with Teresa could only result in an honorable and content union.

The sun began its descent in the western sky, and Antonio bid farewell to his intended in-laws who had never felt as close to him as they had that particular day. After the reluctant parting, Antonio journeyed eastward to the garrison with the scarlet sun setting at his back.

The weeks slipped by rapidly, and months passed almost unnoticed. The routine of army life ravenously consumed the precious commodity of time. Few changes, if any, were made in that region of Calabria. The Calabrian people accepted the presence of the Bourbon army as part of their lives. This attitude seemed to reflect the general opinion of the inhabitants of southern Italy. During this era of relatively quiet times, any action would be considered rebellious and was nearly unheard of. However, hidden from the surface, a mounting restlessness and inner turmoil festered. This was most clearly demonstrated in the cold stares of the locals whenever an armed Bourbon patrol trotted by; the undertones for insurrection were apparent to the discerning onlooker.

For the time being, the true feelings of the disillusioned Italians were suppressed until a more appropriate moment in history.

VI
OPEN HOSTILITIES

It had been almost a year since the day Bourbon troopers were ambushed at the half-dismantled bridge; the time seemed to have passed almost too peacefully until the spring of 1860 when a series of events took place near the town of Catanzaro which catapulted the entire region into open warfare.

On a beautiful, sun-dazzled morning in the second week of April, three wagons loaded with supplies had just crossed the reconstructed bridge and headed toward the garrison. They were not yet one hundred yards past the bridge when a massive tree fell to the rear across the road and cut off any retreat. Within seconds, another tree obstructed their path to the front. The armed guards assigned to the wagons raised their weapons in anticipation of an attack, but despite their hurried shots, rebels swung down ropes hanging from the tall trees lining the road and pounced upon the guards with sudden fury. Two Bourbons along with a driver were killed instantly. The remaining Bourbons were taken as prisoners and the supplies confiscated. The rebels loaded the goods onto pack horses and vanished into the mountains.

When the supply wagons failed to arrive by a certain hour, a patrol was dispatched from the garrison. The troopers had not ridden more than two miles when they came upon the fallen trees and the empty, over-turned wagons. The men dismounted their horses and carefully proceeded with their carbines drawn and discovered the bodies of the guards and the driver.

With the aid of their horses, the patrol dragged the trees aside, making the road passable and then drove the wagons with the dead back to the safety of the garrison. Enraged troopers crowded about and demanded swift vengeance with no quarter given.

The patrols were doubled that evening, and for the first time in more than a year, extra sentries were assigned at the fort.

The morning light found two wagon drivers and the remaining Bourbon guard released without harm, shuffling along the dusty road that led to the garrison. When the disheveled men entered the compound, they informed their superiors that the reason for release was to deliver a message to the commander of the post: the ambush was only the beginning. The troopers knew they could not let their vigilance wane, not even for a moment, or suffer the consequences.

Three days after the ambush, six brazen rebels rode up to the garrison gate and shot both sentries. Again, the Italians were too quick and methodical to give the Bourbon army even a second to react. By the time the fort was alerted and patrols were sent out, the assassins were a good distance ahead, but the ensuing chase brought both closer. The rebels rounded a bend in the road and temporarily disappeared from view. Antonio and the other pursuing troopers came around the curve to find the six rebels waiting patiently in the middle of the road. The patrol slowed to a halt, and the sergeant ordered the men to draw their sabers. Antonio glanced at his friend Giacomo and raised an eyebrow with misgiving. He knew something was not right and expected what would come next.

Twenty or so armed rebels emerged from cover and fanned out, leaving the patrol to take stock of their precarious position. The sergeant turned in his saddle and pointed to the rear patrol with his raised saber. For a moment, the troopers in the rear were puzzled by the sergeant's motion until Giacomo turned to see the road behind them blocked by ten mounted rebels.

From the front, one of the assassins addressed the cavalry, "Bourbons, what is the matter? Are the rats trapped with nowhere to go? I have a bargain for you. Hand over all of your weapons and your horses, and we will let you walk back to the garrison in one piece. What do you say to that?" The proud sergeant had no reply and spat on the ground. He then spoke in Spanish and ordered his men to divide into two equal groups; the first were instructed to attack straight ahead while the second would charge to the rear.

Without wasting an instant, the tough veteran sergeant extended his saber and pointed it toward the disbelieving faces of the rebels who apparently interpreted the move as a futile, last-ditch effort to escape. Spurring their horses, Antonio and Giacomo spearheaded the attack to the rear as a volley of shots erupted from both flanks. Joined by the rest of the rear patrol, the brave troopers charged at a full run in two ranks of three toward the waiting rebels blocking the road.

The first three Bourbon horsemen fired their carbines as they approached the rebels, knocking two of them from their horses. They quickly returned their spent carbines to their scabbards and drew their sabers as the gap between them and the Italians shortened. The rebels did not hesitate any longer and fired a volley of shots which knocked a charging Bourbon from his horse and wounded a second trooper who managed to remain mounted. The four unharmed Bourbons continued to charge and clashed blades with the opposing insurgents; the decisive thrusts of their sabers inflicted quick and serious injury. Though outnumbered, they were skillful enough to put six insurgents out of battle while the four remaining rebels ran for their lives.

On first instinct, Antonio and his three companions

wanted to charge down the road to help the forward patrol, but with further consideration, they realized that by the time they reached their comrades, the four of them could be reduced to zero. Instead, they decided to head back to the garrison for help and return with more men.

Antonio and the other three men arrived at the post and enlisted the aid of fifty troopers who had been on alert for hours. Antonio and Giacomo led the way, and the troop of cavalrymen hurried back to the scene of the battle. As soon as the soldiers were in sight, the rebels retreated and disappeared into the woods. The reinforcements continued to ride at breakneck speed to where the courageous sergeant and his men were last seen fighting. When the small army of soldiers turned the bend in the road, they were stunned to see the number of men, dead and wounded. Antonio and Giacomo dismounted immediately and began to comb through the moaning, pain-wracked men. To their despair, they came upon four limp bodies of their comrades with weapons still in their hands.

Two troopers, including the sergeant and a young corporal, remained unaccounted for. After further searching, Giacomo discovered the two missing men behind a large boulder where they had fled for cover. The younger soldier was on his back and still breathing. Blood oozed from a bullet wound in his shoulder and a saber slash on his thigh. Behind the wounded trooper, the valiant sergeant sat with his back to a tree, unconscious with his head hanging forward. His left leg had taken a bullet and a great deal of blood loss was evident, but he was still alive.

Antonio and the other men picked up the dead along with wounded and returned to the fort.

Things quieted down during the following weeks, but the daily patrols were reinforced and a watchful eye was kept. Sudden danger lurking behind the next tree, bush, or boulder was anticipated. The entire garrison swore to the Almighty God that they would never be lured into another ambush and decided that utmost caution would be used before reacting to a situation, and when possible, force the rebels to fight on their terms; seeking out insurgents had already proved to be too costly to the Bourbon Cavalry. The commandant, along with the rest of the officers at the post, was racking his brain trying to devise methods to coerce the rebels out into the open and fight in a more orthodox fashion.

Wagons carried goods from Bourbon supply ships anchored in the Gulf of Squillace and were increased from three wagons to seven weekly. As a result, additional ammunition and weapons were added to the ever-swelling stockpile of military hardware. Along with the wagons came a company of much-needed reinforcements who escorted the heavy laden wagons to the garrison. These new cavalrymen were fresh from the Bourbon training camp in Sicily. Nonetheless, these untried troopers would be welcome help to the veterans at the post.

The wagons were so heavy with supplies that they were barely able to make the trip. Four-horse teams were assigned to pull each wagon, but the load was still burdensome over the fifteen-mile uphill journey to the fort at Catanzaro. The road harbored numerous places ideal for an ambush, but protection from a full company of cavalrymen thwarted any attempt to intercept the wagons which would have proven to be suicidal for any would-be attackers. Trailing behind each wagon was the extra burden of an artillery piece mounted on the carriage. These new field pieces had been requested by the commandant to bolster the garrison's firepower.

When the escort of new troopers and the supply wagons arrived safely at the post, the entire garrison turned out to greet them and get a look at the new artillery pieces they had brought with them. The commandant was jubilant over the safe arrival of both men and equipment. The colonel personally welcomed the new men and inspected the new brass cannons with enthusiasm. Standing on one of the wagons, he addressed the assembled troopers, "Gentlemen, today we have tipped the balance of power to our advantage. Our firepower capability has greatly increased with the arrival of these artillery pieces. Even though we are as an island surrounded by a sea of rebels, I feel we now have the edge. However, do not fool yourselves! As I am speaking to you this very moment, I am very sure that the ambushing insurgents already have knowledge of the number of cannons that have arrived here. Indirectly, this is exactly what I wish, for they might think twice before starting any further trouble if they know fully of our destructive capabilities." The colonel paused, turned to the soldiers newly arriving, and then continued, "I would like to welcome the new men who have joined our ranks and wish them good fortune. I know we veterans will demonstrate our gratitude to them for joining us. Again, welcome aboard. Let us now resume our normal duties. Good day, gentlemen."

Never had the garrison been so optimistic about the future. The following three weeks were uneventful and a pleasant reprieve for the troopers. Their minds were still fresh with the tragic events that occurred just weeks earlier. During this lull, rebel activity had ceased to be a thorn in the side of the garrison; even the verbal attacks from the not-so-violent townspeople gradually dwindled, but in no way were the Bourbons planning to relax or let down their guard and become vulnerable to the ever present threat of rebellion.

Giacomo had been assigned to early morning reconnaissance and was instructed to scour the fields and countryside for potential trouble. One morning, during a routine patrol, just four miles from the garrison, he caught a glimpse of smoke rising from a heavily wooded area. He alerted the other patrol members, and they quickly dismounted and approached the area on foot. A few hundred yards into the woods, they began to hear the dull sound of wood being chopped. Soon they heard the faint sounds of conversation accompanied by noises of a large and busy campground. The patrol advanced another hundred yards and came upon a wide clearing. The troopers approached silently, close enough to recognize some of the rebels' faces. Three or more of the men were recognized as participants in the recent, brutal conflicts. The Bourbons continued to move around the perimeter of the camp and were able to estimate the number of insurgents. Judging from the size and number of fireplaces scattered about, they determined the opposing force to be between ninety and one hundred and twenty in strength.

The troopers took in as much information as they could and then quietly retraced their steps through the dense trees until they reached the road.

The colonel, upon hearing the news about the rebel headquarters, was excited to have inside knowledge so they could devise a scheme which would ensnare the entire lot.

The commandant did not have to wait too long, for within two days' time, the rebels presented him with the opportunity to do just that. The conniving Italians had initiated their own plan, believing that the Bourbon soldiers were unaware of their hideout so close to the Catanzaro garrison.

A dozen brazen mounted rebels assaulted the fort in broad daylight. The soldiers were astounded by this action, for the insurgents must surely have realized that the post's complement of men had nearly doubled in number with the recent arrival of reinforcements. The colonel saw through the façade of the so-called attack by the inadequate number of rebels besieging the post. The screaming malcontents, waving their rifles and shooting wildly, were obviously attempting to goad the Bourbon soldiers into chasing after them as they had in the past. The troopers hesitated before they played along, and four patrols were ready to chase after the scoundrels. As anticipated, the ten or so rebels quickly ceased firing and began their retreat westward in hopes of being followed by the irate troopers. Their plan was to stay far enough ahead of the pursuers but in easy sight of them so they could lure them to the road adjacent to their wooded hideout. Once there, the rebel comrades would be waiting to ambush the patrols. Unknown to the rebels, the soldiers executed a counterplot. The colonel, intending to use the impending attack to his favor, dispatched the newly-arrived artillery pieces to the north of the region. His plan was to shell the woods behind the ambushing insurgents and force them out of hiding and out into the open fields to the south. Another much larger group of cavalry was to follow in support of the first four patrols and pursue the fleeing rebels.

As the rebel horsemen approached a section of woods, a few riders turned about to assess the distance between them and the soldiers; to their surprise, the following patrols slowed down to halt as they approached the edge of the adjoining woods. The rebels continued to ride past their hidden comrades, hoping to see the soldiers resume the chase. Instead, the patrols stopped entirely and waited for something. The rebels were puzzled and unnerved as they fumbled for their next move. Suddenly, the signal was given, and the colonel's carefully positioned cannons north of the woods commenced firing.

The first shells landed directly on the rebel encampment in the center of the woods. Fortunately for the rebels, most of them were toward the road and south of the camp, but the entire encampment was demolished after two cannon bombardments. The smoking artillery pieces were then calibrated three hundred yards south and then reset to strike another hundred yards beyond in an attempt to drive any hidden insurgents from their camouflaged positions.

When the first cannon shells struck the interior of their wooded refuge, the startled rebels moved their positions closer to the road. They hoped the bombardments would stop after the Bourbons realized the rebel encampment had been destroyed, but when the next barrage of shells struck further south, some of the insurgents realized what was happening. The rebels had little choice and retreated closer to the road for safety. The shells landed still nearer, bursting with ferocity and fragmenting into hundreds of small death-delivering pellets. Only a hundred yards from the exploding cannon fire and the open road, the rebel ring-leaders realized that the next barrage of shells could come hailing down on their heads if they didn't move from their position. The word was passed to move out to the open road where they outnumbered the four Bourbon patrols six to one then they burst forth from their hidden posts. The soldiers turned off the road and trotted into an open field when the shouting irate rebels emerged from the dense expansive woods and pursued the soldiers with swords and rifles. A third of the rebels were mounted and led the chase with the rest of their men on foot. Surprisingly, again the Bourbons slowed and came to a halt, this time turning to face the oncoming insurgents who were still a hundred and fifty yards away. The rebel leaders were bewildered by the actions of the outnumbered patrols. The sixteen Bourbon cavalrymen were no match for the entire opposing band of one hundred plus, yet they were not going to run, thus waited patiently for the onslaught of screaming insurgents. To the rear of the attacking rebels, the full complement of troopers from the garrison slowly made their way to the edge of the battle; the hundred or so troopers had waited a mile away until the artillery bombardments had ceased before they began to trot behind the charging rebels. They had taken their time, and the large rear guard of troopers patiently followed the insurgents; their arrival was utterly unforeseen. The slow, advancing rear column of Bourbons picked up the pace as they prodded their horses to a faster gallop. The gap between the rebels and waiting patrols began to shorten, and the soldiers prepared for the siege by drawing their sabers. The troopers looked beyond the attackers and were encouraged by the sight of their comrades advancing on the heels of the rebel army. The rear column of cavalry sounded a bugle charge when fifty yards of separation was between the two forces; it was a sudden surprise to the rebels. The insurgents tried to react, but of course, it was too late and their fates were sealed. The men floundered about as the two ranks of Bourbons closed the trap. The cavalry and the rebels finally made contact, the sound of clashing sabers and the screams of fallen men reverberating. Both sides were almost equal in number with the rebels having a slight edge. Regardless, the well-disciplined troopers quickly disseminated the ranks of their foe with precision. The rebels, realizing their defeat, began to disperse and run for their lives.

In a short time, the insurgents were completely routed, scattering in all directions with the cavalry in hot pursuit. Within an hour, the returning troopers had managed to capture thirty-seven rebels; these prisoners, along with twenty-three wounded and twelve dead, accounted for almost half the number of men who took part in the battle. In comparison, the Bourbons suffered light casualties with eleven wounded and three dead.

The rebels' defeat led to the complete breakdown of the insurgent movement, and as a direct result, the local inhabitants never again supported such an extensive rebellion. The wiser and more sensible people feared the Bourbon might.

It would not be until August of 1860, with the arrival of

Garibaldi, that the inhabitants would ever think of overpowering the Bourbon military.

VII
CROSSING TO THE MAINLAND

The army of Garibaldini volunteers had increased to twelve thousand as they assembled at the northeastern tip of Sicily around the village of Faro. Here Garibaldi planned to assault Reggio and Calabria on the opposite shore. Across the strait on the mainland, opposite Faro, were two small Bourbon forts, Torre Cavello and Altifiumara. The strategic locations of these forts commanded an unobstructed view of the narrow passageway to the straits. From these two positions the Bourbon gun emplacements could easily demolish any attempt made by invaders venturing near the coast. A possible invasion would be quite difficult with the massive firepower and sixteen thousand Neapolitan troops camped nearby. Regardless of these factors, Garibaldi had a plan to send two hundred men across the turbulent narrows under the cover of darkness in an attempt to capture one of these forts. If he could seize the heavy guns at Altifiumara he could then force Bourbon warships out of the strait. This would insure the safety of his remaining volunteers in their crossing of the narrows. With the aid of hundreds of fishing boats and two old steamers, they would make the crossing.

A Calabrian was chosen from Garibaldi's army to cross to the mainland. Dressed in disguise, he arrived a few days before the rest of the men. His mission was to devise a way of having one of the fort's gates to be opened from within, insuring the easy capture of the fort. Hopefully by daybreak and before the Bourbon troops could gather and resist, the main part of the army of volunteers would be across; this was the plan, and Garibaldi waited for the ideal time to carry it out.

Finally, on the night of August 8, 1860, the general got his chance. With a small army of two hundred men in rowboats under a clouded sky, they moved quietly out toward the strait. The volunteers made their way in the dark past several Bourbon warships and were able to land undetected near the fort. As they got closer, they realized that the main gate was still closed. Evidently their Calabrian friend in disguise was unable to get the gate open in time, and their presence was discovered as shots rang out. Without an alternative, the rebels began to retreat toward the mountains.

With great difficulty, each man helped the one below,

fleeing up the steepest terrain, deeper into the highlands. By the morning of the next day they found themselves thousands of feet above the fort.

The volunteers were now positioned on the summit of a mountain which was part of a range known as Aspromonte meaning *harsh mountain.* The elevation was so significant that the men baked under the brutal summer sun by day and shivered with cold by night. They lit bonfires in the darkness to prove their presence and to frighten the Bourbons below.

Local mountaineers in their knee pants and conical hats joined the ranks of the freedom fighters. In a display of support, mules loaded with food supplies were sent up by the volunteers from Reggio to the rebels. With this helping hand, the Italian volunteers began to take action once again against the Bourbons.

They came down from the coast one night feeling confident and brazenly took over the town of Bagnara for several hours and then returned to the mountains.

On August 18, a second wave of volunteers consisting of thirty-four hundred men boarded two steamers anchored just south of Taormina, Sicily. Their objective was to come ashore fifteen miles south of Reggio, Calabria at Melito. This wave of men was comprised of the union of two armies that had fought throughout Sicily.

Leaving his men at Faro, Garibaldi took command of the second wave along with his second in command, General Bixio. The two old steamers sailed easily to the mainland. They found it deserted when they landed at the port of

Melito. The next Bourbon garrison at Reggio was fifteen miles north where a thousand men were stationed. The steamers landed undetected in the dark of night.

Two Bourbon warships spotted the docked steamers the following day and destroyed one of them. That night, in the mountains above, the second expedition of Italian volunteers was joined by the first group of freedom fighters. This formed a more substantial army to continue the fight.

At the Reggio fort, General Galotti, along with a thousand Bourbons, believed the enemy would attack from the sea and failed to acknowledge the warnings of a possible invasion by other means. He was unprepared and left the walls and gates of the fort guarded by disinterested locals who had been organized into a makeshift army. Thus, on midnight August 21, 1860, Garibaldi and his rebels marched through the gates of the fort and advanced to the center of Reggio without a shot being fired. Eventually, the Bourbon army was alerted and fought fiercely and to no avail against the Garibaldini, for they were greatly outnumbered. The Bourbons retreated back to the castle and stood fast, prepared to last for weeks within its walls.

It was not too long before reinforcements of two thousand Bourbons arrived, but they suddenly retreated from view when they had been ordered by their general to not fight the Garibaldini.

The Bourbons defending the castle became disoriented and were easy targets for the Italian freedom fighters who had positioned sharp shooters on the high ground above the rear of the castle walls. They killed numerous Bourbon soldiers at their battlement positions. Within hours, Reggio was seized with little effort. The fort surrendered to the rebel army not long after.

General Enrico Cosenz—Garibaldi's third in command—and his fifteen hundred men crossed the strait with success but were quickly surrounded by two Bourbon armies. The encircled Cosenz and his men fought their way through the Bourbons and escaped into the mountains. Eventually, he and Garibaldi with two armies of rebels were able to divert and split the Bourbon resistance and their effectiveness.

With the surrender of Reggio, Garibaldi was seen as an invincible leader, who until then had led a charmed life. Because of this victorious image, he and General Cosenz were able to capture fort after fort along the southwestern coast of Italy. Operating from two different bases, they managed to successfully divide the Bourbon armies. The enemy soldiers became easy targets for both liberating generals; many of the garrisons were now taken without firing a shot, mainly because the Bourbon armies consisted of sympathetic drafted Italians. Once captured, these Italians were given the choice to go free and return home or join forces with Garibaldi; the majority chose the former.

Groups led by wealthy land barons emerged from Calabria and Basilicata and joined forces with Garibaldi. With this support, Garibaldi was able to defeat many Bourbon strongholds in southern Italy. The enemy soldiers surrendered their forts and quickly retreated northward and hurried back to the large Bourbon garrison at Naples. On this retreat, twelve thousand Bourbon troops were caught between an army of six thousand Calabrian rebels led by local land barons and an army of veteran Garibaldini in the northwestern part of Calabria. Felled trees both to the rear and forward positions prevented the Bourbons from either advancing or retreating. Having evaluated their position as desperate, the trapped army chose not to fight and gave up their weapons and surrendered to the rebels. Though, the Bourbons had a very good chance of overpowering the rebels, they were too demoralized to fight. The surrendering soldiers were allowed to join the rebel volunteers after they had given up their horses and weapons.

With the defeat of the Bourbon forces in southern Italy, Garibaldi set his sights northward on the city of Naples.

VIII
CAPTURE

Antonio and the rest of the Bourbon brigade rode from Monteleone intending to escort routed Neapolitan-Bourbons retreating northward. They made an attempt to out-distance the quickly advancing Garibaldini. The demoralized army believed they were a full day's ahead of the pursuing Italians and had halted their march on the outskirts of the town of Nicastro where they set up camp for a few hours to rest and care for the wounded. The Bourbons' apathy led them to leave the perimeters unguarded. Garibaldi's army, though outnumbered three to one, managed to outflank the resting Bourbons on three sides. This left only the position facing the mountains as the sole means of escape.

As the army relaxed in their vulnerable position, a high-pitched bugle charge shattered the silence, and the red-shirted Italian cavalry swept through the stunned enemy. The defenseless Bourbons dispersed in every direction. Foot soldiers were captured or forced to surrender while cavalrymen took their horses and fled toward the mountains.

Antonio, Giacomo, and two other Calabrians were badly routed by the rebel cavalry and became separated from their unit. Disorder and chaos overran the helpless Bourbon officers. The entire brigade had been divided into small confused bands of fleeing men. Antonio and the three other bewildered Bourbons paused to assess their dilemma in the hills above Nicastro.

The cavalrymen discussed possible alternatives while hidden behind a stone outcropping. Two of the four men had been superficially wounded during the surprise attack; Antonio had been slashed across the bicep even before he could have drawn his saber from the scabbard. Giacomo was also wounded during the charge and received a deep gash on the calf. The other two Bourbons—Francesco Bozzi, the son of a shoemaker from Sambiase and Giovanni Scatlolla, a cabinet-maker's son from nearby Nicastro—remained unharmed.

The men, unaware and still mounted on their horses, huddled together and barely had time before they were besieged again by eight Italian Red Shirts who had charged from the thick woods nearby. Again, before any of them could draw their swords, they were staring down the barrels of a half dozen carbines. Regretfully, without a choice, the cornered Bourbons handed over their weapons to their captors. They were immediately bound with their hands behind their backs.

The sergeant was unmistakably from northern Italy, his dialect strange to his Calabrian captives. The wary prisoners were informed that they would be taken to the closest Garibaldi headquarters for interrogation. The nearest camp was located on the coast, a dozen miles to the west.

Four of the eight Italian soldiers soon departed, leaving the other four horsemen to guard and escort the captured Bourbons.

As the captives and their guards traveled westerly to the sea, darkness was imminent. Being from the north, the Italian soldiers became increasingly cautious, for their knowledge of the Calabrian geography was limited. On the other hand, the four captives had traveled the same roads on countless occasions during their early years.

As they approached a turn in the road ahead, one of the Italian rebel guards dropped back to have a word with the others. After a few muffled sentences were spoken, the prisoners were ordered to halt. The sergeant asked his comrades if that particular place would be a suitable to stop for a break. Three of the guards agreed and dismounted, disappearing behind some thickets to relieve themselves. They left one Italian guarding Antonio and the other prisoners. The guard asked the captives if they, too, needed to relieve themselves; they all declined. He responded by shrugging his shoulders then casually lifted his right leg over the pommel of the saddle and rested his carbine on his crossed leg. He struck a match and lit a small cigar. Antonio realized that there would be no better chance if they were ever going to make a run for it. Once he got Giacomo's attention, he motioned to him to alert the other two. They responded immediately and were aware of what they must do in the following moments.

A few seconds later, Antonio shouted, "Escapare! Run!" Simultaneously, the prisoners spurred their horses and then bolted away into the dusk. Sparks flew in their wake as the steel-hooved horses struck the stones beneath them. Before the startled guard could squeeze off a hurried shot, the escaping prisoners disappeared into the shadows of the woods with their hands still bound behind them.

The fleeing captives crouched low in their saddles as their frightened horses ran for their lives through the mountains. It was a harrowing ordeal for the men to maintain their balance with their hands tied behind them. It was an almost impossible maneuver to remain aboard the runaway mounts. The half-crazed horses twisted their way along a dim and winding mountainous trail but began to tire from the blazing pace they had set for themselves.

They finally slowed to a trot with the comforting reassurance of their riders. Slowing further to a walk, the valiant beasts snorted and breathed heavily as they ultimately came to a halt. Miraculously, none of the four men had been thrown. Feeling grateful, they dismounted and managed to free themselves by loosening each other's ropes in back-to-back fashion.

They hadn't the slightest idea how far they had traveled or whether or not they were being pursued. There were no sounds of horses behind them, so they felt a temporary feeling of safety. They huddled together to discuss their next move. It was not an option to try to rejoin the brigade, as it was now dispersed. More than half of the cavalry had been captured by the Italians and the remainder of the routed brigade had split up into small groups and scattered into the hills and mountains for refuge. If the fugitives ventured westward to the coast, they would undoubtedly run into searching patrols as the Italian army would be pushing their way up Calabria's coast. To go southward would be suicide for the area had already been overrun and was controlled by the Italians. It was a unanimous decision that the four of them, now fugitives, would ride northeastward further into the mountains.

They did not wait for daylight and quickly headed for higher and more rugged country. They rode most of the night and only halted when exhausted. The hours of hard, monotonous riding had not helped Giacomo's or Antonio's wounds. Antonio's injured arm was only a surface wound, but it began to throb nonetheless. Giacomo's slashed leg had been seriously affected by the long-strenuous hours on horseback and had to be helped to the ground when he attempted to dismount by himself unsuccessfully. His companions gently lifted him from his horse and set him on a blanket.

The morning sun began to rise in the eastern sky as the men finally made camp. It was the end of August of 1860, and the warmth of the sun was a comfort to the tired, saddle-weary men. Rest for a day or two was what both injured men desperately needed in order to heal.

In the meantime, Francesco and Giovanni did the camp chores and made an effort to make their wounded comrades as comfortable as can be. Antonio was very obstinate and tried in vain to help prepare the fire for cooking of what little food they had with them. He had lost quite a bit of blood, and the slightest exertion made him feel faint. Giacomo, on the other hand, had little if any choice; his loss of blood and the pulsing pain in his leg made him feverish. It was evident that both men needed to remain idle for an indeterminate amount of time.

At the same time, twenty miles west near Nicastro, the irate Italian horsemen whom the four Bourbons had escaped from were joined by other cavalrymen and began to search for the fugitives' trail. Painstakingly, these red-shirted cavalrymen retraced the steps of the escaped prisoners. By mid-afternoon the following day, the Italians had progressed only four miles on the elusive trail left by the fleeing men. The hard, rocky terrain made it very difficult for them to pick up the tracks of the Bourbon horses. Time went by too quickly for the pursuing Italians, as they had managed only a total of six miles before darkness halted their efforts. At that rate they would never catch the fugitives.

The Italian cavalrymen continued their search at the

first sign of light the following morning. All through that day, as the one before, their progress was frustrating, but they were able to cover two miles further than the preceding day. Nevertheless, the disheartened Italians agreed to continue for another twenty-four hours before giving up. They knew two of the fugitives had been wounded in the battle and hoped their injuries would slow their progress.

Once again, at the dawn of the third day of the search, the steadfast Garibaldini cavalrymen picked up the Bourbon prisoners' trail. The terrain became even more rugged as the steep, craggy mountainsides and precipitous gorges greatly slowed the pursuing party. Only four miles had been traveled by one o'clock, and at that point, dissention broke out among the men. More than half of them wanted to give up the futile trail and believed the prisoners were surely many miles away and would never be caught. Compromising to some degree, the Italian sergeant who led the patrol, agreed to end looking for the Bourbons if they were not found by sunset. A few miles further, they would be entering an isolated and heavily forested region known as La Sila. Had the fugitives made it that far, the chances of finding them would be improbable.

Unaware of the approaching search party, the four outlaws were in the process of breaking up camp and getting ready to leave. The wounded men, having been idle for almost three days, rallied back to health considerably, thanks to the care and patience of both Francesco and Giovanni. Antonio's arm was stiff, but the wound had healed well. Giacomo had also recuperated considering the very high fever that ravaged his body for almost twenty-four hours. He was also fortunate that the tendon in his leg had not been severed. Another half an inch and he would have lost the use of his leg. Somehow Antonio's high-spirited friend was already trying to walk about unassisted. Giacomo provoked sharp criticism from his friends by leaning on a make-shift crutch and hopping about on his good leg. They all thought it was much too early for him to be walking, but the hard-headed young Calabrian would not have it any other way.

As they gathered up their meager belongings, the hunted men proceeded to load their gear onto their rested and well-fed horses. They agreed it would not be safe to spend another night at the same camp, and they certainly did not want to overextend their good fortune. They had planned to ride four or five miles further to the safety of La Sila. Their current camp site was situated on a rocky, treeless mountain that overlooked a twisting valley below. Francesco was placing his canteen of water into his saddle bag when it slipped from his hands. It bounced and rolled a few feet from the mountain's edge. Annoyed with himself, he walked around his horse to pick up the fallen water jug, and as he bent forward, his eye caught the flash of sunlight reflecting off a metal object far below. He quickly alerted the others to come over to have a look. Antonio uncased a small telescope and carefully scanned the valley beneath them. Francesco pointed to the area when he saw the reflection once again. Antonio was then able to focus and pick up the movement of figures below. He easily made out the images of a dozen or more Italian horsemen. He also recognized two of the men as the ones who had guarded them the night they had escaped. He closed his telescope and suggested, "My friends, we had better move quickly for in less than half an hour we will be entertaining these Red Shirts. They do surprise me, I must confess. I thought they would have given up our trail by now. They are a determined bunch. Quickly, douse the fire. Andiamo, let's go."

Without further hesitation, they mounted their horses and slipped down the opposite side of the mountain and escaped into the forest below. They set a brisk pace, for their horses were rested and could have ridden well into the night if necessary; whereas their pursuers would never be able to maintain such a pace on their already-tired horses. In a few hours it would be dark and it would make it impossible for them to follow the fugitives' trail.

The Italian cavalrymen entered the recently vacated outlaw camp twenty-five minutes later. The weary searchers were encouraged by the realization that the hunted men had just departed; the embers in the fire were still glowing hot. The sergeant paused for a moment before making a decision. He was well aware that the fleeing men had the advantage. It was obvious they had been encamped there for a number of days indicating their horses were rested and fed. It was five o'clock in the afternoon with approximately three to five hours of remaining daylight. The greatest disadvantage facing the search party was the fact that they had been riding since daybreak, and both they and the horses were fatigued.

The disheveled pursuers reluctantly followed the fresh trail down the mountain. Their hopes were rekindled by the discovery of the camp, but they would travel only eight miles before night fell and their horses became exhausted. It would have been useless to follow the trail in the dark, and the Italians were forced to make camp for the night. In the back of the shrewd sergeant's mind he knew very well that the fleeing Bourbons were outdistancing them with every passing minute. He realized that darkness would prevent him from following their trail, but it would not inhibit the fugitives from continuing their escape.

At eleven o'clock that night, the four escapees finally stopped riding. They had estimated they had traveled twenty miles since they had left the camp six hours earlier; they had ridden as far as they could. A chilling wind suddenly began to brew as they searched the mountains for an overhang or ledge so they could get out of the icy gusts. The mountains were well over four thousand feet in elevation, and the temperature was much cooler than they were accustomed to. Soon the gusting wind brought a shower of cold rain as they continued to look for some kind of shelter.

Night came upon them as they dismounted and led their frightened horses by the reins. They were almost reduced to feeling their way, for there was very little visibility in the driving rain and total darkness. Any sizable nook or overhanging ledge that might shelter them would do. They carefully made their way around a bulging promontory as rocks were kicked loose by their frightened horses; the stones plummeted downward and disappeared into the black ravine. The men pressed their backs against the face of the mountain and continued until they fortunately stumbled into a large opening in the rock. Both men and beasts hurried into the protection of the cave.

The tired travelers managed to light a fire then looked in awe at the mammoth-size cavern. It could have easily sheltered twenty men and their horses, if need be.

The grateful fugitives looked for more dry kindling to burn a larger fire. Again, luck was with them. Giovanni came upon a pile of old branches behind a boulder, possibly placed there by the last tenant to inhabit the cave. Before long, a large, blazing fire warmed the cold, wet bodies of the tired men. Then Giovanni had a brilliant idea as he grabbed a piece of flaming kindling and decided to explore further back into the cavern. The others were too exhausted to accompany him, so he proceeded alone. Five minutes had not passed before they heard him crying out for help. Startled and believing the worst, his three companions quickly snatched up their carbines and ran toward their screaming friend.

In less than a minute they stood over him as he lay on the floor with his torch beside him. He was pinned under half a dozen heavy wooden beams. The three men glanced at each other and looked down at the ridiculous expression on his face. They began to laugh uncontrollably. Giovanni became irate and responded with a score of curses which only intensified their laughter. Apparently, he had found a pile of ancient shoring timbers and decided one of them would supply enough wood for their fire for the entire night. When he tried to pry one loose, the others rolled down on top of him. Luckily, only his pride was damaged; so much so, while his friends removed the timbers, Giovanni ungratefully insulted their ancestry. Ignoring Giovanni's comments, Antonio and Francesco managed to carry one of the timbers back for the fire where it could burn through the night.

Once again, the tired men bedded down to sleep close to a crackling fire. They were thankful to have a safe, dry shelter and a warm fire to comfort them.

Outside the ancient cave, the wind and cold rain continued to inflict havoc on the land. Twenty miles west, their pursuers did not fare as well and were caught in thin canvas tents which the driving rain thoroughly soaked through. All possible chances of finding the fugitives washed away with the rain.

The storm raged through the night; creeks became rivers, and mudslides obliterated trails leading westward. The deluge subsided by morning, making its way toward the coast. The violent rains had left the land dripping wet and the air exceptionally clear and invigorating.

When the sergeant emerged from his soaked tent at dawn, he knew there was only one decision to be made. The fleeing prisoners and all traces of them were gone. He accepted fate and rousted his men from their tents and ordered them to break camp immediately. His prime concern was to return to the nearest Italian garrison as quickly and safely as possible.

IX
MEN OF THE MOUNTAINS

To ensure their safety, the four fugitives left the cave days later and rode deeper into the forest. Their meager food supplies had run out, and they were anxious to find a deer.

The men split up and scoured the area. Only Giacomo had been lucky enough to find a large rabbit. The other three came up empty, but luck was on their side when Francesco's horse ran over an injured grouse. They all had a good laugh and accepted the unexpected bounty, though it wasn't much.

They decided to look for a place to settle for the night and hoped to find a location with fewer vipers that were indigenous to the area. The asps were always a danger, especially to their horses.

That night they ate and were thankful for it. The sky was exceptionally clear when the stars appeared that evening. Occasional meteors streaked by, and the men gathered around a fire as they watched the celestial show.

The men slept exceptionally well, and when the sun rose the next morning, they heated the meager leftovers from their evening meal. As planned, they left as early as possible.

They rode through a piñon and hemlock forest and continued to travel, determined not to get caught by the ever-pursuing patrol now well behind them. Antonio and the others desired to increase the distance between them even further.

Food supplies were completely exhausted the following day, and the men came up empty handed in their hunting. By nightfall, their bad luck continued as no wildlife had been seen. They fell asleep uncomfortably with only some tea or coffee in their bellies, and morning arrived not soon enough.

They left early again to have more time to hunt. The morning crept by; noon came and went, and still, no game. Evening found them famished. The hungry men had only hot tea for a second night. They went to sleep early and hoped the next day would bring them better fortune.

The weary four slept through the night dreaming of food and family.

Some rabbits had been seen the next morning, but none

were shot. Circumstances went from bad to worse as the men weakened from lack of food. It was past noon when the starving four rode in single file and Francesco, who was leading, spotted a column of smoke up ahead. All became hopeful that their prayers would be answered but were very cautious as they followed the smoke to a cabin in the middle of nowhere.

They saw no evidence of horses or any other pack animal as they approached the house. They encircled the cabin, and Giacomo got off his horse and looked through the window. No one was home. He knocked on the door and received no response. He then raised his carbine and opened the door to find a sparsely-filled room. A heavy large iron pot rested on burning coals. Antonio almost burned his fingers when he reached into the pot and found half-baked bread dough. The famished men forgot what was right and divided the bounty. It had been nearly three days without food of any kind, and the dough seemed God-sent. Giovanni took his portion outside while his three friends stayed inside to devour their share and sat on real chairs which seemed a luxury.

Giovanni heard voices coming toward the cabin. He quickly alerted the others and then they took their horses to the rear of the house and hid as best they could. Two older men soon emerged from the trees dragging a freshly killed deer. Antonio showed himself without hostility, but his large frame unintentionally frightened the smaller men. They dropped the deer and backed up, wanting no trouble. "My friends, do not be afraid," he said, greeting them, "I wish you no harm. Is this your cabin?"

"Si, signore, it is indeed," one of the men answered with hesitation as Francesco, Giacomo, and Giovanni appeared behind Antonio.

"My men and I apologize for trespassing and for eating your baking bread. We have not eaten in days," Antonio continued.

"Look, you seem like a good man having hard times. Why don't you help us skin and butcher this animal and then we can all eat?" the other man said, stepping forward. Antonio and the others smiled with relief and then offered to do all the butchering.

The older gentlemen agreed whole-heartedly and watched in fascination how quickly the four unexpected visitors dressed the deer. The cabin owners stoked a larger fire as chunks of meat were skewered on a spit to be roasted.

"This would be a perfect time to introduce ourselves," Antonio suggested. "I am Antonio, and my friends are Giacomo, Giovanni, and Francesco."

"I am Angelo, and my good friend here is Franco. We came here months ago to escape the craziness of the war. We wanted to live out our lives here in the peace of the forest." The four younger men understood and agreed with their reasoning and then told them their story. The succulent venison had finished roasting by the time they all shared what had led them to that place and time.

Angelo and Franco were delighted to have the company as they watched their four guests devour the food with gusto. They brought out a gallon of wine that they had been saving for a special occasion.

In a while, after an evening of good food and new friends, one by one, they found comfortable places inside the cabin to sleep, and for that moment, all was right with the world.

Antonio opened his eyes and saw dawn slip through the shutter of the cabin. He was thankful the feasting had not been a dream. He looked toward the fireplace and saw Angelo making a pot of tea while Franco was busy making biscuits.

Soon everyone was awake and talking. They all joined together around the table once again and shared breakfast.

After eating, Antonio and the others agreed that they should leave in a short while. He did not want to take the chance of a patrol following their trail and bringing trouble to their kind hosts.

Soon the visitors said their goodbyes to Angelo and Franco and went outside to pack their already-saddled horses. As they were about to leave, Franco rushed from the cabin with a burlap bag filled with a larger portion of their roasted deer.

Antonio and the others were eternally grateful as they left the safety and hospitality of these good men.

The rejuvenated wanderers continued into the forest. Rugged escarpments and deep ravines were common for the area. Wide rushing streams cut through the mountains before cascading as powerful waterfalls and merging into cool, dark pools far below. It was nature at its most magnificent. They slowed their pace, almost ambling, to enjoy the beauty surrounding them. But in reality, the necessary isolation, both welcoming and challenging, was one that none of them had ever experienced.

At that time, they aimlessly traveled north toward the remote area of La Sila. The high elevation was a good indicator that they were going in the right direction. The numerous lakes provided good fishing and were perfect refuge for the weary men. The abundant game gave them the choice of staying as long as they wished.

Time slipped by almost too quickly, and they moved their location every week to avoid being detected. They managed to stay within a thirty mile nucleus. The days they spent in this region were a welcome interlude as they replenished their bodies and spirits.

While they were making their way around the shoreline of some unnamed lake, they were startled by the howl of a wolf. They instantly halted and glanced at each other. To their knowledge, wolves had been hunted almost to extinction. Antonio's horse, as well as Giovanni's, bristled at the sound. The creature was apparently quite a distance from them, so they cautiously continued their trek around the lake. A rifle shot unexpectedly rang out, and the four men quickly jumped off their horses.

They surveyed the area with their carbines cocked ready to fire as Giacomo went ahead of the others to investigate the situation. The others, out of sight, heard his sudden scream for help. Without hesitation, they rushed in Giacomo's direction and burst into a small meadow where they saw him on his back with a large wolf gripping his arm. Antonio and the others aimed their carbines at the predator. "Per favore! Don't shoot!" someone implored from somewhere near the meadow's edge. "Basta! Mico, let the man go!" The animal obeyed, watching his owner emerge from the tree line. Giacomo and the others sighed with relief. Though still growling, the wolf went to his master's side. Giacomo jumped up and brushed himself off. Fortunately, the wolf's grasp did not penetrate the sleeve of his jacket.

"What is this, Signore?" Antonio asked with outstretched arms.

"I am deeply sorry. He was only protecting me. Come, let's calm down and talk some," the stranger beckoned. With all the commotion, Antonio and the others hadn't noticed that one of the man's arms was missing. It was evident that he was truly sorry as he went on to tell them how he had saved Mico from a bear when he was just a pup; he had raised him as his loyal companion and Mico had become his self-appointed protector, better than any dog.

While the stranger told his story, his devoted Mico rested his head on his outstretched paws and lay calmly at the man's feet. "I am Gino Pirelli," he informed them, adding, "I've lived here almost eleven years. Come with us and stay a while. Now you tell me your story and what has brought you to my meadow."

Antonio and his friends followed Gino and Mico to a sturdy cabin. They marveled at its workmanship knowing that a one-armed man had constructed the well-built stone and timber dwelling. It contained two rooms and a large stone hearth. Bunches of tied herbs hung from the rafters, and their scent permeated the cabin.

By this time Mico was becoming more familiar with the visitors and permitted them to pet his pale, gray fur. In no time, he was licking their hands and nudging them for attention. The four outlaws were asked to stay for supper and to rest overnight. They accepted the offer with gratitude.

Gino had shot a deer a few days earlier and was eager to share his good fortune with his guests. Large portions of venison along with vegetables from his garden were placed on the table. To say the least, they feasted well that evening.

The guests filled Gino in on their interesting and challenging experiences, and their conversation broadened to days gone by. This camaraderie and contentment continued well into the night. Finally, everyone became too tired to talk and unrolled their blankets on the floor. Mico was no different and sprawled out contentedly in front of the fire. They all soon fell into a peaceful sleep.

At approximately two in the morning, shadowy figures

slinked toward the cabin. Apparently familiar with the location, six silhouetted forms deliberately moved toward the house. Out of a sound sleep, Mico's ears instantly perked up before he made his way to the door and scratched to go out. Giovanni, who was nearest to the door, stretched over and let him out. The other sleeping occupants were unaware of what was happening. Soon a desperate cry was heard from outside, and it was apparent that Mico had jumped upon an intruder. A volley of gun shots followed. Antonio and Giacomo were the first to respond and grabbed their guns before crawling out the door. Francesco consequently followed. Giovanni stayed back to assist Gino if someone tried to force their way in.

Two more shots rang out and were followed by a yelp. Gino assumed Mico had been hurt and ran to the door, but Giovanni intercepted him. Giovanni had no intentions of letting him go out into the dark with his physical disadvantage and put his arms around him to prevent him from acting further. More shots were exchanged. Someone's yell for help was heard before a seemingly-eternal silence dominated the scene. A sound came at the door, first a whimper, then scratching.

Giovanni opened the door with caution, and Mico limped in. The animal immediately went near the fire to lie down. Gino rushed to his devoted companion and discovered a gunshot wound to Mico's right front paw. Gino inspected the leg more closely and was relieved to find that the bullet had passed right through. Mico struggled for a comfortable position and then fell sleep.

Both men tended to the injured Mico as best they could but knew that rest would be the only remedy.

The silence outside was broken by Antonio letting them know it was safe to open the door. When they did, they found Antonio carrying a still-conscious but wounded Giacomo. He had been shot in the shoulder. Antonio put his friend down on a cot. Soon Francesco emerged at the door holding his head and leaning on his carbine. A bullet had apparently grazed his scalp, and the wound was bleeding profusely. Giacomo and Francesco were tended by their two friends while Gino stayed near Mico.

Antonio then told Giovanni and Gino that when he and Giacomo left the cabin they found six men heading toward the house. Each had a weapon and joked to one another about how easy it would be to overtake a lonely, one-armed man. Apparently, that soon changed when Mico found one of the culprits and attacked him. His cohorts had started blindly shooting as their friend was being mauled. "Then we found where the shots were coming from," Antonio continued breathlessly, "We saw three men reloading their weapons, and we started firing. We killed one and wounded another. The third dragged one of the bastards away. Meanwhile, Mico went on with his business attacking his victim." Antonio paused to catch his breath and rinse a bloody rag in a basin of water. "More shots came, and we knew from Mico's cries that he had been hurt. Then Francesco came out and the three of us cornered the *putans* by the edge of the trees. Bullets flew from both sides, and Giacomo was hit. Another round of fire, and that's when Francesco was grazed. I fired two more times and heard a groan. It was evident that the men were hell-bent on getting away and headed back to their horses. On the run, I fired one more time and hit another. How many were left, I don't know, but they all finally rode off. After they left, I surveyed the area and found three dead. I don't think that any of the survivors will return, for they gained nothing. Losing three men was a high price to pay."

"Mil grazie, for your bravery and for putting your lives on the line for us," Gino expressed with gratitude as he stroked Mico by the fire.

"You do not have to thank us for doing what is right," Francesco answered as Antonio continued to tend to Giacomo. The bullet was imbedded in his shoulder and had to be removed as soon as possible. Fortunately, Giovanni had experience in the military medical corps prior to being assigned to the cavalry unit.

Knowing they would need a very hot fire, Gino threw some heavy pieces of oak onto the tired embers. The fire caught and was left to burn until the proper heat was attained. In the meantime, Gino and Giovanni gathered a few crude implements they would need to remove the bullet and placed them deep into the red hot coals until they were white and sterilized from the intense heat. Fortunately for Giacomo, he was now unconscious from blood loss. A leather strip was placed between his teeth in case he came to before the end of the procedure. To keep Giacomo immobilized, Antonio held Giacomo's head securely from behind while Giovanni straddled the wounded man.

Giacomo only had a momentary flicker of consciousness during the procedure and then returned to oblivion. Giovanni did what he could to remove the imbedded bullet. After much concentration and anxiety, the piece of lead was successfully taken out. To everyone's relief, all went well under the dire circumstances. They made Giacomo as comfortable as possible and hoped for the best, and as in Mico's case, it was evident that sleep would speed his recovery.

Francesco's head wound finally stopped bleeding; he would recover fully, albeit with scars.

Dawn came silently, and all had an opportunity for much needed rest. They were relieved the ordeal had ended and they all survived.

Due to the constant attention from his caring friends, Giacomo finally stirred after ten hours. Antonio and Giovanni propped him up so he could swallow some hearty broth. They hoped infection would not set in, but their meticulous precaution gave him a good chance.

Another day and a half passed, and with the constant changing of Giacomo's dressing, the wound was clear.

Mico was also managing to get up on his three good legs and hobble around the cabin with a good appetite. Soon he was scratching at the door as a grateful Gino let him out. Giacomo, with his arm in a sling, was able to navigate about and feed himself. Time had also helped Francesco to heal; he only suffered from a minor headache as his scalp began to heal nicely.

The four outlaw friends stayed at Gino's cabin another week before the two wounded men were able to ride. All were eternally grateful to their new friend Gino. In return for his generous hospitality, Antonio and Giovanni smoked and salted some hunted game and stockpiled the meat which would supply Gino and Mico for weeks to come.

What had begun as a bad introduction by Mico had blossomed into an endearing relationship. Both man and wolf had grown to trust and care for these four good men.

The night before they were to leave, Antonio sadly informed Gino during the evening meal that he and the others would be leaving the following day; Giacomo and Francesco were healthy enough to travel. A sad look appeared on Gino's face, but Giovanni assured him that they would not forget him and would return someday.

The remainder of the evening was subdued, the men knowing too well it was their last night there. They all tried to put on a good face, but it was difficult. Even Mico detected something in the wind and was more affectionate than usual. After casual conversation, they all retired with bittersweet contentment.

The sun seemed to rise earlier than usual, and morning found Gino with a dish towel over his shoulder as he busily prepared breakfast. The aroma of meat sizzling in the pan prompted the others to awaken. In no time at all, everyone was laughing around the table once again. As always, Mico was by the fire and relishing his portion of meat.

Antonio and Giovanni cleaned up after the meal, and within half an hour, the men started to pack the few things they possessed. Francesco saddled the horses and then the others secured their gear to their mounts as well as a few days' worth of meat. Gino and Mico both stood in the doorway and watched them preparing to leave. Each of the departing men then went to Gino and embraced him with thanks.

"Gino, may God bless you and buono fortuna! May we all meet again!" Antonio shouted as they turned to ride away. In a slow trot, the four riders soon approached the edge of the meadow and before they entered the forest, stopped to pivot in their saddles to take one last look and wave goodbye. With tears, Gino and his devoted Mico watched their dear friends disappear from view.

X
HOSTAGE VILLAGE

Seeking a more secure area, Antonio and the others journeyed far into La Sila. The four men rode in single file gradually, higher and higher into even more rugged terrain. They managed the steep climb and were relieved to see the way ahead finally becoming more level which made it much easier for man and beast.

Giovanni was the first to notice smoke rising above distant tile-roofed dwellings, and they soon came upon a village perched on a precipitous ridge with sweeping views of ochre valleys and jagged mountains of isolation and beauty. The buildings were a far cry from their medieval glory; centuries of ill-repair had played havoc on the structures.

What first appeared as a single house was instead a row

of seven dwellings. The small stone buildings were so close to each other that they appeared to be attached. The narrow roadway in front was eerily vacant of activity; there were no horses, mules, or any other animals in sight. The only sign of life was smoke rising from a few chimneys.

The four men were in dire need of water and thought they could fill their water jugs there. Giacomo got off his horse and knocked on the door of the first house. There was no response, even after a few more attempts. He then went to the next one and knocked again with the same results. There were no sounds of life, even after they called out.

Antonio gently opened a door to have a look. No one was in sight, but a fire was burning. Remnants of cooking were evident. Apparently, the inhabitants had left in haste.

The men then tried the other houses without seeing a soul. They realized the people could not have been too far a distance, for their families and animals were apparently in tow.

Francesco then suggested that he go on foot alone to see what he could find. He left the others behind and quickly picked up an easy trail left by animals as they had passed through. In a short time, he observed a group of twenty or so peasants with their horses, goats, and other animals. They huddled in a small evergreen clearing. At that time, Francesco did not make himself known, and instead, quickly returned to Antonio and the others.

Back at the abandoned village, he told his friends what he had seen. They decided to approach the people and inquire about their situation.

Francesco led the way, and they headed toward the clearing, dismounting and calmly walking in on the obviously frightened people. Some villagers cowered and tried to hide while others stared with fearful eyes. When the four fugitives approached further, the people drew closer together, circling back to back for protection and expecting the worst. Antonio's intimidating appearance and stature made many of the peasants shrink back even further. "Please, do not fear us. We mean you no harm," he said with apology, "We want nothing from you except water and to purchase some food, if we may." An older man standing next to a younger man finally broke away from the huddling group and walked toward Antonio.

"We do not know you. In the past, evil robbers inflicted injury and took from us. How do we know you are not the same?" the older man asked with hopelessness.

"We are not the same as the low life you speak of. We have no intentions of taking from you or inflicting harm. I am sorry if we frightened you. All we want is water and a little food," Antonio tried to pacify them.

"Grazie Dio," replied the old man, "We have suffered much. We saw you coming into the village, and we feared the worst, gathered up everybody. The last ones took without mercy and anyone who fought back was beaten and our women..." The man trailed off with the implication. "This has been our Hell here in Monte Vista the past few months. They ride in once a month to take and hurt." His eyes softened a bit. "I can see you men are not the same. Come, and we will try to help." Everyone nodded with agreement and relief and then went back to the village with the four outlaws.

After a while, one by one, the people accepted the strangers for who they claimed to be. An underlying malaise and defeated attitude were reflected in the people's daily activities, and it was obvious that their vulnerability left them as easy prey to marauding brigands.

Antonio, Giacomo, Giovanni, and Francesco were shown a clear stream of water emanating from a sheer rock wall which supplied the people with more water than their needs demanded. The men refilled their jugs, and the villagers offered them simple food which they accepted with graciousness. For this, the four visitors gave them a few small silver coins for their kindness.

Antonio and his comrades decided to make camp within a few miles from the village. They liked the hunting prospects in that section of La Sila as well as the idea of having some good people nearby. The high elevation was also favorable to observe the landscape below for any passing patrols. Upon leaving, the fugitives told the people that they would only be a few miles away and if they should ever need their assistance that they should light a signal fire on the hill above the village.

The outlaws traveled on and recognized an area they had briefly passed through months earlier. Remnants of a stone fire pit were still discernible. The site fit their needs-a flowing brook nearby and a vantage point of the mountain trails below, even a serene view for their tired spirits.

Satisfied with the location, the men prepared their site for an indefinite stay. Within a day, they made a more substantial shelter of stone and timber; Antonio's talents with stone and Francesco and Giacomo's carpentry experience quickened its completion.

Three weeks passed easily for the sought-after men who kept themselves occupied by hunting, fishing, and basic survival. They also explored a good portion of the surrounding territory. Trails were discovered and taken note of to be used for possible escape routes.

One day, late in the morning, Francesco and the others thought they had heard gunfire in the direction of the village. Antonio pointed his telescope toward Monte Vista to see if there was any sign of trouble. He was startled to see smoke billowing from the signal area. He alerted the others and prepared to leave immediately.

Giacomo was the first to burst out of camp; Francesco and Giovanni followed a minute later. Antonio was the last to leave, for his horse was tethered some distance from camp. They darted down the trail, taking the turns dangerously fast as they maneuvered along the serpentine path. The village was approximately three miles from their position; the ride was difficult, down a mountainside then up a steep terrace. The horses responded to their riders as they dug their hooves into the winding curves and quickly descended the ridge.

Fortunately, all four riders were able to stay mounted without being thrown. Ascending the terrace was especially arduous for the horses, and the sound of gunfire exacerbated their distress.

They finally arrived on the plateau and chose to approach the village from the south which would be the least anticipated side for attack. They sneaked around the perimeter and halted to have a last minute word before they made their next move.

A gang of thieves had taken eight people hostage in one of the houses while their cohorts ravaged the remaining homes and took anything of value. Two armed brigands guarded the captives while the others continued to ransack the village.

Antonio and his companions had agreed to overtake the marauders one house at a time instead of splitting up. They inched up to a window and spied two thieves overturning the meager contents of the house. The robbers were oblivious to any impending danger and went about their nasty business. Francesco motioned to the others, indicating he wanted to be first in.

Bursting through the half-open door, Francesco stunned two dumb-founded men as Antonio, Giovanni, and Giacomo followed with equal force. Only one thief was able to react and attempted to raise his rifle, but it was too late as Giacomo ran his sword through him. The other robber received the butt end of Francesco's carbine.

The avenging foursome quickly moved to the next house which was windowless. The door was ajar, and the sound of smashing pottery and glass reverberated loudly. Antonio and the others rushed in, catching three men by surprise. Antonio jumped on two of the thieves and sent them sprawling to the floor as his large body crushed them senseless. The third robber was quick enough to spin around and strike Giacomo in the shoulder with the end of his carbine. Giacomo collapsed to the floor instantly. Giovanni responded by slashing the man across the neck and chest, totally disabling him. Giacomo tried to stand, but he was in too much pain.

Antonio, Francesco, and Giovanni resumed the elimination of the rogues throughout the rest of the village. Wasting little time, Francesco led Antonio and Giovanni to the corner of the fourth building and looked through the partly open shutter. Five thieves, feeling unchallenged, sat around a table eating and joking like there was no tomorrow.

The cocky rogues had the presence of mind to keep their weapons on the table within arm's reach. Giovanni suddenly crashed through the door with his carbine leveled to the nearest man who tried to lunge. Giovanni fired and hit him in the neck. Another thug then attempted to pull a pistol as Antonio jammed the butt end of his carbine on man's hand, crushing his fingers. The third man was able to draw his sword in time while his partner lunged at Francesco with a bayonet. Firing from the hip, Francesco shot him in the chest. He then used his spent carbine to slap the sword free from the other man and cracked his skull. The last culprit ran out the door to alert the others before Antonio or Francesco could stop him. Pulling a stiletto from his belt, Giovanni quickly ran after him and threw the knife. The blade found its mark, penetrating the back of the thug. He stumbled to the ground, and Giovanni did not hesitate to bludgeon the man before he had a chance to cry out and warn the other marauders.

The only surviving thieves were the two standing guards who held the villagers captive; Giovanni approached the house with careful steps. He signaled Antonio and Francesco to follow his lead and then burst through the door. The force sent the two jolted guards reeling to the floor along with their weapons. The frightened hostages scattered. Antonio and Giovanni pounced on the stunned guards and pounded them before they could react. Francesco assured the villagers that they would be fine and no further harm would come to them.

The people of the village soon realized they had been rescued from a near-tragedy. The villagers who had been fortunate enough to escape into the outskirts of the hamlet gradually returned when they realized it was safe to do so.

Of the dozen or so marauders, eight had been killed and four wounded. Antonio and Giovanni survived with little injury. Francesco, not as unscathed, had received a shallow gash on his forearm. Giacomo's hard blow to the shoulder was more serious and made his arm painfully immobile.

The villagers, more than happy to show their gratitude, treated the four honorable men with hospitality. They remained in Monte Vista for ten days while Giacomo healed from his injury, and his three friends helped the villagers mend the destruction. Despite all of their sufferings at the hands of the thugs, the people did not hesitate to tend to the thieves who had been wounded. Antonio was awed and a bit dumbfounded by their gracious charity.

The injured thieves had healed enough to walk and eventually ride a horse, and Antonio suggested that he and his friends escort them out of the area. Struck by the villager's compassion, one of the injured men had a change of heart and asked to remain with them and make amends. His request was accepted.

The day arrived when Antonio and the other three avenging angels had to leave. It was concluded that the healed villains must leave with them. It was difficult for the villagers to say goodbye to the brave men who had saved their lives and few possessions.

With Francesco and Antonio leading the rogues and Giovanni and Giacomo in the rear, they slowly filed out of Monte Vista with a fresh supply of food and water. Giacomo, before reaching the bend in the road, shouted to the villagers behind him, "Signal us if you should need us, and we will be here!" The people of the village were grateful for these honest men and their unselfish bravery.

The somber group of men rode through the tedious and rugged trails until dusk and then finally halted. Antonio and Francesco turned their horses around and faced the three weary marauders. "The three of you are very fortunate to be alive," Antonio announced. "I cannot say that for your eight other partners in crime. We are going to let you go free. I am going against my own better judgment; if it were up to me, you would have joined your deceased friends. Nevertheless, I am going along with the others and have decided to let you live. I hope you all have learned something and will change your ways. But most of all, I want to advise you: if you have any future ideas to ever return to Monte Vista to harm those good people again, we *will* find you and kill all of you. Leave and never return if you value your pathetic lives." With that, Francesco reached over and slapped the hind quarters of the horse nearest to him, and the startled animals bolted away with their riders barely hanging on.

XI
AFTERMATH

Garibaldi and his army victoriously entered the city of Naples to thousands of cheering Neapolitans. Politicians in the north had already formed a new regime which would rule an area from Naples to Sicily. These political positions in the government were to be filled by advocates from the North. They would inflict laws which they believed to be appropriate, but these political puppets never once reflected the desires and needs of neither Neapolitan people nor the poor people of the south. These peasants had revolted against Bourbon domination but were once again faced with the same situation with a new system in power.

In most instances, the enforcement of laws by the new authorities was much harsher than under the previous

Spanish rule. Newer and more sizable taxes were imposed. Consequently, the people were in the same frustrating predicament as they had been under foreign domination.

Dissatisfaction spread throughout southern Italy, and a fresh counter-revolution emerged. Groups were formed to protect the defenseless people from the inequitable treatment dealt from the new northern rule. The Camorra was formed to defend the people of Naples from the carpetbaggers of the north. In the meantime, the Mafia had its beginnings as a society in Sicily; the intention was to protect the poor from the same injustices.

Three resistant groups—the brigands, the Camorra, and the Mafia—all set out to avenge the unfair treatment of the people of the south. The outlaws or the brigands, as they were called, were looked upon as heroes and champions of justice. Many of these outlaws had been accepted as allies of the Church and the ex-Bourbon supporters. Many of the clergy were persecuted by the new regime for their outward stand against exorbitant demands on the poor.

This was the pathetic situation that existed after Garibaldi had liberated the Italians from Bourbon tyranny. Because of these conditions, brigandism spread throughout the south including Sicily. Between 1861 and 1865 an army of one hundred and twenty thousand soldiers were sent into the region in an attempt to disband the new counter-revolutionaries who took refuge in the rugged nearby mountains. These fugitive groups of disillusioned men were comprised of ex-Bourbons, ex-

Garibaldini, dissenting clergymen, and peasants who were tired of being exploited.

These circumstances drove good but desperate men to find sanctuary in the rural region of Calabria. Our quartet of ex-Bourbon cavalrymen did likewise and hid in the very heart of the remote forest areas of the province. They could remain there with some degree of security and freedom. The tall pines, crystal-clear lakes, and abundant wildlife offered them easier hunting which they relied on for their survival.

For their first undertaking, Antonio and his companions built a sturdy shelter on the leeward side of a mountain which possessed a commanding view of a verdant valley below. The hunted men settled down to a blissful existence for three to four weeks. The absolute freedom experienced by the men taught them a new respect for nature. To give up the so-called luxuries of civilization was not such an ordeal; the benefits far outweighed the harsher conditions. They were amazed they could live rather comfortably with only the basic necessities of life. The warm and aromatic days and pulsing star-filled nights passed quickly as they became more adapted to living a Spartan life.

After they spent a month at their campsite, they agreed to venture further south toward their homes in hopes that conditions might have changed there. It would have been easier to remain where they were with an abundance of game, but they chose to leave their haven for the uncertainties of more familiar ground. They knew they could never help their oppressed people if they chose to remain safe and hoped to influence a change for the better for their loved ones.

They departed from their camp that had served them well for almost a month, and a feeling of loss overcame them; their mountain shelter had provided them with many hours of secure contentment. The independence had been a welcome change from the months of battle and the strain of war. Nonetheless, they realized they would eventually have to leave their care-free life behind and return home to loved ones and unknown conditions. Antonio was anxious to not only return to his family, but to his beloved Teresa.

After four days of riding, the fugitives began to descend the steep mountain trail overlooking Nicastro where they were captured a month earlier. They approached the road leading to the town with caution.

Giacomo was selected to scout ahead and reconnoiter the area. He noticed the scarcity of any occupying military presence as he neared the edge of town. Life appeared normal, people walking the narrow cobblestone streets and shopping at the many small, bustling bodegas. Giacomo could barely detect any evidence of Italian patrols. Without revealing his Bourbon identity, he removed his military cardigan and stuffed it into his saddle bag and then unfolded a shepard's sheepskin vest which he had found in an abandoned mountain hut a few weeks earlier. He slipped it over his shoulder and appeared to be one of a dozen transient young men making their way through the busy town. He exercised extreme caution as not to bring too much attention to himself.

He trotted by the first row of shops and sensed an atmosphere of openness which was reflected in the manner which townspeople moved and spoke. It was a far cry from a few months earlier, when under Bourbon domination, the very air seemed ready to ignite from the ever-present hostility. The people were now speaking more freely as they had years before tyranny had been forced upon them. The happy sounds of children at play brought joy to Giacomo's heart as he lost his unwarranted feeling of apprehension. Some locals glanced with curiosity at the young man on horseback and acknowledged him as they would any other stranger.

Giacomo felt safe enough and dismounted. Eager to engage in conversation, he walked into a dry goods store and picked up a pouch of tobacco. He handed the owner a small gold coin. The proprietor remarked with great surprise, "I haven't seen a gold piece in almost six months. Is there anything else you might need?" Giacomo paused before he answered.

"Well, I'm wondering if you could give me some information. I have journeyed from Catanzaro and want to join up with the Garibaldini. I heard that a month ago or so a battle was fought not too far from here and the Bourbons were routed. Where can I find the Red Shirts?"

"They must be in Naples by now," the owner said, "Garibaldi left his troops behind and raced to the Bourbon city by himself. His soldiers followed a day or so later. If you want to join the liberators you had better travel north; there are only three or four patrols remaining here in Nicastro." Giacomo obtained the information he wanted and smiled.

"Thank you. I am in your debt, signore." He turned and walked from the store back to the street once again and could hear raised voices coming from across the way. A group of townsmen had gathered before a newly-posted decree. It was obvious that the onlookers were very dissatisfied with the new town ordinance which banned the possession of firearms within the town limits. One angry citizen remarked, "We have just driven the Bourbons from our land only to have them replaced by a form of authority that does the same. Any system that denies the possession of firearms must have unworthy motives in mind." The other men standing about nodded in agreement. Giacomo took note of what was said and continued to walk and examine the town more closely. After a short while, he decided it was time to leave. Above all, he did not want to arouse any kind of suspicion.

He got back up on his horse and slowly galloped through town toward his anxious comrades waiting in the foothills above. They were surprised to hear that only a dozen or so Italian troops were occupying the town and the townspeople were already disenchanted with the month-old regime.

Upon the conclusion of Giacomo's narrative, they all agreed that they would neither join Garibaldi's army nor accept a life under the conditions set by the new tyrannical authorities. It was decided that it would be far better to act as a small group in an effort to rectify some of the injustices being thrust upon their defeated people. Therefore, they chose to return to the safety of the mountains and establish a base camp for the near future.

The headstrong men of conviction were determined to not relinquish their principles to any dictatorial system. They turned their backs to Nicastro and journeyed back to the uncompromised tranquility of the high country. In the back of their minds, they hoped to join other dissatisfied Italians who also refused to knuckle under the new form of oppression.

They carefully retraced their trail through the mountains and avoided the well-traveled roads. They did not wish to accidentally run into Italian troops patrolling the countryside. They left Nicastro far below and climbed higher, again ascending the hills under a veil of gray clouds.

Upon their return to their refuge, they immediately planned their course of retaliation. The main objective was to incite the already disgruntled populace against the cruel establishment. The four men needed time to organize themselves and hopefully enlist the aid of like-minded men.

The weeks rapidly slipped by for the busy outlaws. Each man became more familiar with the lay of the land within a twenty-five mile radius. They realized such knowledge would be a very valuable ally for their future plans. While in this region, the isolated men never once caught a glimpse or a sign of another person. They were beginning to think they were the only active adversaries in the region until one morning when Francesco discovered a footprint in the moist soil while washing in the stream.

It was unlike his own print and that of his three friends who were still asleep a hundred yards away. He was a little startled at first but quickly regained his composure as he took up his carbine and investigated further. He moved with caution through the underbrush beside the water and proceeded to uncover other boot prints in the damp earth. It was obvious that others too had drawn water not more than an hour earlier. Francesco continued to follow the prints further downstream as they indicated an undetermined number of men on horseback. The distinct trail then abruptly took a ninety degree turn toward a nearby mountain range. At that point he thought it would be foolish to continue alone and returned to alert his companions.

Back at camp, Giacomo had just awakened and was concerned about Francesco's absence, though his horse was still hobbled with the others. Giacomo stirred Antonio and Giovanni from their sleep and informed them of their friend's disappearance.

They were about to saddle their horses when they heard the sound of someone approaching. They grabbed their weapons and hid within the perimeter of the camp and waited for the intruder's appearance. Suddenly the thick foliage parted, and a man stumbled and fell face-down onto the ground of the clearing. Antonio instantly stepped out from the thicket to confront the intruder. He walked closer for a better look with carbine in hand and then slowly approached the prone figure on the ground. He addressed the still unidentified man, "Who are you? What do you want?" The breathless man finally raised his head.

"Have the three of you gone crazy? It is me, Francesco!" Antonio rushed toward him with apology and helped him up.

"I am sorry, good friend, but we had to prepare ourselves for the worst when you came bursting into camp." His three friends gathered around and listened intently to Francesco's discovery of the strange prints by the stream. Once they heard the whole story, the men began to break camp. They doused the fire, gathered their belongings, and prepared to leave. They had one goal and that was to find and identify the strangers.

They swiftly saddled their horses and followed the trail, using utmost caution; there was a good possibility that there was an Italian militia patrol scouring the mountains looking for them. They picked up where Francesco had left off and followed it to a nearby summit. They paused to study the topography below. The path seemed to lead into a rugged valley. Antonio scanned the forest with his telescope, but surprisingly, there were no signs of the men they were after.

The four descended the face of the mountain and spotted a pale gray column of smoke rising from the far side of the valley and decided to travel toward it.

Once in the general vicinity, they dismounted and approached the rest of the way on foot to avoid being detected. They neared a small oval clearing after they hiked a hundred yards into the forest. A group of unidentified men were seen crouching near a fire and speaking softly to one another. Antonio instructed his companions to separate so they could surprise the unsuspecting men from four directions.

Giacomo signaled, and they charged the startled men. The men were caught off guard and refrained from resisting as it was evident that their position was hopeless. "Pardon our intrusion," Giacomo questioned with sarcasm, "Who are you? And what are you doing here?" One of the bewildered men stepped forward to respond.

"At the moment, we are men who have no ties to any cause." The man paused for a moment to take a closer look at the four armed men surrounding them. "It seems to me that you are in a similar position."

"There, you are wrong, my friend," Antonio remarked sharply, "Our loyalties lie with our oppressed countrymen who are constantly being taken advantage of. First, it was by the Spanish house of Bourbons, and now by our own Italian brothers. We have made it our mission to chip away at the roots of this new, corrupt government."

"Do my ears deceive me, or do we have the fortunate opportunity to be among men who are also disgusted with the injustices put upon all of us?" another disheveled member of the vagabond bunch replied. "We fought with

Garibaldi from the beginning at Marsala to the surrender at Naples. We realized, to our dismay, that once a town had been taken, it was quickly turned over to a few favorite northern Italians who governed as they wish. They never gave a single moment of consideration to the sufferings of the poor who were in their trust. We have seemed to replace Bourbon tyranny with Italian tyranny."

Antonio, Giacomo, Francesco, and Giovanni were less suspicious after the stranger spoke and lowered their carbines to their sides. "I think we have common ground here. We can help each other if we join forces," Antonio commented. "As you served for Garibaldi, as troopers we served for the house of Bourbon. I do have to confess that our sympathies have always been with our own people for we are born Calabrians. Since the collapse of the Bourbon army in the south, we have acted as free men. We refuse to knuckle under any form of domination. I believe I can speak for my friends that we would consider the union of our two small groups as an honor." The spokesman of the band turned to his companions for their decision.

Some nodded their heads with approval while others voiced their opinions, but it was unanimous that the two similar-thinking groups were to join forces. The seven strangers, who minutes earlier had been held as captives, were now members of the same band.

The eleven united men would be labeled as brigands and rogues; before long, rewards were posted for their capture or information concerning their whereabouts. At that time, throughout Italy's south, many other rebellious men also took safe refuge in the dense interior. Their rank swelled in number from hundreds to thousands in a matter of six months after the new regime was established. The unfair laws turned normally law-abiding citizens into bands of malcontents. These wronged hordes of people sought restitution of equitable rights for all. In some instances, they desired revenge for suffering numerous hardships. Brigandism flourished on a wide scale as a result of the post-war conditions. Local officials of most towns and villages were kept busy in their efforts to keep the outlaws from seizing control. In most cases, the majority of the people supported and aided these gallant rogues as their champions of justice. Their fortitude was envied by the meek as they fought to defend their rights and beliefs.

To avert the complete loss of control in the South, an army of a hundred and twenty thousand Italian regulars were dispatched to quell the rebellious tide. This amount of military was equal to half the entire army of Italy. Each town and municipality received a contingent of soldiers that supplemented the existing local military. The direct result was a larger military presence which enabled more numerous patrols to scour the hills and mountains in search of the ever-increasing number of outlaws.

The bands of ex-patriots advanced deeper into the rugged interior to avoid being captured. Though they penetrated the forest further than ever before, the increased

Italian patrols were still unsuccessful in capturing any of the fugitives. At best, they uncovered a handful of abandoned outlaw hideouts but never saw their former inhabitants. The wary brigands maintained a system of sentries that quickly relayed the existence of any approaching patrols in a matter of minutes. The army's attempts were numerous but all in vain. The majority of the outlaws had been raised in the area, and they knew it all too well. The army, comprised of northern soldiers, did not have the slightest knowledge of the local geography. This in itself was a very important advantage for all those who fought against the new oppressors.

Giacomo and another member of the newly-formed band were assigned as lookout sentries to guard against the many probes by the Italian militia. The new comrade had positioned himself at the base of the mountain hideout while Giacomo was stationed approximately a hundred yards above him. At this range, they were to keep in sight of each other.

It was a warm spring day as both men made themselves as comfortable as possible, for it would be a long watch until dark. Each had brought food and drink as it would be many hours until they were relieved. The morning passed very slowly and uneventfully, but they remained steadfast in their lookout positions. The sun was soon directly overhead, and hunger forced Giacomo to unwrap his food. He looked forward to eating which would break the monotony.

He wolfed down a large wedge of formaggio and a small

piece of crusted bread and quenched his thirst with half a bota of cool wine. Within a short time he became very sleepy. He took a quick look at his friend who was in position overlooking the trail and seemed satisfied that his partner was very much alert down below and settled back and relaxed. Since there had been no sightings of Italian patrols for two weeks, things appeared to be relatively calm. Giacomo used the half-filled bota with wine as a headrest and stretched out on the soft, moss-covered ground and soon dozed off.

An hour and a half went by when the sentry on the boulder below suddenly jumped to his feet. He had seen a number of riders approaching his position, and he waved his carbine to signal Giacomo who would in turn alert the others in the camp. He soon realized there was no acknowledgement from his friend above and waved frantically to get his attention. When there was no response, the sentry crouched behind some large rocks as the riders came closer. He had a dilemma; if he fired his carbine to alert his friends he would certainly be captured, but if he did not, his friends would be in jeopardy. He planned to let them ride by and find a shorter route back to camp to alert the others.

Within moments, twelve uniformed soldiers trotted by at a slow but deliberate pace, unaware of the concealed sentry. They continued to climb higher to Giacomo's position. The corporal who led the patrol turned to his men and remarked, "I hope today we find some of the bastards instead of just another deserted camp." They continued on the trail in full view of Giacomo who was in a very deep sleep. The two point riders spied his outstretched form and pulled to a halt immediately and informed the others of their discovery. At first glance they thought the man was injured but a closer look revealed he was just fast asleep. It was an unfortunate stroke of bad luck for the happy-go-lucky Giacomo. They surrounded the content young man as a few soldiers dismounted and then prodded him with their gun barrels. In response, the snoring outlaw quickly and angrily awoke and cursed the intruders as he jumped to his feet in disbelief. The situation was very amusing to the corporal of the patrol who commented, "Signore, I am very sorry if we disturbed your pleasant dreams, but I was wondering if you could direct us to the camp of outlaws." The other soldiers roared with laughter as the red-faced Giacomo stood there fuming.

"I wouldn't be so smug if I were you. You might have caught me off guard, but I can guarantee you that my friends have already been alerted and are making tracks as we speak," Giacomo replied irately.

"That, my sleepy friend, remains to be seen," the corporal responded and then commanded his men, "Let's go. The trail will probably lead us directly to the others."

Giacomo, the new captive, was pulled up behind one of the mounted cavalrymen after his hands were bound. The patrol then continued to climb in the direction of the hideout. A scout was sent ahead and returned minutes later to tell the others he had found the outlaw camp, but it had been abandoned. The corporal then boasted smugly, "We may not have apprehended the entire band, but I think we can make this one tell us what we want to know."

"Corporal," Giacomo retaliated, "I do not think you will have the pleasure of me revealing anything which would endanger the safety of my friends."

"We shall see, my impetuous fool. Only time will tell," the corporal sneered.

The patrol slowly galloped down the mountainside toward Nicastro with their prisoner. In the meantime, Giacomo's companions had been alerted by the other sentry who had managed to circle quietly around the soldiers and warn his friends before they were all captured.

Antonio and the others had escaped. They halted to regroup and discuss the strategy they would use to free their unfortunate comrade. They feared that Giacomo would be harmed during the melee and decided it would not be wise to ambush the soldiers; instead, they followed the patrol at an undetectable distance.

The group of outlaws cautiously made their way behind the returning militia to the edge of town. They stopped and allowed the red-shirted patrol to enter into Nicastro without interference.

When the soldiers arrived at headquarters, Giacomo's hands were untied as he was shoved into an old jail cell. The space contained a straw mattress in the corner under a small barred window facing the rear. From his cell window, Giacomo could peer out at the distant hills and beyond. He thought of his predicament and wondered the whereabouts of his loyal friends.

The hours passed; soon it was dark as the imprisoned outlaw made himself as comfortable as possible. He pondered his fate as he rested on the tattered bed and waited for an unpredictable outcome.

Later that evening, he was awakened by the sound of gunfire. He then heard anxious soldiers shouting to one another. From what he could decipher, a group of unknown riders, obviously outlaws, had taken positions directly across the street from the jail. They fired through the windows as the besieged guards were pinned to the floor by the constant barrage of bullets. In the midst of all the commotion, Giacomo's attention was diverted to his cell window. A thick hemp rope began to inch its way down between the iron bars, and then he heard the unmistakable baritone voice of his friend Antonio, "Giacomo, fasten the rope tightly to one of the bars." The imprisoned outlaw grasped and secured it. He stared into the night for a glimpse of his rescuers, but it was much too dark. Again, another rope was slipped through the window which he secured to another iron bar. "After you have tied the ropes, step back clear of the window." Giacomo stepped aside while the rope stiffened and the slack was taken up. The other ends of the ropes were attached to the saddles of his friends' horses. Soon, the thick ropes became tighter and tighter. Giacomo's eyes remained glued to the cell window as he watched for the first signs of the bars weakening. Within a few moments, the mortar surrounding the bars began to crack and powder under the pressure of the straining ropes. He suddenly heard a sharp, quick sound as the bars finally snapped free.

When the dust cleared he saw that the bars were removed entirely. Pushing away the loose mortar, Giacomo lifted himself to the narrow window ledge; within seconds, he dangled his legs outside and let himself slip into the outstretched arms of his loyal friends below.

Meanwhile, the rain of bullets continued to rip through the jail, distracting the attention of the soldiers to the front of the building. Giacomo quickly pulled himself up behind the already-mounted Giovanni as his outlaw rescuers swung around to the front of the building and rode past the rest of their outlaw companions who had realized the escape was successful and had ceased firing. They then sprang up onto their horses and rode off after their friends who had already fled into the darkness.

XII
VOWS AND RESTITUTION

Four months after Giacomo's rescue in Nicastro, Antonio was able to persuade his three companions to break away from their alliance with the other bandits. Distinct difference of opinion concerning the band's motives and methods of action had caused a split. Antonio and his friends had become dissatisfied, but nevertheless, he was anxious to leave the area and go see his family and betrothed Teresa once again. It had been months since he had seen everyone.

Early one morning, he and his friends informed the others in the band of their decision to leave. The other outlaws were genuinely sorry to see them go, but they understood and respected their wishes. Before the four departed, they were made aware that they could depend on the group if they ever needed their assistance. With this understanding, Antonio and the others left the mountain compound.

They descended from the higher elevations and rode southward to Nicastro and then to the sloping hills surrounding Antonio's Maida. When they left the security of the mountains behind, they unavoidably increased their chances of being discovered, but there had been talk that the militia patrols had become fewer and less frequent, an aspect which was encouraging.

They arrived at the outskirts of Maida by early afternoon. Antonio, though anxious, thought it wise to visit his family after dark. The returning men made a temporary camp in the hills above the town and waited for the sun to set. When it was finally dark enough, Antonio departed and left his companions behind. He cautiously took the familiar road homeward. In a short time he found himself approaching the north side of the family home where the faint light of the kitchen lamp was easily visible. He arrived at the rear of the house, dismounted, and walked the remaining distance. When he was close enough, he peered through the window and saw his mother cooking as always. In a few steps, he was at the back door. He paused for a moment when he saw his father and younger brothers seated at the table about to eat their evening meal. He then lightly knocked on the door which brought an immediate response. The door swung open with caution as Don Fortunato took a step backward when he saw the huge figure of a bearded and bedraggled man. But within a moment's time, a wide smile broke out across his face as he recognized his oldest son. The men embraced each other and were soon joined by Angelina who almost dropped a pot of beans as she ran to him in haste. Not to be outdone, his two younger brothers gathered about to welcome Antonio. To the side, his bewildered little sister Rosa, who was at first frightened, reached up and hugged him around the waist. After tears of joy were wiped away, the reunited family sat at the table as they had so many times before and shared a meal together.

There was a lot of catching up to do. The conversation flowed easily as hours passed too quickly and Antonio brought his family up to date with the events that had taken place in recent months. Soon his brothers and sister were reluctantly sent off to bed. It was the opportunity for Antonio to talk with his parents about something he had given much thought to.

In the dim light of the kitchen, he beckoned the advice of his father and mother and informed them, "Recently I have devoted much thought to asking Signore Riccio for Teresa's hand in marriage."

"I hope you have considered the unsettling times that exist and the fact that you cannot show your face for fear of capture," his father replied, before continuing, "I know you love her very much, but do you think it would be fair to her?"

"I have thought of this and realize marriage at this time would have its disadvantages, but at least it will give us something to cling to," Antonio said and then paused. "For God only knows how long it will be before things will be right again. I know our marriage would not be under the best conditions, but it is a future life to hope for."

"I see," Don Fortunato said, "that you have given the matter very serious thought. However, what do you think Teresa and Signore Riccio will have to say about it?" Antonio hesitated.

"As far as Teresa is concerned, I am sure she will agree. Her father could present some opposition. Regardless of this, I am going to ask for his permission for her hand."

"If the two of you do marry, I am sure you would not ask her to go with you and also become a fugitive of the law," his mother stated.

"Of course not, Mamma," Antonio replied, "do you think I am mad? She would stay with her family until the time comes when I can come home to her."

"This decision, my son," advised his father, "will rest on your shoulders and hers. I will support your choice as I have in the past if it is approached with reason."

"Thanks, Papa. I appreciate your faith in my judgment and hope to also earn Signore Riccio's approval."

It was after midnight when Antonio left his parents' home. He returned to his friends in the hills as they slept soundly beside a glowing red-ember fire. The next morning he informed them of his decision to marry. They were all happy for him and Teresa.

That same night, under the cover of darkness, he left once again and went to the Riccio home. He had feelings of apprehension concerning Signore Riccio's possible reaction to his proposal of marriage. When he approached the large, familiar home, his heart quickened. His insecurity was out of character, for he was courageous in the heat of battle. At that moment, nonetheless, he felt very meek.

He knocked, and the door opened promptly. Signore Riccio answered and was somewhat shocked at the disheveled stranger before him. It took a few moments before he recognized the unkempt young man, but when he did, he threw his arm around Antonio's shoulder and escorted him inside. It had been months since his last visit. From out of nowhere came the impetuous dark-haired Teresa who stretched up to fling her arms around his neck. The nervous Antonio smiled. Not knowing what to say, the embarrassed young man was rescued by the loud voice of Signore Riccio. "Young lady, have you lost your mind? Use a little restraint. You have been raised properly," her father criticized. The red-faced Teresa reluctantly drew to the side as Antonio was invited to join them at the dinner table; to this Antonio did not need much coaxing.

Teresa's father had heard of the numerous bands of ex-soldiers who had chosen to become brigands. He was in total sympathy with them for they refused to live under the new dictatorial officials. He did confess he was ashamed that newly-freed Italians were becoming the new enemy of the poor. Teresa hadn't spoken much, but she didn't have to; the expression on her face and the glow in her lovely dark eyes gave her away. At that time, Antonio decided to ask her father for his daughter's hand in marriage.

The apprehensive young trooper explained the situation as he had done the previous night with his parents. At first, Signore Riccio was taken back but softened when Teresa expressed her desire to marry him. The fact that she would not be leaving the house after the wedding was the determining factor in her father's approval.

All too soon, Antonio left feeling very happy.

Arrangements for the marriage ceremony had been discussed and agreed by both families that attracting the least amount of attention would be prudent. Therefore, they arranged to have the marriage performed at La Chiesa Matrice Santa Maria, a local church where a personal friend, Father Umberto, would officiate. On a Wednesday night, at nine o'clock, the two families met at the old church to witness the secret marriage. Giacomo served as best man, and his two other companions witnessed the vows.

After the ceremony, the newlyweds spent their first night together in one of the many rooms in the spacious Riccio home. Unfortunately, as a safety precaution for all concerned, the honeymoon was agreed to be very brief.

Though somewhat naïve, the predestined couple reached deeply into themselves as they melded into each other. They became one as they experienced blissful love. Time was not an ally, but a spiritual bond emerged, bringing forth a pristine, enduring union.

Too early the following morning, Antonio was forced to return to the safety of the mountains, taking with him the memory of his beloved Teresa.

In the weeks that followed, the wanted men were forced to deal with the ever-mounting efforts made by the military for their capture. Those who sided with the new regime stood to gain but shuddered at the very mention of the bold brigands. The brave foursome took it upon themselves to right the many wrongs inflicted upon the helpless and elected themselves as avengers of the oppressed which was demonstrated in their nightly raids. In many towns rich land barons and other people of wealth supported the unfair government and hoped to obtain special privileges. They openly aligned themselves against the peasants and the working class. In reprisal, Antonio and his companions made repeated attacks and inflicted financial havoc upon the feudal landlords. Many a well-stocked barn—the direct result from honest toil of the hardworking poor—was a target for the bandits. The crops from these storage places were carted away and distributed among the needy or ruined, rendering them worthless. The self-appointed avengers would strike an area one night and then spring up in another location ten miles away the following night. Panic was surely spreading among the greedy barons who had become fat and content from the sweat of the poorly-compensated workers.

The rich saw to it that these laborers were constantly in debt to them and took advantage of their lack of business sense. The fate of the poor was to work all their lives and never once come close to repaying their wealthy lieges.

As a result, large rewards were offered for the capture of the notorious men responsible for the damaging, nightly raids. Meanwhile, many a peasant was the lucky recipient of a sack of flour or beans placed at their doorstep by some unknown, gracious benefactor. In rare instances, a horse or mule would appear tied out front as to no explanation of its source. The simple, defenseless people who were the beneficiaries gave thanks and accepted their good fortune.

The outlaws, constantly on the move, terrorized an area from Nicastro to Maida, as far east as Catanzaro and as far north as Tavernia. They were never at a hiding place for more than a few nights for fear of being betrayed or discovered by a searching patrol.

Weeks progressed and became months, but the authorities still were no closer to apprehending the elusive bandits than when they had begun pursuing them. At the same time, the unholy four continued to menace the rich and the corrupt town officials. Time after time, the patrols anticipated the moves of the wanted men, and as in the past, their efforts were futile. Many a night, a nobleman discovered his livestock run off while the next night, miles away, a bank would be set ablaze. Never establishing a pattern to their raids, the outlaws caused the enraged authorities to be forever in a state of confusion. This was worsened by the obvious fact that the peasants in the surrounding countryside supported and heralded the deeds of the Robin Hood-like bandits. Never once did the local officials receive any information which led to the location of the lawbreakers. This particular fact of not being able to depend on the cooperation of the people greatly hindered the militias' chances of apprehending them. The nightly raids were relentless, causing ever-mounting losses to the already-furious land owners. This was not allowed to continue, for it would be the ruination of many a baron.

A meeting of the noblemen of the surrounding area was arranged in an effort to find a solution which would end the damages being inflicted upon them. A scheme was devised which would surely flush out the marauding culprits. Information was to be intentionally leaked out that three supply wagons and an undetermined amount of gold coin was to be shipped from Maida to the town of Pizzo, fifteen miles south.

An area was selected by the militia between these two towns which was most likely to serve as the best scene for an ambush. They positioned themselves high above the road to have a clear, unobstructed vantage point. The road was primarily in the open except for a span of a hundred yards of huge boulders that blocked their view. From an elevated position, the authorities could easily swoop down upon any unsuspecting villains.

It was a little past midday when the three heavily-laden wagons and their drivers started out from Maida. Hoping to entice the outlaws, the wagons had been loaded in full view of everyone in the town square. It evidently worked, for one of the spectators in the crowd was Giacomo. He had gone to town to purchase a few much-needed supplies. Once again, he was selected because his identity was unknown in Maida.

When Giacomo returned to his friends, he informed them of the well-stocked cargo wagons. At first, Antonio and the others were skeptical about attacking them in broad daylight, but they soon agreed to have a try it regardless. They didn't want the rich barons to feel too secure in the shipping of their goods during the daylight hours. Antonio insisted they should scout the surrounding countryside before making the attempt. Since his companions thought it unnecessary, he volunteered to survey the roadside alone before they proceeded further. He approached the area they would use as an ambush site and chose a location just below the ridge of hills. As Antonio looked down toward the road, he started to have second thoughts about his overly-cautious attitude. He thought maybe his companions were correct and he was wasting time inspecting the area. No sooner had he relaxed his surveillance when he caught the sunlight reflecting off something metallic some distance below.

Again and again, the object flashed in the bright midday sun. As far as Antonio determined, it was emanating from a ledge overlooking the road. Upon closer inspection, he was able to see figures of at least a dozen armed soldiers. It was evident they were lying in wait for an ambush to occur. It was now all beginning to fit together. The big show of loading the wagons in the center of town was for their benefit. Antonio's first reaction was that of anger, but he started to smile as he pondered the situation. He took a closer look at the road below and noticed a section that was hidden from the view of the armed men. An area of huge stones blocked their sight. After evaluating the situation, he quickly turned his horse and reported back to the others.

When he arrived back at camp, his friends were quite surprised to hear of the averted trap and were very grateful for his suspicion. He informed them about the part of the road hidden from the militia. At first, the others thought he had gone mad when he suggested they continue with the ambush. He assured them that if they could make their way to the protection of the huge stones without being detected, they could still proceed to capture the wagons. First, the four of them had to surprise the drivers, bind them and then take their positions on top of the wagons wearing the drivers' hats and jackets. From there they were to drive directly past the soldiers and continue until they were completely out of sight. Antonio explained that the position of the soldiers overlooking the road was far enough away for them not to be able to recognize the faces of the drivers. It all sounded too daring, but because it was such a bold plan they went ahead with the challenge.

Within minutes, the outlaws were riding to the ambush site. Antonio feared his huge stature would signal something amiss; the four approached as closely as they could on horseback, dismounted, and then left their horses behind with Antonio. Giovanni, Francesco, and Giacomo made their way on foot, crouching behind the colossal boulders that bordered the road's edge. The three paused in the shadows and waited for the wagons.

Not more than thirty minutes later, they heard the rumbling of heavy wagons traveling closer to their position. The trio prepared themselves to leap upon the unsuspecting drivers. As the wagons entered the hidden section, each driver was immediately pounced upon. It all happened so suddenly that not one cry of help sounded. The drivers were promptly rendered unconscious by the fast-moving outlaws then bound and gagged by Antonio. The three other men then donned the drivers' hats and jackets and took their places aboard the wagons.

The nervous soldiers on the ridge above waited then breathed easier when they saw the wagons reappear from the behind the boulders. The three bandit drivers, with their heads bowed low, rode past the unsuspecting soldiers. The very brazen Giacomo then waved to the militia above. Fortunately, the soldiers smiled and waved back at the amiable driver. Six to seven minutes later, the wagons were completely out of sight as they headed southward to Pizzo.

After the supply wagons passed, the soldiers decided that the outlaws had skipped this opportunity for an ambush. They speculated that the road afforded very little cover and obviously scared them off. The militia felt somewhat frustrated and disappointed as they headed back to Maida.

The bandits turned off the road when they believed they were safe and far enough away. They rode into the hills as far as they dared and stopped to unload the cargo. In a short while, Antonio joined them, bringing their horses with him. Having taken a roundabout route, he avoided being followed. He and the others then decided to stash the captured goods, along with a small amount of gold in an abandoned, tumbled-down mountain cabin.

They released the three teams of horses and pushed the empty wagons over a ravine and watched them careen, smash, and then splinter into hundreds of pieces as they finally came to rest at the bottom of the gorge.

The soldiers reported back to the anxious barons that the drivers had passed by unmolested and they would probably arrive in Pizzo by late afternoon. The wealthy noblemen were a bit surprised that the wagons had gone through without incident. Their scheme to capture the marauding bandits had failed, but they did not know to what extent.

Early the following morning, the same barons, along with a few officers of the militia, assembled in the piazza and waited for the arrival of a messenger from Pizzo. Within the hour, a fast-moving rider approached. Those standing about were skeptical of his expression and knew something was amiss. The breathless rider dismounted and informed them that the wagons and the drivers never arrived in Pizzo. The barons were not at all surprised, but were infuriated at the inefficiency of the local military. All were appalled that a few outlaws could pillage and destroy at will without fear of ever being apprehended. There was no doubt that the culprits were Antonio Lochetto and Francesco Bozzi for they had been sighted by the son of Baron Rota on a mountain road a week earlier.

Baron Rota instigated the other land owners to devise a scheme to trap the outlaws for he had a deep hatred for Antonio and his family that went back many years. He resented the Lochettos and anyone else in the area who did not depend on him for their livelihood. The group of angry affluent men continued to argue with the military and demand protection of their homes and property. They could not understand how a few bandits could continually outmaneuver the local authorities.

Baron Rota added to the fervor of the situation as he remarked, "There may be a band of renegades in the mountains, but I can assure you the one most responsible for the damage is that *figlio di puttana* Antonio Lochetto. Somehow, someday, I will get my chance for revenge. This, I guarantee."

The following few weeks proved to be a windfall for the

local peasants. Fortune smiled at their front doors in the shape of urns of olive oil, sides of beef, and gifts of money. Through some remarkable quirk of fate, much to the consternation of the rich, all the bounty pillaged from the surrounding baronial estates was finding its way into the hands of the needy.

XIII
AIDED BY TERESA

As a result of the many raids aimed at the wealthy and the powerful, it was becoming increasingly difficult for the renegades to show themselves during daylight hours. The ever-mounting rewards that had been offered did not help their situation. It was only a matter of time before some weak-hearted soul would try to cash in on the easy money. This forced Antonio and the others to stay close to the camp by day and venture forth only under the cover of darkness. Shackled by this restriction, they had to seek out some outside emissary, one who would not be tempted by the increasing bounties.

Whoever it would be had to have knowledge of the area as well as be able to ride a horse with seasoned skill. It was this thought which convinced Antonio and his friends to choose Teresa for the role. She knew the country well from years of riding with her father during her adolescence. She had been known somewhat as a tomboy, much to her parents' dismay. Antonio agreed with the others that she would be the ideal person and that she could always be trusted and depended upon.

Teresa jumped at the opportunity. After this, she had to convince her worried parents to agree with her decision. They did so, albeit reluctantly.

As to not arouse suspicion in Maida, she purchased much-needed supplies—tobacco, cartridges, and canned goods—in surrounding towns because everyone in her own town knew of her betrothal to the notorious Antonio Lochetto. She employed every precaution in an effort to avoid being followed but it was impossible on some occasions. The local authorities had hoped she would unknowingly lead them to the outlaw hideout.

It was on one such occasion, while she was returning with supplies from Borgia, that she unsuspectingly rode by a patrol. They were hidden from view behind thickets by the side of the road. One of the local soldiers recognized her as Antonio's sweetheart. Informing the others of her identity, they decided to follow her. They traveled far enough behind her to remain undetected as they pursued her over mountain trails. After riding for some time, Teresa was still unaware of her followers. She brought her tired horse to a halt by a rapidly moving stream, dismounted, and drew a cold refreshing drink of water. The pursuing patrol continued to close the gap between them. Having quenched her thirst, she leaned back against the tree to rest a while before continuing. She closed her eyes for a few moments as the sound of the rushing water and the chirping woodland birds lulled her into a reverie. Then—almost undetectable at first, the muffled sound of horse's hooves interrupted her peaceful interlude. Fortunately, the riders had not seen her turn off the road and kept going. Teresa realized she was being followed and swiftly remounted her horse.

Hoping to lead her followers astray, she took the way that led to her home instead of the outlaw camp. She maintained her distance and soon drew up in front of her house. The patrol had halted some distance away and waited for her to reappear. To their frustration, an hour passed, but she was nowhere to be seen. They surmised that she had detected their presence. With resignation, they gave up their futile vigil and returned to town.

Before the sun rose the following morning, Teresa selected a fresh horse and rode quietly toward the mountains. She checked and rechecked her back trail to make certain she was not being followed again. She arrived at the camp long overdue. Antonio and the others had been worried sick over her long delay. He realized she was a resourceful person, but nonetheless, they were still apprehensive. She reassured her husband, "Cara Mia, you shouldn't worry so. This isn't the first time that the patrols have tried to follow me, and it will not be the last. I have always managed to lead them on a chase to nowhere. Do you forget the times I lost you on the same trails when we were young?" Antonio smiled and nodded his head.

"True, but I do not want to put you in any more danger than what is necessary. If something should happen to you, I would never forgive myself."

"Remember, I can ride as well—if not better—than most men. But if it will please you, I promise not to take any unnecessary chances." Her words calmed Antonio's anxiety.

They gathered around the campfire to discuss the strategy of their next raid and agreed upon who would next receive their wrath.

Most of their menacing escapades were confined to the evening, but there were occasions where they were forced to act during the daylight. One such incident occurred when a patrol was sent into the interior whose prime mission was to make contact, if possible, with the elusive bandits. The wanted men had just returned to camp when they heard the approaching soldiers. It was decided by Giacomo to draw them into a chase. Unknowingly, the searching party had almost stumbled upon their hideout; had they continued further, they would have ridden straight through the camp. Their main objective was to lure the soldiers as far away from the area as possible. The fugitives managed to stay just ahead of them, but close enough to lead them further astray.

There were times during the chase when the outlaws intentionally exposed their position to taunt the pursuing patrol. This was done only when the renegades thought they were well enough ahead and knew they could not possibly be caught. Again and again, they outdistanced and outsmarted their pursuers. Revealing their location, they appeared a few hundred yards above the laboring cavalry. They whistled and waved their arms, beckoning the flustered Red Shirts; they knew they would be long gone by the time the search party would reach their position. At times the persistent soldiers came very close to apprehending the fleeing bandits, but within moments, the outlaws would miraculously appear on another mountainside out of reach. Indeed, it was very frustrating for the militia to have the culprits in sight and never be able to reach them.

The soldiers, after riding across half of Calabria, decided to slow the pace but continue their pursuit. The elusive outlaws realized the tenacious militia and their horses were tiring; the renegades plotted to embarrass them further. Antonio and the others concealed themselves on both sides of the mountain road and waited for their unsuspecting prey to ride into their ambush. The weary patrol never anticipated that the bandits would halt and confront them, especially when the soldiers outnumbered them eight to four. Unaware of the hidden outlaws, the agitated party galloped closer. When they came within range, Antonio and Giacomo burst forth from road's edge into the direct path of their stunned pursuers. The fugitives confronted them, leveling their carbines at the heads of the first two soldiers, and received the undivided attention of the remainder of the patrol. Simultaneously, Francesco and Giovanni appeared to their rear, also wielding their weapons. Completely taken off guard, the weary militia offered no resistance and threw their weapons to the ground. When they picked up the firearms, Giacomo remarked, "It seems a little ironic that you are our captives instead of the other way around."

"That may be very true," Antonio added, "but we do not want you as our prisoners. Our vengeance will come from the ridicule you will receive from your peers. Gentlemen, please do me the favor of dismounting from your horses. They will no longer be any use to you. If you start walking now you will be able to reach town by tomorrow morning at the latest. Think of it as a health benefit. The fifteen mile hike will do wonders for you." The disgruntled soldiers muttered obscenities in response.

"Oh, stop your crying. Consider yourselves fortunate, for if I had my way, you would be walking back without your boots. Leave before we change our minds!" Giovanni exclaimed.

Grumbling and stumbling, the eight disillusioned soldiers began their long trek back to Maida. In the background, the four outlaws shook their heads in disbelief at the spectacle before them. They laughed wholeheartedly as they watched the humiliated men make their way on foot along the dusty, rock-strewn road knowing they would spend an uncomfortable night in the mountains.

When the patrol finally arrived at the edge of town the following morning, the forlorn group hoped to enter as inconspicuously as possible. Adding to their embarrassment, they had been spotted by two old men who happened to be the town's biggest gossips. One of the old-timers soon darted off to inform the local authorities about the missing militia while the other man summoned the attention of whoever would listen. By the time the ruffled men lumbered their way to head-quarters, half the townspeople were following in their wake. Many a spectator snickered at the sight of the horseless cavalry patrol. Like dogs with their tails between their legs, the men approached the headquarters in disgrace. Their commander stood on the steps before them with his hands on his hips with a disturbed expression. Every returning man wanted to shrink from his penetrating stare. "I am glad you men finally thought it was time to return, but aren't you all missing something?" the irate commander remarked, unable to contain himself. "Did you not leave yesterday on horses?"

"But commander, we were completely taken by surprise and could not help the consequences that followed," one of the belittled men bravely rebuked, "You know how elusive those outlaws can be."

"You were taken by surprise by four men. Well, I have another little surprise for all of you. Since you prefer to go about on foot, this will continue to be your future means of travel. Italy does not have a surplus of good horses, and therefore, cannot replace the ones that were lost." The thoroughly degraded and dejected men were dismissed promptly.

"Antonio Lochetto, this time I think I have a way of smoking you and the other vermin out from your lofty place," the commander muttered to himself with agitation.

More than ever, the wanted men depended increasingly more on Teresa for her assistance. She frequently made trips to and from camp and always managed to lead the soldiers astray. One day, as she was returning from her errands at Nicastro, she was followed by three militia men. This in itself did not alarm her; it had become almost routine, though this time, the trio of riders stayed much closer than usual. She had already decided which direction she would lead them and increased her horse's pace. Her followers did the same which seemed unusual to her.

Again, she spurred her horse's gait even quicker and again, the men did likewise. She sensed the situation would not go as it had in the past. She desperately attempted to outdistance her pursuers, but it was to no avail; they were already too close. Adding to the dilemma was the fact that her mare was tired from the trip to Nicastro, whereas the soldiers were on fresher horses. This became very apparent when they gained distance with every stride. Teresa frantically tried to lose them and pushed her mare to her limits. It was all in vain, for the riders had closed the gap to only a few horse lengths behind her. Within moments, they were riding alongside and one of them leaned over and snatched the reins from her hands. The three soldiers drew to a halt and surrounded her. "The army of Italy now makes war against women? Or is it because the outlaws are too tough for you? So now you take your vengeance out on a woman? Next you will be against young children and the defenseless old," Teresa chided them.

"Silence. It is not you we seek. It is your bandit boyfriend who we want. Maybe now we can persuade him to meet us in the open. I think when he hears that you are being held hostage, he will leave the safety of his hideout and rescue his precious woman. You are just the bait for the trap," one of the soldiers rebuked.

"I would not be so sure that your plan will work out. It might turn out differently than anticipated," she warned.

The patrol escorted their female prisoner to town and made no attempt to hide the fact that they were taking her to jail. It was obvious they had been instructed to create as much attention as possible. The authorities hoped some outlaw sympathizer would bring the news of her capture to Antonio's ears.

Hours later, at the mountain camp, Antonio was seen pacing back and forth, obviously worried about Teresa being long overdue, but it was not the first time this had occurred. He prayed it was the same situation and she would arrive soon.

It was well after midnight when the outlaws were suddenly awakened by the sound of an oncoming rider. None of the four men demonstrated any real anxiety, for they all believed it was Teresa returning. To their surprise, it turned out to be Vito Franciosa, a trust-worthy friend who had ridden with them once before when they were all members of the same band. He drew up forcefully and dismounted in haste. "Vito, my good friend, why do you ride as if your life depends on your every stride? What could be so important that it could not wait until morning?" Giacomo asked with concern. Their loyal friend looked at Antonio.

"I don't know how to tell you, but they have imprisoned your Teresa." Antonio flushed with immediate anger.

"Who has done this and why?" he asked.

"The soldiers from the town captured her yesterday afternoon. They caught up with her then forcibly escorted her to jail," their friend explained.

"Well, that will be remedied soon, I assure you," Antonio declared.

"This is exactly what they want you to do. Can you not see? They want to provoke you into making some kind of foolish mistake. Please, my friend, don't let them have their way," Giacomo interjected. Antonio paused and fought to control his rage.

"The way I feel at this moment, I would like to ride into town and tear the jail down with my bare hands. But I must admit, this all sounds like a really desperate scheme. I better control my temper and think about this more rationally." He contemplated his next move as he walked away from the others. At that point, Giacomo took time to thank Vito who brought the information concerning Teresa. He reached into his cardigan, withdrew a gold coin, and threw it to their loyal friend. Vito caught the coin in his hand and then tossed it back.

"Please, don't insult me. I came to notify a friend, not to collect a fee."

"That, my good man, is the truth. You are a good friend, indeed," Giacomo said with a grateful smile. Vito shook his hand and rode back toward town.

After almost an hour of being alone, Antonio rejoined his companions by the fire. He squatted down before the flames and told the others of his plan to free Teresa. He would slip into town at night and set fire to a nearby building and leave a note warning the authorities that he would burn down the entire town to the ground if they did not release her. His friends reluctantly agreed that it might work and it sure beat storming the jail and foolishly endangering more lives.

The following morning and through the remainder of the day, the local militia waited for Antonio's arrival. They waited in vain. The authorities were bewildered, for they were well aware of his raging temper. A response was not initiated until that night.

Under the mantle of night, the avenging outlaws slipped into the slumbering town. They stuck close to the sides of buildings as they managed their way through the dark streets. Undetected, Giacomo and Antonio carried metal containers of kerosene while Francesco and Giovanni stood guard with their carbines.

Edging closer to the jail, the unseen men paused for a last-minute check of their intended objective. Once again, they decided on the local dry goods store as their target, for the building stood directly across the street in full view of the jail. The two men carried the kerosene as they crawled on all fours until they were directly beneath the large windows of the store. They stuffed oil-soaked pieces of cloth into the openings of the containers and hurled the fire bombs through the glass. Flames spread rapidly through the first floor and the entire building was soon engulfed in flames.

Astonished soldiers came running from the opposite side of the street. A water bucket brigade was hastily formed but proved to be useless from the start. The raging fire was too far gone for the business to be saved. They barely managed to contain the fire from spreading to other buildings.

By dawn, only the supporting beams, still smoldering, remained of the charred structure. Later that day, one of the soldiers discovered a message that had been tacked to a door of a nearby storefront. It was addressed to the commander of the militia:

The destructive fire is only a sample of what will happen if you don't release Teresa Riccio. If she is not freed soon and unharmed according to my demands, the entire town will be put to the torch. Don't think this is an idle threat. At precisely 3pm on Wednesday, I want you to raise and lower the flag on top of the records building three times signifying her release. In the event that this is not done, I promise you that the consequences that will follow will rest upon your shoulders. You will set her free if you have the welfare of the town in mind.

The commander read and re-read the message then paused and looked at the still-smoking remains. He was thoroughly convinced that Antonio was not making idle or empty threats. Soon the shopkeepers and businessmen got wind of the message and demanded that the authorities release Teresa immediately. They were joined by others of the town and agreed that she must be released.

As a result of these pressures, the authorities had little choice in the matter. At three in the afternoon, Teresa was released in compliance, and the flag was raised and lowered as Antonio instructed.

Meanwhile, on a nearby hilltop overlooking the town, anxious men looked for the anticipated signal. Antonio focused his telescope toward town and watched at the precise time to see if the flag would come down and rise again as he had requested. It did, to his relief.

Antonio was glad for the townspeople; he did not want to resort to such a heinous act, but most importantly, his beloved Teresa was safe.

XIV
FINDING THE GOLD

On a routine errand, Teresa thought she heard the sound of many horses closing in and pulled to the side of the road. She hid behind some tall brambles and waited to get a glimpse of the riders. The sound grew louder as the first few soldiers filed by. Realizing it was not the usual patrol but a much larger group, she counted the number.

A little while later as the last of the riders rode past, Teresa had estimated that between seventy-five and eighty troopers were heading toward Maida. Apparently, these men were reinforcements for those already stationed there; the column of soldiers was traveling south while she was journeying northward.

After the dust cleared, she cautiously returned to the road and set an unhurried pace. It was an exceptionally beautiful day. When she resumed riding, her eye caught the image of something in the center of the road up ahead. She slowed her horse to halt. She dismounted and crouched down to brush the road's dust from the indiscernible object. A closer look revealed it to be a locked black leather satchel. Curious about the contents, she lifted it, and to her surprise, it took the effort of both her hands to move it. She barely managed to put the handles of the satchel over the pommel and then continued her ride.

When she arrived at the hideout, she told Antonio about the column of troopers that had passed her on the road to town. Surprisingly enough, he had already known of their presence, for Giovanni had spotted their dust earlier that morning. Teresa told her husband about the heavy satchel she had found. Curiously, Antonio walked to her horse and lifted the bag from the saddle. He placed it on the ground, and he was immediately joined by the others who wondered about its contents. The lock on the bag held it tightly shut. Antonio motioned to Giacomo who quickly produced a long, thin bladed stiletto from his boot. The sharp knife easily pierced the leather as the side of the bag was slit. Antonio dumped the contents to the ground. The clinking of scores of gold coins falling at their feet stunned the small group as they stood motionless in disbelief. Finally, Francesco broke the silence. "My friends, pinch me. Tell me I must be dreaming. This cannot be real."

"If it is a dream, we are all having the same one!" Antonio exclaimed. Giacomo knelt on the ground and touched the coins. "Ah, you are right, Antonio," Giacomo marveled, "These are gold ducats from King Emmanuel himself. There is enough here to give each of us a small fortune! Let's divide it."

"Just a minute," Antonio interrupted, "let us think about this awhile. Have we lowered ourselves to where we have become nothing but common thieves? You know as well as I do who this gold belongs to. The King's seal is the emblem on the bag. Evidently, this money belongs to the company of troopers that had passed by this morning. Think of the consequences that could arise by us withholding it. They must realize by now that it's missing, and I assure you they will waste no time in dispatching a number of patrols to search for it. Instead of finding the gold, they might find us. This we do not need. And what about the people who put their trust in us? They will think we are nothing but common highwaymen."

"As you said before," Giacomo responded, "let's take some time before we make a decision about the fate of the gold."

"Alright, my impetuous friend, we will give ourselves twenty-four hours to think about it," Antonio commented with annoyance. He was apparently upset over Giacomo's over-zealous attitude. "Then we will take a vote among us, including Teresa, for it was she who found the money. I will abide by the will of the majority as I am sure all of you will."

A few miles away in town, the commander of the garrison and the captain of the troopers were furious over the loss of the company's gold. A patrol was immediately dispatched to retrace the route taken by the soldiers. They were to go as far east as the town of Catanzaro where the reinforcements of troopers originated. Clods of earth flew from the hooves of the horses as the men departed with hopes of retrieving the gold.

There were many people in town who had their own opinion concerning the fate of the soldiers' lost pay. It was general knowledge that Teresa Riccio frequented that particular road on her errands for her infamous Antonio. Therefore, it was more than likely that she had found the money.

The following morning the search party was midway to Catanzaro but still had not yet uncovered one clue concerning the satchel of money. Back at the outlaw camp, Giacomo was still adamantly in favor of dividing the gold, as was Giovanni who quickly seconded his motion. Antonio and Teresa were in favor of returning the money. This left the deciding vote to be cast by Francesco. "To tell you the truth, I would like to keep the gold, but if I take it, I am no better than a thief, and this I am not. I say we give back the gold," he said with conviction.

Upon hearing Francesco's decision, Antonio smiled broadly and slapped his friend on the back. But it was obvious that Giacomo was very upset as he turned without saying a word and rode off on his horse in a fit of anger.

Giovanni, who had sided with Giacomo said, "He'll be back. He may be fuming now, but come tomorrow, he will come back smiling."

"I hope you are right," Antonio remarked, "We have been close friends for a long time."

By nightfall, the patrol had ended their search and arrived in Catanzaro empty-handed. They immediately sent a message back to the commander in Maida informing him of their unsuccessful trip. The commander went into a rage when he received the message. As the senior officer of the garrison, he was solely responsible for the safety of the payroll; undoubtedly, he would have his career cut short if it was not found. In desperation, he appealed to the people for any information concerning the lost money. A handsome reward was then posted.

It was this incentive that motivated a poor peasant two days later to inform the distraught commander of what everyone else already knew. The peasant told him of Teresa's frequent rides along that particular mountain road. When the commander was made aware of this, he immediately sent a rider to the Riccio home in hopes of contacting her. With words that appealed to the virtues of charity and fairness, the courier relayed the urgent plea to Teresa's parents. Though she was not home at the time, they would see to it that she received the message.

Meanwhile at the camp, Antonio, Teresa, and the other two men waited for Giacomo's return; many hours had already passed since his disturbing departure. Darkness began to enshroud their camp. Teresa had waited as long as she could and then left to return home. The three remaining men gave up their vigil for their friend's return as they wrapped themselves in blankets and bedded down beside the fire.

Hours later, just beyond the light of the campfire, the shadow of a man slowly advanced toward the sleeping men. He inched his way closer as the firelight revealed his identity. It was Giacomo. But why was he lurking in the dark?

He moved carefully to avoid waking his friends. He sneaked past them to where the saddles were kept, and deftly and soundlessly, went through the contents of the saddle bags. It did not take him long to withdraw a fistful of gold coins and leave the major portion still in the bag. With haste, he slipped back into the shadows to his waiting horse. *They cannot say that I took more than my share of the gold. What they do with theirs is fine with me, but I do not wish to be a righteous fool*, he thought as he gently tugged on the horse's bit and trotted away into the night.

Early the next morning, Antonio was awakened by the chirping of birds. He shook his blanket free of any debris and then walked to the nearby stream to refresh himself. Not quite fully awake, he almost overlooked fresh footprints alongside the water. Taking a closer look, he realized they belonged to his small friend Giacomo. He followed the tracks back to camp and was puzzled. Why hadn't he made his presence known? Then remembering the disagreement over the gold, Antonio hurried to the saddle bags where the money was stashed. He discovered that the strap of the bag had been unfastened. He anticipated the worst. He was relieved when he opened the bag and saw the gold. He then dumped the contents and began to count the coins.

He realized that approximately one fifth—which represented one full share—was missing. Even though it was voted upon to return the money, Giacomo apparently was not going to accept that decision.

Antonio alerted his slumbering friends and informed them of their comrade's thieving visit during the night. They were surprised to hear of his larcenous act, for he had never before attached such importance to possessing money. They thought the many months spent living as a fugitive must have affected his sense of ethics. Nonetheless, the others were determined to see the safe return of all the gold; they did not wish to be regarded as robbers who would steal from the pockets of poorly-paid soldiers.

The three men agreed to send someone to overtake Giacomo. It was to be Antonio, for he had known him the longest and also knew his ways and habits.

Antonio picked up Giacomo's trail just beyond the camp and then started to track his double-crossing friend. The tell-tale prints led deeper into the central highlands. Avoiding the main paths as much as possible, Giacomo had traveled from one mountain to another. The way he chose had taken him across precipitous ledges, through valley streams and gullies, all in an effort to reduce the chances of being followed. He left as few signs as possible which made tracking him very difficult.

By 7a.m. Giacomo had a five-to-six hour lead and was twenty miles ahead of his persistent friend. He had tired from the hours of riding through the night, and feeling secure of his distance, stopped to rest and eat something. With a few dried twigs, he quickly made a smokeless fire to heat a mug of tea. He then withdrew a piece of cured ham from his saddle bag and ate and drank until he was satiated. True to his character, he felt quite content and leaned back against a large rock and was soon very drowsy. He decided there would be no harm in dozing off for a while.

Not long after, he was in a deep sleep, and hours slipped by unnoticed while Antonio continued trailing him and gaining ground with every passing minute. Though the trail was difficult to uncover, Antonio had a very good idea where his friend was headed. Based mostly on a gut feeling, he raced in a straight course to a campsite that he and the others had used almost a year earlier. It was a high promontory overlooking a lush valley. He had ridden more than six hours without pause but pushed himself and his horse to their limits without stopping. He soon arrived at the base of a mountain and then rested his stallion before making the final ascent to the top.

The shriek of a low-flying osprey momentarily disturbed the sleeping Giacomo. He opened his eyes half-heartedly to see the squawking bird swoop behind a nearby tree. His curiosity was satisfied, and he closed his eyes to sleep once again.

Two thousand feet below, Antonio remounted his horse after resting for a while. He found the narrow path leading to the top and resumed his ascent. After thirty minutes of arduous riding, both horse and rider popped their heads above the edge of the summit. He then got off his horse and began to look around.

His eye caught a glimpse of Giacomo's horse tied to a small scrub bush as he approached a group of large pines. He carefully encircled the trees and almost stumbled upon his snoozing friend. With his hands resting on his hips, Antonio stood above Giacomo and was reminded how his lazy vigilance had gotten him into serious trouble once before. Then with his foot, Antonio kicked his friend's boot. This only stirred Giacomo but didn't wake him. Antonio finally let out a loud, shrill whistle. Giacomo was so startled that he almost jumped to his feet. He squinted and saw the large frame of Antonio standing over him. "Once again, my little friend, your dozing off has gone against you," Antonio chided, "When will you learn to stay awake? You know damn well why I am here."

"Truthfully, I did not think you would follow me, for I only took *my* share of the gold."

"But that is exactly it! It's not yours to take. Had you found the payroll instead of Teresa, you might have some claim to it. We cannot return only four fifths of the money. More or less, Teresa and the rest of us are responsible for its entirety. Therefore, please hand over the gold willingly. I do not want to take it from you."

Accepting fate, Giacomo reached into his saddle bag and reluctantly took a bulging, knotted handkerchief full of coins and tossed it to Antonio. Giacomo, having relinquished his share, remarked, "Well, I probably would not know what to do with that much money anyway. And to tell you the truth, my conscience was beginning to trouble me. I don't think I would make a very good thief." Antonio reached over and gently held Giacomo's shoulder.

"My friend, I think these uncertain times have forced us to forget our true values, and frankly, the first time I saw the gold, I also dreamed of what I would do with a small fortune. I fought feelings of greed but persuaded myself to not give in to these selfish desires. I don't think we have reached that low yet, and I hope we never do."

The two reunited friends shook hands and turned their backs from the summit and decided they would travel south to return to their companions.

They rode into camp side by side as they had done scores of time before. Their friends were waiting when they arrived and were happy to see the two men together again.

Giacomo got off his horse and called out, "Francesco! Giovanni! I bet you thought you were rid of me. No such luck! I am back and here to stay." He smiled broadly. The other two men laughed and shook the hand of their returning prodigal brother.

Teresa had returned home after deciding with Antonio and the others on what to do about the gold. She was informed by her parents of the desperate commander's plea. She responded bravely and decided to ride to the garrison and offer to help with the return of the soldiers' pay.

The distraught commander once again appealed to Teresa's sense of charity, for this would certainly save his career if she knew the location of the gold. He expressed that he would be eternally grateful for its return. She told him she could not make a definite promise until she heard from Antonio and the others. After having secured the commander's word that she would not be followed, she mounted her horse and headed out of town toward the mountains.

She took a circuitous route to make sure she was not being trailed. Sometime later, she saw her husband and Giacomo in the familiar clearing near their camp. They seemed to be friends as before. When Antonio saw Teresa enter the camp, he walked briskly toward her carrying the black pay satchel and greeted her with an embrace and a kiss on the cheek. "Cara Mia, now you can return the gold to the nervous commander. Tell him not one coin is missing and he is very fortunate that the money found its way into the hands of honest men, for if anyone else had gotten possession of it, I am sure he would never see a single gold coin again."

Teresa nodded in agreement as Antonio secured the

heavy satchel to her saddle. "Please promise me you will be very careful and ride directly to town without stopping. I am sure there is more than one desperate person who would give his right arm for this."

"I know," she answered, "I will stop only when I have reached the militia headquarters where I will personally hand it over to the commander."

"Very good, go now, and have a safe journey." After one more kiss, she spurred her horse and bolted out of camp toward town.

The long-striding steed swallowed up the miles between the high mountains and the town of Maida. It was not too long before she was galloping toward the piazza in the center of town. The sharp sound of iron hooves striking the wet cobblestone echoed throughout the town.

She reined up in front of the garrison, and before she could dismount, the anxious commander was standing in the doorway to greet her. He did not have to say a word; his eyes said it all—pleading—hoping—that she had returned with the gold. Teresa slid from the saddle and asked him to help her remove the heavy satchel. His face lit up joyfully as he lifted the leather bag from her horse. "My dear young woman, you are a saint. You do not know it, but you practically saved my life. All my years of service and my future pension all depended upon the recovery of the money. I am so ever grateful and would do anything in my power to help you if you should ever need it. Mil grazie, signora."

"Do not thank me. It was the so-called evil brigands your rich friends hate so who decided to return the gold. You owe your thanks to them," Teresa remarked.

"Signora, please extend my gratitude when you see them. Tell them they have nothing to fear from me in the future, and that I know they are honest and gallant men," the commander said, clutching the bag.

So ended an era of hostility between the four ex-Bourbon brigands and the local authorities, but the rich barons and conditions were as such that they would remain adversaries. Whether it was true or false, there were too many acts of plunder accredited to Antonio and his friends. As a result, the barons posted new bounties for these men, increasing the amount each passing week. Consequently, Antonio and the others had little choice but to remain in mountain isolation to hide and endure.

XV
RENDEZVOUS AND TROUBLE FOR THE RICCIOS

In only a couple of years, Antonio Lochetto had gone from boy to soldier and soldier to brigand. He had relinquished his own well-being for what he saw as the greater good and in doing so, became accustomed to living on guard, moment to moment, with very little allowance for emotional latitude.

At age twenty-one, he was also a husband who had not been with his wife for more than a few hours at a time. Teresa still stole away from the safety of her parents' home to visit her beloved renegade, but both she and Antonio were in desperate need of a few interrupted days together where they would have time and freedom to be young and their true selves.

Signor Riccio gave his consent to the weary newlyweds to spend time at the family hunting cabin in the verdant foothills of La Sila.

"Don't you let that wife of yours turn you into a sad-eyed goat," Giacomo teased as Antonio packed supplies for a five-day rendezvous with his beloved. "You had better come back to us, Romeo," the others warned him as they tugged at his shirt and slapped him on the back with affection. Antonio ignored their comments and rolled his eyes with embarrassment as he stuffed his saddle bags with necessities and tried not to dwell on his inner conflict. He was torn between the voice of reason telling him that leaving the current campsite was reckless and the quieter voice telling him to follow his heart. Antonio sided with the latter and mounted his horse with a shy smile. He waved to his teasing, albeit good-intentioned friends and then rode out of sight.

"Cara Mia, relax. They will not find us, not here," Teresa whispered against Antonio's bare shoulder as rain darkened the twilight beyond the stone refuge of her family's humble but warm cabin. He was finally with his Teresa, her long hair glistening like a raven's wing in the fire's glow. But he found it very difficult to breathe easy. His cavalry life and survival in the mountains had heightened every nerve, and out of reflex, felt an inclination to pursue the slightest creak in the old house.

"Forgive me, but I have forgotten how to be a normal

man. It is a fact that I do not even know who I am, patriot or brigand," Antonio confessed with hesitation as he wound her hair around his index finger with affection.

"Tony, my Antonio, you are neither of those," Teresa said as she lifted her face to look at him. She had known him all of her life, yet seeing his gray-blue eyes in the dim light was like seeing them for the first time, and she paused with happiness. "Don't you see, occhi azzurri, you are *mine*. That is who you are. You belong to me and the beauty of these mountains." Her mouth found his, and their smiles melted into a kiss.

"Thank you for reminding me," Antonio whispered, holding her tighter as the rain poured in sheets beyond the shuttered windows. The sweetness of the storm blew between the slats and for a moment, deceived them into believing it was spring instead of autumn.

"Tell me, what do you dream about while you lie under the stars every night?" Teresa snuggled closer against him until their bare forms melded in seamless harmony.

"The day I have my freedom to give you the life you deserve, Cara Mia. Sometimes I think it may never come. These times make me doubt even my own plans."

"I will wait forever, Antonio Lochetto," Teresa said, holding him even tighter.

"Sometimes I think you are stronger than I."

"I will wait forever if I have to. And then someday, I will give you blue-eyed sons." Her eyes filled with tears, and for the first time in a long time, Antonio felt his mind let down its guard and his heart open with bitter sweetness.

"In the meantime, you cannot act old before your time. Come!" Teresa added, leaping out of bed with sudden mischief.

"Where?" Antonio asked, laughing and not worrying if his voice was too loud.

"Come!" Teresa flew out the door and lifted her face to the fragrant rain. Antonio hesitated but then followed his wife's playful beckoning. Soon, the storm washed over their bareness, and they laughed like they did when they were children when they chased each other through meadows on horseback. "You see, my Love, we are still young!" Her voice rang like a bell between claps of thunder.

"You are always right!" Antonio exclaimed, stretching his arms out like a boy, melting into the present moment with joy and without reservation.

Upon returning from his blissful time with Teresa, Antonio rejoined his friends at the hideout camp, and Teresa headed back to her parents' house.

When approaching her home, she noticed three horses tied in front and two others near the barn. She thought it quite odd; any of their friends or relatives who usually dropped by would arrive by buggy or carriage.

For caution, she rode to the rear of the barn and slid off her horse quietly and walked around the front. She heard two strangers speaking softly. She continued to sneak her way to the house to have a closer look. Pressed against the side of the house, Teresa was able to peek through a parted shutter and was startled to see her parents sitting with their hands bound behind them and men ransacking the premises. One of the men shouted loudly to the two others near the barn, asking them if they had found anything of value. She could not believe her eyes and ears and quickly realized she could do nothing without help. Undetected, Teresa made her way back to her horse and quickly rode off.

It was almost nightfall when she rode into camp to Antonio's surprise. He looked over the fire and saw that his wife was obviously very troubled. Teresa jumped off her horse and ran to him. "Antonio, strange men have my mother and father as hostage in their house. I am deathly afraid that they will be harmed!"

"Don't worry, Cara Mia. We will leave now," Antonio said, turning to his friends. "Will you help us?"

"Of course," Giacomo replied, "You insult us by even asking us. Let's go!" Francesco and Giovanni immediately responded with their support.

They departed with haste and rode toward the Riccio home. There was a full moon that night which helped illuminate the way. Fortunately, all had traveled that particular path hundreds of times and could navigate it almost by instinct. With the moonlit night, conditions were favorable, and the miles passed swiftly.

Before long, the anxious riders descended the hills above Maida. A single light dimly flickered from the Riccio home. The riders approached the house silently, left their horses, and proceeded on foot to the rear of the barn. Francesco and Giovanni slipped through the half-open door into the dark barn. They emerged within a few minutes and reported to the others that everything seemed normal. Giacomo then suggested that he and Giovanni go to the house, for both of them were much smaller in size and less likely to be seen. Antonio, Teresa, and Francesco agreed to remain hidden nearby.

Giacomo, with his back against the outer wall, crept closer to look in. He saw no one in the low-lit room. Meanwhile, Giovanni was around the front of the house and saw no one. They both entered and searched the premises with the same result. There were no horses about; every single one had been taken. Giovanni yelled out to the others that is was safe to enter. The house had been ransacked with furniture overturned, drawers pulled out, and rugs rolled halfway up. Evidently, they were looking for anything of value.

Teresa could not contain herself when she walked in and went into a hysterical rage. Antonio tried his best to calm her worst fears, but it was futile. A note had been tacked to the wall with a knife, confirming their conclusions. It was apparent that her parents had been abducted. The note stated that if Teresa ever wanted to see them again that she would have to follow their instructions to the letter. One way or another, she would be contacted the following day. Any deal would be off if she went to the authorities and she would never see her mother and father again.

Antonio was outraged and did not want to wait to be contacted. He suspected that it was a gang of thieves who had been robbing and extorting money from local farmers. He had an altercation with one of them months earlier when the ring leader approached him about joining forces. When Antonio emphatically rejected the offer, the entire band was insulted and made a few idle threats toward him. At the time, Antonio had thought that their anger was passing and then soon forgot the incident until he stumbled upon their hideout when he had been looking for Giacomo. They were intoxicated and riled up about getting revenge on the locals. Antonio heard enough and then left the half-crazed brigands.

Antonio had more than a hunch regarding the whereabouts of the kidnappers. They all presented ideas which could work and be the safest for the Riccios. They finally decided to have Antonio, Giacomo, and Giovanni leave in pursuit as soon as possible. They rode westward while Francesco remained behind with Teresa to receive any further instructions from the kidnappers.

The bright autumnal moon illuminated the night, aiding the three men in their search. They maneuvered through many familiar mountain trails; after many hours, Antonio finally recognized a large rock escarpment where the kidnappers had camped last. The position had a strategic bird's eye view of the canyon below.

The three searchers agreed to leave their horses behind for the narrow trail to the top was very steep and treacherous for the animals to maneuver. Slinging their carbines on their backs, the men climbed hand over hand, pulling their way to the crest. Antonio recalled that the campsite was hidden behind two mammoth boulders, and they moved closer until they saw the thieves' campfire flickering in the darkness. They heard loud laughter and voices speaking of the large ransom they would receive.

Antonio and the others moved nearer and saw Teresa's parents sitting on the ground with their hands and legs bound. They were positioned on the perimeter of the camp with their backs to the fire. The kidnappers continued to boast, saying that the bonus would be the fact that the money would be coming from Teresa, the girlfriend of the big choirboy Antonio Lochetto. Upon hearing this, the irate Antonio was set to lunge forward, but his two friends restrained him and whispered, "Let's move a distance away and think about this."

Back at the Riccio home, Teresa and Francesco waited for a message from the kidnappers. Around three in the morning, a sharp gunshot rang out followed by another, and shortly after, the sound of hooves fading into the distance. They waited long enough after the mystery rider rode away. Francesco slipped out the door to see what he could discover. He ventured toward the direction where the gunshots had been fired and looked about with caution. He saw a glint of light, a knife stuck into a tree and shining under the moon. It held a scribbled note. Francesco removed the knife and slanted the paper to the moonlight to read. The note demanded ten thousand in gold ducats to be deposited at the base of the tree, emphasizing that if the gold was not delivered to the spot within forty-eight hours, Teresa would never see her parents again.

Meantime, the rescuers set their plan into motion. Giacomo circumvented the camp and came in behind Teresa's parents and approached their backs. The two older captives were startled. They quickly realized it was a rescue attempt and cooperated as best they could. From out of nowhere, Antonio and Giovanni appeared from two opposite directions and caught the villains totally off guard. One of the men reached for his rifle, but Antonio was able to kick the weapon away. Another rogue made a move for his sword, and again, Antonio thwarted the attack, this time using his forearm. His victim careened to the ground. From the opposite side, Giovanni popped up and knocked two men off their feet. Three others, drunken and stunned, were too slow to react and dropped their weapons. Giovanni and Antonio then aimed their carbines and held them at bay. One kidnapper turned to flee but stopped dead in his tracks when he saw Giacomo emerge from the other end of the camp.

All went as planned, and the men were captured without firing a single shot. The captives were bound and the Riccios set free.

Teresa's parents happily expressed their gratitude for the rescue; they had given up hope of ever seeing their daughter again. Giacomo suddenly put his finger to his lips to quiet them and motioned for them to take cover when he heard a rider approaching at a fast pace. It turned out to be another member of the band who was unaware of what had just taken place. He rode obliviously straight into camp, jumped off his horse, and looked about. He was quickly surrounded and physically coerced into revealing his identity; that he was the messenger who had left the ransom note on the tree for Teresa to find.

Dawn was soon upon them as the group of the good and the bad traveled the winding road back to Maida. Once they arrived on the outskirts of town, Antonio breathed a sigh of relief and was only interested in handing the villains over to the authorities.

The three rescuers escorted their prisoners directly to the front steps of the jail. A handful of soldiers dragged the culprits to their new home, glad to finally have the evil band of thieves in custody. The commandant had apparently made good on his promise to Teresa and Antonio for returning the regiment payroll.

The enraged Riccios filed the most severe charges possible and hoped for the worst punishment to be rendered.

Weary but happy, they made the short ride back home. Teresa burst out the front door to join her fortunate and unharmed parents. Antonio embraced his wife and in-laws as tears of joy mingled with their laughter.

XVI
UNINVITED GUESTS

Weeks seemed to pass quickly after the rescue of Teresa's parents. It was an unusually calm time for Antonio and the other three men, but it was not to be enjoyed for long. There were hundreds of brigands in Calabria engaged in scores of raids. The unfortunate result was that Antonio and his companions continued to be blamed for the violent acts of others. The four men decided that incidents were becoming too frequent and too close to their current hideout. Due to the ever-increasing patrols that would eventually discover their position, the men left for a more familiar, remote area and higher ground.

Cooler temperatures prevailed as the four outlaws returned to their already-constructed and previously occupied shelter just outside the village of Monte Vista.

Soon, they began hunting and preparing enough meat to last them through the cold months ahead. The high elevation and rugged geography would make riding to the closest town out of the question during the winter season. Their location and isolation provided them with safety, but it also became their winter prison; however, there was no alternative but to endure.

Their stone and heavy timbered cabin contained a large area with a fireplace at one end and bunks built along the outer walls for sleeping. A large planked table occupied the center of the room. A small window on either side provided light and view. Near the cabin, the men constructed a small stone hut half submerged in the ground which would keep meats cold and safe from any hungry predators.

As the cold days and nights increased, the resourceful men kept themselves busy and productive with their craftsmanship—Giacomo's carpentry, Antonio's stone masonry, Francesco's shoemaking and talents in leather; but it was Giovanni who possessed the most important expertise of all which was cooking. He could make a banquet meal from a few basic staples.

Not far from the cabin was a sturdy shelter for their horses which protected them from the elements and any aggressive brown bears and wolves.

The air was sharp and cold late November, and the first snowflakes made an appearance. The four isolated men did not mind the change in the weather, for they had food, shelter, and wood to burn. A thin pristine blanket of snow covered all, enhancing the already-majestic mountains. The winter air was a welcome relief from the dry and sweltering summer.

Calm nights followed peaceful yet busy days. Most of the nights required a fire to keep them comfortable; it was then that each could busy himself with personal interests. Francesco saved scraps of leather and formed them into wonderful and useful objects. His ability to make knife sheaves, belts, leather shirts, and sometimes boots, was a great asset. On the other hand, Giacomo made chairs and bowls, and indulged in carving small figures of animals. Antonio spent his time molding bullets and shot for their weapons. Giovanni baked crusty breads for the next day's meal from flour and grains bartered from local villagers. The delightful aromas filled the small cabin and reminded them of long-lost home.

During the first week of December, as the evening fire dimly flickered and they prepared to retire for the night, the distinctive howl of a wolf echoed in the distance. "I was wondering when we would hear or see a wolf," Giacomo commented.

"I thought I saw a print near a stream a few miles north, but I wasn't sure," Francesco added.

"We will have to be more alert and wary of their presence in the future," Antonio said. They took note of what they had heard but rested that night knowing they were safe in their cabin.

Days became weeks as the winter intensified. They awakened one morning to find a foot and a half of fresh snow which made moving about extremely difficult. This amount of snow, and more expected, drove home their apparent seclusion. They knew they would literally be prisoners of the mountains for some time to come.

The men dug paths through the snow to the stable and supply hut. Keeping the paths free of deep snow took all of their efforts, but their lives ultimately depended upon it. Everyone pitched in willingly. Thanks to Francesco, their cavalry riding boots were kept in good repair. For deeper snow that was becoming a problem, Giacomo made snow shoes from cut saplings.

They made a small corral for the horses to exercise which became a major concern because of snowdrifts. Each day, one at a time, they would lead a horse around the space for an hour.

Donning their snow shoes, Antonio and Giacomo ventured out periodically with hopes of shooting a deer or rabbit to add to their meat supply. They came back empty-handed the majority of the time. Nevertheless, when they were successful, it increased their chances of an easier survival.

Francesco rose earlier one morning, put on his snow shoes and quietly left the cabin. With carbine in hand, he decided to have a look around the perimeter of the encampment. His breath clung to his beard in the crisp, cold air. Hoping to see a deer, he stopped and leaned against a pine. It was then that he heard sounds of animals fighting within the dense underbrush. Francesco waited for something to emerge and aimed his carbine, but the sounds stopped. Still nothing came from the thicket. His curiosity got the better of him, and he approached the area. He parted the branches with his carbine and saw a wolf gnawing away at a small deer carcass. Upon seeing Francesco, the animal released its grip on the deer and turned toward him. The wolf growled and curled its upper lip, exposing intimidating fangs. Francesco retreated slowly and almost tripped in the deep snow anticipating the wolf to lunge and attack. He backtracked and got further away without confrontation. Agonizing moments went by before he realized he was a hundred yards away and thankfully, no wolf appeared.

Francesco figured that the wolf was too hungry to chance losing his meal to other predators. Feeling a little more secure, he turned his back and headed toward the cabin as quickly as possible.

After hearing about Francesco's encounter, the men knew all too well that having only one shot and wearing cumbersome snow shoes, the odds were much in favor of the wolf.

They remained alert the rest of the day and were cautious of their movements around the encampment, but they found themselves constantly looking over their shoulders. The slightest noise would make them respond nervously. To their relief, the day passed without incident.

That night, the men anticipated the worst and had a

restless sleep. The hours passed slowly for them, and sunrise was welcomed.

Antonio was eager to go out and check on the horses and their cache of meat. Giacomo offered to join him, and with weapons in hand, they trekked their way through the snow.

The two men saw fresh tracks, unmistakably wolves, as they approached the stable. The prints circled the stable, and upon inspection, the men estimated there were six or seven in the pack. There had been no destruction, and the horses were safe.

As the day before, everyone remained alert and ready, for wolves are known to be silent and quick in their attacks. No one left the cabin without their carbine and pistol and did their chores in pairs, one working and the other standing vigilant.

The men survived another day without incident as did the horses. That night's supper was a little more jovial than the previous one; Giovanni had outdone himself and cooked some of their favorites. They all talked and joked about their antics when they were younger.

Toward the end of the meal, their contentment was broken when they heard a howl—and then another. An ominous silence overtook the men as they looked at one another until Antonio slammed his fist down on the table. "I guess they want us to know that they are here and not to rest too easily," he said.

"We'll just have to be ready for them when they do come," Francesco added. They all nodded in agreement and finished their meal in more somber mood.

Afterward, they sat in front of the fire and contemplated what might transpire next. They soon gave in to their drowsiness from working outdoors in the harsh cold and snow. Each crawled into his bunk and kept his carbine close by. They slept in their clothing in the event they had to respond quickly. They were asleep in a short time, numb to the world around them, for nothing disturbed their deep sleep that night.

The next morning was considerably colder, and Giovanni added more wood to the fire. Being that he was the first to rise, he did his chores quietly as the others slept. He grasped a large pot and went outside to scrape up some snow for water. He then noticed an abundance of tracks encircling the cabin. Giovanni woke the others.

They all filed out and were amazed to see the large number of prints, this time indicating no less than sixteen wolves. Giacomo inspected the stable and was happy to report that the horses were fine, but found it odd that there was an absence of tracks near the horses' enclosure. The others were also mystified until Antonio said, "I can't believe it! I think the wolves are playing games, letting us know that if and when they want to, they can get to anything they desire, even us." The others agreed with hesitance, though at first with disbelief. These were no ordinary predators, and the men took the animals' cunning very seriously.

They decided that no one was to be alone outdoors and it would be safer to venture forth in pairs as they had done before. In preparation and readiness, each would carry a pouch with extra cartridges along with a loaded pistol. During their work, half of their attention was devoted to the task and the other half to keeping a watchful eye. The hours passed at a snail's pace.

The men were quiet over dinner that night as the constant vigilance was wearing them out. None of them stayed around the table too long once the meal was over. One by one, they crawled into their bunks and retired early, and once again, slept with their weapons nearby. Soon the only sound was the crackling of the fire as it projected ghostly shadows in the dark.

At two in the morning, Giacomo was awakened by the sound of heavy scratching at the door. His first reaction was to open the door to investigate but then decided to stay on the side of caution. The scratching eventually stopped, and Giacomo decided not to alarm anyone and then went back to sleep. The remainder of the night was to remain without incident, and all slept calmly.

As usual, Giovanni was the first to rise and prepared to make breakfast. When he proceeded to go outside and collect snow for tea, he noticed deep scratches in the door and wolf tracks imprinted in the snow. He wasted no time and went back inside to alert the others.

"This is too close to ignore," Francesco exclaimed as he jumped out of his bunk. "Surely, we and our animals will suffer if we don't do something now." Everyone knew he was right.

"I have an idea. Since the wolves are traveling here at

night," Giovanni said, "when we cannot see them, we should bait them to come during the day. Then we might have a chance to eliminate some of them. Why don't we take some deer meat and distribute it in strategic places around the camp where we would have clear and open shots?"

By midday they had butchered two deer; deciding where to place them required some thought. Fortunately, about thirty paces from the front door of the cabin stood the trunk of an old oak. They decided to hang some of the meat there, for the location offered a perfect unobstructed view from inside the cabin. Twenty paces from the stable was a walnut tree ideal for hanging more meat. This way, both locations could be aimed at from a window or a door.

A length of heavy hemp was threaded through the body of one deer and secured to the trunk of the oak tree. The second deer was attached to the walnut tree with a piece of iron link chain. This way, the wolves would be easier targets and unable to drag the carcasses away.

Everything was completed by early afternoon. Giacomo and Giovanni positioned themselves by each window in the cabin while Antonio and Francesco waited in the stable with a supply of food and water so they did not have to venture out. They knew it would be many hours before the predators would appear. Complete silence and patience were necessary.

The hours dragged. One man would rest while the other remained vigilant. As dusk approached and daylight waned it seemed that their plan was fruitless. Giacomo, frustrated with the vigil, said to Giovanni, "Basta, enough! Let's tell our friends we will try another day." With that, he opened the cabin door just as a wolf streaked by. Giovanni ducked back inside quickly. They peered out and saw another wolf whiz by to be followed by four more. The animals lunged at the meat without hesitation. Meanwhile, Antonio and Francesco were caught off guard inside the stable when they saw the wolves fly past. Shots rang out from the cabin. The ravenous animals were close enough and made easy targets. Yelps were heard as one wolf fell on its side and another leaped into the air and fell into the snow. More shots were fired, while some injured animals started to limp away. Francesco then opened fire from inside the enclosure. His bullet hit a wolf and the animal tumbled to the ground. From the half open door, Antonio shot and badly wounded the wolf closest to him; his second bullet struck another in the side as it stumbled forward. Shots continued as more wolves were hit, and finally, the uninjured of the pack turned and ran out of camp. There was silence for a while until it was broken by the whimpering of wounded wolves as they lay in the snow. In time, all four men emerged slowly and made sure the rest of the pack was gone before putting the injured animals out of their misery.

After the gunfire ceased and the smoke cleared away, there were nine dead—half the number of the pack. The lifeless bodies were dragged out of camp and placed along the perimeter as a deterrent against future attacks.

XVII
THE MISHAP

The four still sought-after outlaws gathered about a blazing fire under a clear, star-studded spring sky. The warmth of the fire was comforting as each man busied himself mending or cleaning a piece of equipment. Francesco and Giovanni applied saddle soap to their dry, course saddles. Then they rubbed and worked lanolin into the leather and softened them.

On the opposite side, Giacomo concentrated on putting a new edge to his hunting knife. The sliding of hard-tempered steel across the rectangular whetstone had become a familiar sound. Nearby and closer to the fire was Antonio bending on his knee, cleaning and oiling his carbine. For the moment, his attention was directed toward the barrel of the weapon. With an oil-soaked cloth patch attached to the end of a cleaning rod, he thrust the rod vigorously into the barrel and then withdrew it. He did this repeatedly. He then raised the gun and peered into it and noticed a small piece of debris still clinging inside. He took the cleaning rod and thrust it once more into the carbine and attempted to dislodge it. This time he achieved his objective and was marginally satisfied. His friends laughed at him for trying to make everything he did perfect. "Basta, enough," Giacomo said to Antonio, "You are going to wear out your barrel." Everyone laughed. Annoyed with himself, Antonio stood up and moved away from the fire.

Still a little aggravated, he picked up an axe and began chopping more fire wood in an obvious attempt to work off some frustration. His first swing was so strong that it sent split pieces of wood flying in the opposite direction and landing close to the others. He apologized when he saw what had happened. Antonio continued to split wood when out of the darkness, beyond the fire's light, came the sharp crackling of a falling tree limb; their attention was diverted, including Antonio who was mid-swing. As a result, his axe glanced off the edge of the chopping block, flew through the air and hit Giacomo's rifle leaning against a tree. The impact was such that the carbine fell to the ground and discharged. Blood instantly spurted from Antonio's left hand.

His hand bled profusely as his dumbfounded friends attempted to stop the bleeding. They made a make-shift tourniquet by wrapping a narrow strip of leather tightly about his forearm. They temporarily succeeded at stopping the flow of blood. Upon closer examination, they realized the index finger of that hand was gone. It was evident that he needed professional medical attention as soon as possible. Giovanni volunteered to ride to the Riccio home and inform Teresa of the accident so she in turn could fetch the aid of the local doctor.

Antonio thought it would be best that he be moved to his father's home on the outskirts of Maida. His parents' house was ideal, for they were miles away to the north at the time on their annual trip visiting relatives.

Giovanni left camp immediately. Antonio and the others decided to wait for morning and then ride to Maida. They figured Teresa and the doctor would already be there when the three would arrive.

With no other choice but to disregard caution, the injured Antonio and his two friends rode toward Maida in broad daylight. They warily surveyed the area for a possible ambush as they approached the Lochetto home. Convinced that the authorities were not lurking about, Giacomo and Francesco helped to settle their wounded comrade and made him as comfortable as possible. "Now, please go before you are found. I will survive," Antonio said firmly. With reluctance, they left him there and rode toward the safety of the mountains. It was Antonio's contention that if he was to be taken prisoner, his loyal friends would remain free. It was bad enough that his temper had been a catalyst for his own maiming. He was angry with himself for allowing the long winter and two years of hiding to take its toll on his disposition. He had been more resentful than he would have liked to acknowledge, and the accident was proof of this.

With his carbine by his side and his back against the wall, Antonio settled himself and waited for Teresa and the doctor to arrive. From his position, he had a clear view of the road as he began his agonizing vigil.

One hour passed then two, and still, no sign of them. He became weaker with every passing minute as he continued to lose blood. It was getting very late in the afternoon, and Antonio was concerned about Teresa's absence.

He periodically went in and out of consciousness and then into a fitful sleep. It was dark when he finally awakened, but there was still no sign of his wife or the doctor. Realizing that something had definitely gone wrong, Antonio prepared himself for the worst. Too weak to ride back to the mountains, he decided to bolt both doors.

While he was asleep, the local authorities had surrounded the house and were now about to make a rush. It was obvious that they had been alerted by the traitorous doctor who Teresa had unavoidably confided in.

Antonio suddenly heard low, unfamiliar voices from outside, "Did you see him yet?"

"Are you sure he is inside?"

"Do not worry. He is inside, alright. And if you continue talking, you will have a bullet between your eyes to prove it."

The sound of rustling leaves in the undergrowth was unmistakable as the men lurked about. For a moment, the dark, low-hanging clouds parted and light from the half-moon illuminated the landscape. Antonio's silhouette was visible as he peered from behind partially-closed shutters. He crouched from window to window preparing for combat. His situation was a desperate one.

Antonio held his loaded carbine in his right hand as his injured left arm remained limp by his side, bandaged and blood-soaked. The rounded tips of cartridges protruded from the faded pockets of his military cardigan. He also clenched a ready cartridge between his teeth which was barely visible beneath his mustache. He squinted, his steel-blue eyes trying to penetrate the dark for a glimpse of his enemies.

Under his breath, he muttered, "Stupido, I should never have let them send Teresa to get a doctor. The rat must have informed the militia, and here I am cornered like a mad dog. As for those so-called men out there acting like a bunch of excited youths on their first hunt, together they are brazen; alone, they would run like scared rabbits."

From the edge of the woods, another voice shouted out, "Antonio Lochetto, we know you are in there! You do not have a chance of escaping. We have the house surrounded, and there is no way out! Throw out your weapon and show yourself!"

"Antonio, don't be foolish. Come out! You do not have a choice," another voice advised. Inside, the desperate Antonio became more infuriated at his dilemma. He aimed his carbine toward the direction of the voices. "Hey, weasel, I will give you my answer!" Antonio shouted back as he squeezed off a shot. He slipped another cartridge quickly into the chamber and fired again. His shots were answered by a score of bullets that ripped through the closed shutters, inches from where he stood. He moved to another window for a better vantage point and fired back with impatience.

After almost an hour of exchanging gunfire, not a single bullet had found its mark on either side. It was almost impossible to distinguish a rustling bush from a man prowling in the dark. The tension of the situation and the loss of blood had greatly weakened him. Fighting off fatigue, Antonio attempted to think of his next move. He knew too well that he could not fend off his attackers for much longer, for he was down to his last few cartridges. His predicament seemed nothing less than hopeless. He pondered whether to give himself up or stay and fight until the end.

Before he could make such a decision, suddenly both front and rear doors of the house burst open. He instinctively jumped to his feet and rushed his assailants with the butt end of his raised carbine but stumbled to the floor unconscious before he could reach them.

Having heard about Antonio's wrath, his captors considered themselves lucky that it had played out this way.

Antonio was on a straw bed behind steel bars in the town jail when he regained consciousness. Almost forty-eight hours had lapsed since his capture. His memory was hazy, and he was disoriented as he heard the sound of keys jingling. Antonio raised his head to see his wife Teresa being let in by the jailor. He greeted her in a soft and weak voice, "Cara mia, that traitorous doctor should be taught a lesson."

"Please, no more. Let the war end here and now. Hasn't there been enough blood spilled?" she pleaded. He nodded weakly and conceded.

"It is the truth. Many a good man has been wasted in Italy in recent years. I guess hiding like a criminal the past couple of years has changed me more than I thought. I knew I would be caught eventually." With tears in her eyes, Teresa sighed with relief.

"I am glad you realize the futility of fighting a one-man war. Let's forget that now. How is your hand? You know you have lost quite a bit of blood."

"My hand feels like a red-hot poker, but I still consider myself lucky. It was a careless, stupid accident. An inexcusable one for me, but enough talk of the past. What are my chances of being tried as a military criminal?"

"I have already obtained the services of Signore Bardini," Teresa announced, eager to inform her husband. "He thinks the judge will be more liberal than you might expect for, after all, it is not a criminal trial but a military one." Antonio flinched in obvious pain.

"Pardonna Cara Mia, but I must sleep now and regain

my strength. I will need it." He closed his eyes as his loving wife kissed his fevered forehead with affection then summoned the jailor and left.

The period of time that followed was anxious for both Antonio and Teresa. Days turned into weeks, and Antonio healed both body and spirit. His wife's daily visits and her nourishing meals that were allowed to be brought to him were the reason for his overall improvement.

The day of the trial was only twenty-four hours away, as Antonio sat on the edge of his bunk and discussed his case with his counselor. "Signore Bardini, what kind of a chance do I really have in front of that judge tomorrow?" he asked.

"Well, as good as can be expected under your unique circumstances," Bardini replied and continued, "He is a hard man, but a fair one. You could do worse. The all-important factor tomorrow is to listen and follow my instructions. It will be to your benefit, for I have your best interests in mind."

"This I know. I am very grateful for the care and time you have devoted to my case. If I lose tomorrow, it will not be for the lack of effort on your part. I realize the outcome will ultimately depend upon the judge." Both men stood and shook hands.

The lawyer departed, leaving Antonio in his cell to ponder the events of the following day.

Morning's first rays filtered through Antonio's cell window as he gathered his information and prepared to leave. A feeling of apprehension permeated the air, but like the sunlight, a ray of hope for the future prevailed.

Teresa arrived within a short time to help him and to boost his morale. They discussed the possible consequences that could arise from the court's decision. Both husband and wife remained optimistic but objective about the outcome. It was almost certain that he would serve a few years in prison for his rebellion against Garibaldi. Even though he had been drafted into the Bourbon cavalry, emotions ran very high against anyone who participated in the opposition of freeing Italy from its foreign oppressors. "Cara Mia, no matter the outcome, you have my heart and my loyalty," Antonio whispered, touching his wife's soft cheek. "If it becomes too difficult, I will understand if you find someone else to spend the rest of your life with."

"Antonio, never. Never!" She held back tears and embraced him.

Signore Bardini arrived not much later. The three of them mapped out their strategy for that morning's trial. Both Teresa and Antonio were in accord that they should rely totally on their counselor's judgment.

The moment finally came when they had to leave for the courthouse across the way. They were escorted by four soldiers armed with carbines.

Upon entering the courthouse, Antonio was amazed to

see the number of townspeople who had turned out for the trial. He also noticed his parents and siblings sitting next to Teresa's parents. It was obvious that loyalties had been divided between the spectators. There were those who were for Antonio one hundred percent and conversely, those who were emphatically against him for the position he chose.

Within a few minutes, everyone in the court stood when the robed justice entered the room. The presiding judge seated himself and then commenced with the proceedings. He declared, "The case between the Province of Catanzaro and the Kingdom of Italy versus Signore Antonio Lochetto begins. Is the prosecution and the defense ready?" Both the prosecutor and Bardini nodded in agreement, and the trial began.

The prosecutor's objective was to prove that the defendant acted in a manner contrary to the best interests of the Italian people. To counter this claim, Signor Bardini attempted to establish the fact that Antonio had been under considerable duress when he was forced to join the Bourbon cavalry. If Antonio had not, severe consequences would have beset his family.

The prosecution was the first to deliberate. A very detailed, articulate attack was launched upon the motives of the defendant serving on the Bourbon side. The prosecutor vehemently accused Antonio of selling out for financial rewards. No evidence of coercion existed on the part of the Bourbon military and the idea of duress was a fabrication in attempt to disguise the true motives for enlistment. The prosecutor did his job very well and nothing was lacking in his style; he was eloquent, forceful but polite in manner, and almost infallible in the way he presented the government's case. Above all, he was so convincing that Antonio began to have doubts about his own motives. The prosecution's deliberation continued for hours until the judge recessed the proceedings for a midday break.

When the court resumed, the prosecutor continued his case against the defendant and called Antonio to the witness box more than once. Finally, the prosecution concluded its presentation, and the trial was adjourned until the following day.

There was no denying that at day's end the situation appeared hopeless for the accused.

The trial was resumed the following morning, and for the second day, the courtroom was jammed with interested parties and curious onlookers. Signore Bardini presented the defense immediately. He attempted with fervor to impress upon the court that Antonio's lifestyle was forcibly altered by the existing law which ruled southern Italy. He went on to say, "The Bourbon law stated that the oldest son of every family, providing he was not the sole offspring, must fulfill a military term in the service of the King of Naples. There was no alternative concerning this matter. If the family refused to abide by Bourbon law, exorbitant taxes could be and would be demanded, and in many cases, physical harm brought upon them. So rather than bring the wrath of Spanish tyranny upon his family, Antonio Lochetto reluctantly did what was according to the law. Being of honorable character, the defendant made an effort from the beginning to be an exemplar soldier. During the course of his service, he distinguished himself in a number of insurrections against Spanish rule, for which he received a commendation of valor. This should not be held against the defendant; on the contrary, it is an example of the man's loyalty to a cause which he had sworn to defend. Had he made a similar contract with the Garibaldini, he would have served in the same manner and been a hero of the Italian Army. His strong convictions and sense of dedication should be praised as an example of his straightforwardness." Bardini paused to sip from a glass of water and then continued, "So when the war between free Italians and the Bourbons came about, he had already served time defending the Bourbon King and therefore felt an abiding loyalty to remain with his regiment. This was not loyalty to the Bourbons as much as loyalty to his comrades who had fought alongside him. So the question is: is it a crime for a man to choose to defend what he believes is right in his heart? I think not." Signore Bardini concluded. His words appeared to have made an impact upon all who were present.

Antonio was recalled to the stand to substantiate what had been stated. Bardini did his best to ask questions that would evoke the most favorable impressions of his client's innocence. Other witnesses were cross-examined by both the defense and the prosecution. These people had known Antonio and his family for years and could testify to his character.

The hours flew by as half a dozen people gave testimonies. The prosecution then made a lengthy summation which was followed by Signore Bardini's rather brief one. This brought the second day of court to a close. As he saw fit, the judge would deliver a guilty or not guilty verdict the following morning.

That night, Antonio's nerves were on edge anticipating the verdict. He barely touched the food which was brought to him and instead paced back and forth in his rectangular cell and pondered the outcome of the trial. He realized the odds were very much against him and to be found totally innocent of any and all the charges brought against him would be fantasy. Even Teresa could not shake him from his melancholy and pessimism when she visited him that evening. She, too, was not naïve about his chances, for it was more than likely that he would be sent to prison. She secretly thought prison would be far worse than the time he spent away in the military; at least he had the privilege of returning home on leave. That kind of separation was bearable. Dealing with a prison sentence would be far worse. Teresa did not know if she could cope with these circumstances. "I have no control over what will be," Antonio said, breaking her disturbed thoughts, "for it is not in my power to change it. Hope is our only ally now."

After Teresa's departure, the time weighed very heavily on the wearisome Antonio. The restless hours moved at a snail's pace as he tried to convince himself into a more optimistic mood. The uncertainty of the future gnawed away at him, and sleep finally overtook the exhausted and troubled man.

At nine the next morning, the courtroom was again crowded to capacity. The same familiar faces appeared among the spectators, and emotions ran high on both sides. Worry darkened the faces of his loved ones.

The noise of people talking busily came to an abrupt end when the judge entered the court for the final day. Within seconds, the room became uncomfortably silent. He wasted no time and began to read his decision. "During the past two days, I have listened to the evidence and the testimonies of those involved. To me, the evidence presented clearly points the way for my verdict. I have arrived at this conclusion beyond a doubt. Therefore, this court substantiates the charge of Antonio Lochetto acted in such a way that was unbecoming of an Italian-born citizen. When the war between Italy and the Bourbons erupted, the defendant should have switched his allegiance to the side of this fellow Italians. This should have been his first and only obligation, even though it was contrary to his own personal beliefs. What compounds his guilt even further are his actions after Italy had won its freedom. Being a brigand along with other holdouts, he continued to taunt the law, cementing his guilt entirely. Because of his incorrigible attitude, I declare the defendant guilty of the accusations set forth by the prosecution. Taking in account the circumstances surrounding the defendant's forcible enlistment into the Bourbon cavalry, I will suspend his sentence on one condition only: that Antonio Lochetto enlist in the Italian cavalry for a tour of duty not less than four years. If the defendant chooses not to serve his native land, I will have no alternative but to sentence him to a term of ten years in military prison." The judge looked toward Antonio and his counselor and continued, "Has the defense reached a decision?"

Antonio stood up and shouted, "I would never serve in your cavalry, not even for one day!" Signore Bardini tried to restrain him without success. "How could I betray my loyal companions, both living and dead? Men who I had fought alongside in battle? My allegiance lies with them, not with your army. I would rather spend twenty years in prison standing on my head than betray their trust and loyalty!"

Upon hearing what his client had just said, the very upset Signore Bardini attempted to stop Antonio from saying anything else that might be even more detrimental. The nervous counselor apologized to the judge, pleading, "Please, your Honor, excuse my client's outburst. He has been under great emotional strain for a long time."

"Another remark from your client, counselor, and I will

hold him in contempt of court," the angry judge warned. "If I wish, I could add more time to his already sizable prison term. Now if I may continue without being interrupted, I will conclude the sentencing. Since the defendant refuses to offer his services to the Kingdom of Italy, I therefore have no alternative but to sentence Antonio Lochetto to a term of ten years in military prison. Upon completion of this time, he will be released to society once again. May God help him." The judge rose from the bench quickly and walked out of the emotionally-charged courtroom.

Antonio's first reaction was one of anger, but deep down he realized that going to prison was inevitable and thus accepted his punishment almost without remorse.

Those against him expressed their zeal without restraint while his mother and his wife, openly weeping, did not make an attempt to hide their devastation. Don Fortunato and Signore Riccio shook their heads in disbelief; their obvious anger at Antonio's bull-headedness eventually subsided to sad resignation.

XVIII
PRISON

Forty-eight hours later, having said farewell to his distraught Teresa and his grieving parents, Antonio rode northward escorted by three Italian cavalrymen. The soldiers were to accompany him to the port of Naples where they would board a ferry bound for a remote island prison.

Miles of open sea separated the island from the mainland, for this prison without walls was practically inescapable, and this would be Antonio's home for the next ten years.

They arrived at the busy port at noon and boarded the waiting ferry. The boat did not leave for another half hour as more cargo was loaded on deck. The corporal of the escort left the others to clear his orders with the captain of the vessel. It would be almost an hour before the harsh tone of the ferry whistle sounded as the last of the freight and passengers were brought aboard. The heavily-laden boat finally started its loud engines and carefully pulled away from the pier.

Antonio, along with his escorts, welcomed the opportunity to rest after riding on horseback many hours. The calm, blue sea and the gentle motion of the ferry induced a drowsiness that soon overtook the men.

Two hours passed quickly, and the weary men were awakened by the sound of waves lapping against the bow as the ferry continued westward. A speck soon appeared on the horizon and eventually took the shape of an island.

In less than an hour, the vessel slowed to a stop approximately one quarter of a mile from shore. The island was inhabited primarily by men who made their living from the sea. Due to its isolated location, it had been converted into a military prison. There, prisoners of war—radicals and enemies of the government—were exiled to serve out their sentences.

The ferry resumed its way to a landing located on the only spot of the island that could accommodate a ferry. Dock workers soon emerged to handle the removal of cargo and passengers. Among the people on shore were four other soldiers waiting to deliver Antonio to his destination.

After unloading cargo and passengers, the whistle-blowing ferry slowly backed away and steamed out to sea once again. It would proceed to deliver its remaining goods and passengers to other ports on its routine itinerary.

The soldiers and Antonio walked along the rough beach to an unknown destination. Rows of fishing nets draped over wooden frameworks and small groups of men spaced apart were visible up ahead. Two deeply-tanned men stopped working and walked over. Addressing the soldiers by their first names, they inquired about the strapping prisoner with them. One of the soldiers informed them that he would be sharing their work and joining their group. One of the two middle-aged men with a gentle face glanced at the somewhat bewildered newcomer. "My huge friend, let us welcome you. Come with us and we will show you around," he said. Antonio was temporarily caught off guard by the stranger's politeness but yielded for the moment and followed the bedraggled men. Turning his head back toward the sea, Antonio saw the soldiers who had escorted him walking away. For a second, he laughed to himself and thought, *the soldiers are gone but what good is that? Where could I escape to?* The irony was an added slap in the face. There were miles of open sea to the mainland inhabited by ravenous sharks. Antonio soon realized that the invisible walls would be the island's isolation and utter remoteness.

He continued to follow the ragged men beyond the beach and took notice of the flowers that were everywhere. A hundred yards further, they came upon a small rise with a cliff overlooking the sea. At the base of this twenty foot escarpment stood what looked like a small wooden shack. At first glance, Antonio was puzzled. He wondered how a small shelter could house four men plus himself. As they walked closer, he noticed that the rear of the shack was up against the base of a steep hill. The gentle-faced man smiled at the newcomer and said, "My young man, don't be so perplexed until you have seen the interior. I think it might surprise you." Antonio ducked his head and followed the men through the doorway of the shelter. They came to a second closed door. Upon its opening, the skeptical Antonio was surprised indeed, for it opened to a tunnel leading further inside.

The torch-lit passageway led to sparsely-furnished rooms. Each was lit by an oil lamp, and one was designated as a kitchen area. It contained an iron cooking stove with a metal pipe extending up through the hill above. But the most impressive and pleasant fact was that the temperature was refreshingly cooler.

The friendly prisoner continued to show Antonio about and finally introduced himself, "Pardon my manners, young man, I've been confined to this island for so long that I have forgotten some of the basic civilities of life. I am Father Battone, though in appearance I probably do not reflect my vocation. You are no doubt wondering what a man of the cloth is doing here. It is because of my convictions concerning the evil deeds of the government plus my low opinion of its integrity and its administrators. Basta, enough about me. What is the plight that has brought you to us?"

"We are alike in many ways," Antonio answered, letting

his guard down, "As a result of my own beliefs, I am also being punished. I was a Bourbon cavalryman for a couple years when Garibaldi began to move against the Kingdom of Naples. I could not bring myself to fight against my loyal comrades. Truly, I would have felt like a traitor had I quit and joined Garibaldi. When the liberating army routed our Bourbon regiment, I and a few close friends retreated to the mountains. There we stayed even after the surrender of our army. For almost two years the four of us waged hit-and-run raids against the new oppressors. Those who shackled the very poor during Bourbon rule continued to do so after their defeat but this time under a new tyranny. The four of us swore we would fight for better conditions for the defenseless. Had I not been so hot-headed, I would still be in the mountains of Calabria helping my people," Antonio paused to compose himself and then continued, "Pardon my anger, Father, for I cannot accept the blatant inequities thrust upon us Italians. The same conditions prevail as they had before the liberation, only the characters have changed." The gray-haired priest studied the face of his new friend for a few silent moments and then gave Antonio a friendly slap on the back.

"My son, let us join the others." He led the way through the dim corridor and then into a larger and better-lit area. Occupying the room were the three other men who had been on the beach a little while earlier. Each man looked up and laid aside what he was doing and greeted the newcomer warmly. His association with these men was one of instant rapport.

Though, they were from different walks of life, their viewpoints were similar. There was Carlo Masino, a small well-built man in his late thirties who had been sentenced to exile for his activism against the new rule. Carlo had been a professor of history at a school for boys in the coastal town of Amalfi. Just a few years earlier, his teachings coincided with the advocates of rebellion such as Mazzini and Cavour. When Garibaldi swept through the south and seized control, the newly-appointed administrators began to misuse their power. Once again, Carlo could not remain silent to the injustices that were being inflicted. Authorities attempted to stem the tide of anti-government criticism, and Carlo was falsely accused and quickly tried by a rigged court. He was found guilty and sentenced to a term of five years.

Sitting alongside Carlo was Giuseppe Scali, a journalist from Naples. He was also in his third decade and of smaller build but very instrumental in swaying the opinions of the people of Naples. He openly and brazenly attacked the Bourbon regime, and before long, was forced to go underground in order to continue his campaign against them. When Garibaldi triumphantly took Naples, Giuseppe was considered one of the many heroes that overthrew the foreign Bourbons. However, soon after, a provisional government was substituted, and he again became impatient, this time with the same pre-revolutionary conditions. Frustrated with the unsympathetic new regime, Giuseppe once again launched verbal and written attacks against the indifferent administration. It was the same situation that existed before, dictatorial control by Italians instead of Bourbons. Aware of Giuseppe's influence with the people, the Neapolitan administrators arrested him for his anti-government views before he could go into hiding. He was arrested and convicted for his actions against the powers that be.

The remaining person in this trio of inmates was Mario Grassi. It could be said that he was most like Antonio. Mario was the same age but smaller in physical proportions. He was also a soldier in the cavalry but had served on the side of Garibaldi. He fought very bravely with the Red Shirts, first in Sicily and then Calabria. In most of the fighting between the two cavalries, the Garibaldini were greatly outnumbered by the larger and more experienced Bourbons. Mario, as his friends, was lauded as a hero of the revolution. After the surrender of the city of Naples, he had found it increasingly difficult to remain in the military. It had become repulsive to him to have to police his own people he fought to free with such diligence. Mario refused a well-paid position with the city's police department and chose instead to ride off into the mountains to think things over. After three weeks, he returned to the city only to find it in worse turmoil than before. He then made up his mind that it was not for him and returned to the tranquility of the mountains. Mario eventually met and joined up with other dissatisfied soldiers. Most of these malcontents were unable to adjust and accept the type of life under the same conditions that had existed prior to the liberation. Therefore, in defiance, many of the former Garibaldini turned to banditry rather than knuckle under. Mario's life mirrored Antonio's as he entered the life of a brigand until he and his companions were also apprehended. He, too, was sentenced to prison.

Antonio felt he was with kindred spirits, for these social outcasts would be his constant companions for years to come and this alone gave him much-needed hope.

Antonio retired to bed early that evening and immediately began to condition himself to the harsh reality that he would be there for a long time. He slept well and in reasonable comfort considering the circumstances.

That night he dreamed of home and the hills above Maida; most of all, his beloved Teresa. He awakened the next morning shaken and disappointed to be reminded of his reality.

He lit his lamp and took a long scrutinizing look at his room. It was a large area for one man and contained four other empty bunks. He temporarily had the privacy of his own quarters. The other men also had their own quarters, for the hollow caverns could easily accommodate between twenty and thirty inmates. At the time, these five men were the only occupants in the prison.

Antonio got up when he heard the sound of low voices emanating from the kitchen area. He left his room and walked through the dim corridor. He found Father Battone and Mario seated at the table and sipping hot tea. They both beckoned him to join them. The good priest rose from the table to get a metal cup and then filled it. Mario offered him a hunk of bread left over from the night before; Antonio accepted it with gratitude. Both the former priest and soldier informed him that their stay on the island was not all that bad, for there were few guards to harass them. Once a day, around noon, a three-man patrol would come around to inspect as they did the other camps that dotted the shoreline. As far as work was concerned, the entire day was spent on the beach mending and making new fishing nets. Once a week, the nets were collected and ferried back to the mainland. The work was monotonous, but it would now go quicker with the addition of Antonio.

In a short while, Giuseppe arrived and sat alongside the others. Everyone completed their breakfast, gathered up some tools, and walked out toward the beach.

It was a beautiful morning; the orange sun hovered above the horizon as gentle waves unfolded their white foam on the shore. Approaching the water's edge, Antonio noticed how the many nets were draped over wooden frames with care. Hundreds of feet of damaged nets were brought in weekly in exchange for the mended ones.

The men wasted little time inspecting the nets to see how they could best be repaired. Made from very strong hemp for durability, the nets lay before them in abundance. Within minutes the men were busy with strange-looking needles and hooks which flashed in the bright sun. For the moment, Antonio could only observe as the men vigorously attacked the damaged nets.

After a half hour of just watching, Antonio picked up one of the bone tools and proceeded to imitate the others. At first the tool felt very awkward in his large hand while he held the net with his compromised left hand but was soon able to manipulate the work with more ease.

His new companions took the time to teach him the many different knots that were used in their work. By the end of the first day, he had progressed far enough so that he had become an asset to the others. Because of his great strength, Antonio could easily manage the huge bundles of netting single-handedly whereas it took two of the other men to move the same amount.

The heat of the day became intense as the sun rose higher in the sky. Antonio was so engrossed in his new vocation he hadn't realized that his friends had laid down their work and were walking back to the shelter of their living quarters. He finally set his net aside and took a few quick, long strides and was soon shoulder-to-shoulder with the others.

The hot, tired priest commented, "I see our industrious newcomer has finally decided to join us. We thought you were going to stay until you were baked." The others chuckled, but no one was really in the mood for jokes. The sun at that time of the day reflected off the white-pebbled beach and could broil a man before he even realized what was happening.

The heat-weary men entered the shack leading into the friendly confines of the cavern as a wave of cool air met them. The five of them made their way to the eating area and plopped themselves down on the wooden chairs and benches. They rested a bit before preparing something to eat and drink. Everyone but Antonio mysteriously disappeared into the other rooms. Minutes later, Carlo reappeared with a ball of provola cheese. Mario returned behind Carlo with salami in one hand and a slab of prosciutto in the other. Giuseppe followed, cradling three loaves of crusty bread. Not to be outdone and bearing the most important part of the meal, Father Battone carried in a jug of cool wine.

The hungry and fatigued men drew their chairs up to the large table and ate heartily. They soon made fast work of the food before them.

With their appetites appeased and their thirst quenched, each man wandered off to his quarters. Between the hours of noon and three, the relentless, burning sun was unbearable. It was impossible to work on the unprotected beach without having heat stroke. The men who did not sleep took the time to read or write a letter home. Antonio welcomed the chance to rest and fell asleep easily.

A few hours later, the dreams of the slumbering men were interrupted by the noisy efforts of the good priest. It was his task to awaken all. Though quite unorthodox but effective, he struck an iron pot with a metal spoon. The abrasive sound echoed through the corridor. It was so loud that the sleeping men were up within seconds. To avoid the harsh sound from continuing, they quickly made their way to Father Battone's side, some stumbling through the hallway while others, half-dressed, hopped with one leg in their trousers.

By this time, the heat had diminished and there was a cool westerly wind blowing directly off the breaking waves as they pounded against the beach. The breeze was appreciated as the men returned to their nets and resumed working. They were soon busy untangling many yards of snarled netting. They soaked bundles of nets in the briny water and then draped them over the wooden frames to dry in the heat of the sun. Other nets were mended before going through the same process. The procedure was repeated scores of times during a normal work day. Only when the sun began to set did these hard-toiling men halt their work.

As countless times before, the work-weary men trekked up the slope to their underground chambers. Once inside, they all proceeded to pitch in and prepare their evening meal which was consumed in haste by the famished prisoners.

After eating supper they lounged about talking to one another, discussing any latest news from their families back home. It was at this time when Father Battone motioned to Antonio to follow him into the corridor toward his room. He lit a lamp, and the light revealed shelf upon shelf of books. There in the compact space was a small library including St. Thomas of Aquinas, Plato, Aristotle, Shakespeare, and Chaucer as well as the histories of Egypt, Greece, and Rome. It was an abundant source for anyone with a thirst for knowledge such as Antonio.

Father Battone explained that his friends and relatives had sent him books through the years that would interest him. Antonio expressed his surprise at finding such a cache of literary volumes, especially on a remote little island. He was elated to have such a bounty of knowledge at his disposal, for he certainly would have time to take advantage of it. He was very eager to improve his mediocre education as it had ended when he was sixteen years of age. The priest grinned with happiness and remarked, "If you have the desire to learn, my meager library is yours. And if you think I can assist you, feel free to call upon me. In past years, I did teach, and I would find it rewarding once again to help someone who wants to learn." He then handed Antonio half a dozen books.

Antonio returned to his quarters and anxiously opened one of the volumes and began reading with enthusiasm. He did not lift his head from the Greek history text until three hours later and was a little annoyed with himself for allowing the time to slip by. The sun would rise too early the next morning, and he would need to get his sleep.

XIX
ENDURANCE

Thus a pattern was set; Antonio spent the daylight hours laboring on a sunbaked beach and reading during the evening. Only the changing weather signaled the passage of time as the sun grew weaker with each fading day. In many aspects, the coming of autumn was a welcome relief from the unmerciful summer heat. The men were able to work longer hours in the cooler weather without tiring as much. They kept very busy as they met their weekly quotas.

The cooler temperatures, on the other hand, posed a serious problem with the natural moisture of their underground quarters. Fires were lit and sustained in all of the chambers both day and night to combat the chilling dampness.

Two men from each camp were chosen to cut firewood in the interior of the island. Mario and Antonio were selected for this job and were joined by others from nearby camps. A small army of woodcutters armed with axes hiked to higher elevations for timber. Their objective was a tree-covered hill a few miles away where there was an ample supply of lumber. They cut only enough wood that would see them through the colder months ahead.

The men loaded the firewood onto horse-drawn wagons and distributed it to the camps below. The seven hours cutting timber seemed to end too quickly as the reluctant prisoners returned to their respective and monotonous routine.

In contrast to the overburdened spring and summer months, the uncomfortably damp winter between November and March provided little activity. Most of this time was spent inside usually near a small iron stove which helped to heat the caves. There were few fishing nets to mend that time of year, so the Antonio and the others filled their hours carving driftwood into pieces such as sailing ships, whale boats, and fishermen at work.

They all read a great deal to ease the boredom. Antonio was no exception and used the time to read many of the volumes in Father Battone's library. His thirst for knowledge was insatiable. He was so obsessed with learning that his head was buried in a book even when he ate with the others. The subject did not matter, for his enthusiasm was the same. Before long, his new friends jokingly called him *tarlo* or book worm. However, this did not deter him in the slightest, and he continued despite the ridicule.

Thus the uneventful winter days were spent attempting to stay warm and combating boredom. The time passed slowly, days into weeks, weeks into months. Spring finally arrived, and the sun cast deep shadows along the beach. With the advent of the warmer season came the unending supply of fishing nets to be mended, and the pace of life quickened.

The men's idleness soon disappeared and was replaced with not enough hours in the day to complete their work. Despite the enormity of the labor before them, their morale lifted as their daily activity increased.

And so the predictable cycles of life prevailed with the hope of spring, the toil of summer, the respite of autumn, and the idleness of winter. In the beginning, the years passed at a snail's pace but with each succeeding year, life became a little more tolerable than the one before. Letters to and from home sustained Antonio. His hope depended upon hearing from his family and beloved Teresa. He was happy to read how his brothers had taken his place at home and were now working with their father and uncles. His sister Rosa was coming of age and on the threshold of marriage. Teresa counted the days until his eventual freedom and return.

Nonetheless, years passed and Antonio spent much of them reviewing his misspent life. It was also a bittersweet time when deep friendships were made. He was glad half his sentence had been served, but at the same time, sad to see two of his friends leave. Years earlier, Carlo and Giuseppe had arrived on the island the same week and were to be released at the same time. They were both eager to return to the mainland and their loved ones. Their last day arrived and both Antonio and Father Battone would soon bid farewell to their close companions.

On the brink of freedom, Giuseppe and Mario walked with two armed guards along with Antonio and Father Battone to the idling ferry. They said their last goodbyes and embraced each other.

When the boat finally pulled out, the two remaining prisoners stood on the pier and never took their eyes off the fading ferry until it dipped below the horizon and was out of sight.

With the absence of their good friends, Antonio and Father Battone spent the following two and a half years somberly and quietly; there was a great emotional void to deal with. Antonio tried to take advantage of the subdued atmosphere and continued to educate himself, but it had become wearisome and dull.

The passing of another six months brought the conclusion of Father Battone's sentence. The priest prepared for his departure with anticipation of returning to society and reclaiming his rightful place in it. Though the good father was elated about his release, he was also deeply saddened to leave his devoted friend behind on the wretched island.

On that final day, both men avoided speaking. Their sullen faces said it all. Antonio assisted his friend in the packing of his meager belongings. Not much could be said. These two men had shared their lives for over seven and a half years. In that length of time, they had gotten to know and care for each other as family. Words seemed too inadequate and cumbersome to convey their deep bonds.

The minutes and hours rushed by, and then the shrill whistle of the ferry sounded its arrival. Antonio and Father Battone carted a small trunk loaded with books along with two cloth bags to the pier. Of the two thousand or more days they had spent mending nets together, this would most likely be the last time they would be with each other. After loading the trunks and bags aboard the ferry, Father Battone turned around and faced his loyal friend for the last time and said, “You've been like a brother to me.”

“And I could not have asked for a better mentor and friend,” Antonio answered. The tearful men embraced each other.

One of ferry's crew members motioned that they must be leaving. Antonio once again stood on the pier, this time alone. He watched the boat disappear from view.

Antonio, broken-hearted, walked back slowly to the empty caverns.

The next few months were especially melancholy for him. The loneliness was absolute; it hung as an anchor around his neck. He fought the isolation by devoting more time to reading, learning, and writing home.

One particular week, when the mended fishing nets were to be picked up, Antonio inquired about why there hadn't been any new prisoners transferred to the island. The guards informed him that since the end of the war had been almost nine years past, the number of inmates had diminished considerably with no additional prisoners coming from the mainland. Those who remained would finish out their terms, and when the last man served his time, the prison would be discontinued and returned to civilian use.

Antonio was beside himself; he did not know whether he could endure the agony of isolation much longer. Fortunately, Teresa continued to write weekly, her letters helping to bolster his fading morale. This was the closest thing he had to human contact aside from the soldiers who brought him food and picked up the nets every Saturday. His wife's letters and his continued thirst for learning saw him through the empty months ahead.

Two years had passed since Father Battone's release, and a different and more resolved attitude began to emerge from Antonio. The unsure person who stood on the lonely pier had been transformed into a stronger and more positive individual. What he once looked upon as solitary confinement was now reassessed as an opportunity to advance.

Going at his own pace through the subjects of his own choosing spurred him on to continue learning. He had a natural aptitude for mathematics and attacked the field of study with gusto until he became proficient in it. He realized that had he not been confined to prison, he probably would have remained uneducated throughout his life. But with the tools of new knowledge, he had a chance for a better life when he returned home. He saw the remaining years of his sentence as two more years of schooling.

It was not long before Antonio exhausted the books Father Battone had left behind. Antonio decided to enlist the aid of two soldiers who came to the island weekly. These good-hearted souls had empathy for Antonio's circumstances and would collect books for the solitary prisoner. Greatly indebted to these simple men, he vowed that when he was finally released, he would somehow repay them for their kindnesses.

Fortunately, the months began to slip by more easily as one season's end heralded the next. At last, his final day of confinement had arrived. What had been eagerly anticipated thousands of times in his mind was a reality. Though he was happy about leaving, he did not experience the elation he had anticipated. There were ambiguous emotions as he gathered up his many books and other personal articles and crammed them into two large trunks.

The time arrived when the two soldiers came to escort him to the docked ferry. Both soldiers helped their departing friend load his heavy gear onto the deck.

Once aboard, Antonio turned to take a last solemn look at the island where ten long years of his life had expired. Most people at this time would have nurtured feelings of contempt for the individuals and judicial system that were responsible for all those wasted years. But instead, this unique man was resolved to the fact that circumstances of the times had cast him upon the shores of the desolate island.

After a long while, the island finally diminished from view and disappeared behind the swells of the sea. Antonio continued looking in its direction and remembered the faces of Mario, Giuseppe, Carlo, and most of all, Father Battone.

XX
RETURNING HOME: A NEW BEGINNING

The ferry slowly eased into the harbor at Naples as dark clouds of smoke belched from its stacks. The vessel pulled alongside the pier, Antonio realized that there had been few changes on the busy waterfront in ten years.

He felt excited when he set foot on the mainland again, this time truly a free man. Anxious to make his trip south toward home, he searched until he found someone willing to sell him a good horse. Luckily, his father had sent him some money months earlier in anticipation of his release.

Somewhat disappointed with his final purchase, he nonetheless wasted little time in beginning his journey homeward. He made arrangements to have is belongings sent by wagon to Maida where they would arrive at the latter part of the week.

Antonio mounted his horse and deftly maneuvered through the streets of the city and left Naples behind. Once again, he enjoyed the experience of riding. This simple act had played such an important part in his former life. The feeling of the wind in his face and the motion of a quick horse beneath him began to rekindle buried feelings of exhilaration.

He took the old coastal road south and rode west of the mountain volcano Vesuvius and then passed the silent, buried city of Pompeii. Continuing southward, Antonio rode through beautiful coastal Amalfi; there, he turned east toward Salerno. He had almost forgotten the simple rustic beauty of Italy's southwestern coast.

Antonio stopped every three or four hours and paused to rest and drink in the natural splendor surrounding him. His appreciation for nature had intensified greatly during his years of exile; even the grass was greener and sweeter, the sky a deeper shade of blue, and the clouds fewer. The air was pleasant and pungent with the scent of orange and lemon trees growing in abundance on the terraced hills.

He rode ten miles further and reached the town of Battipaglia where he thought it would be wise to spend the night. He settled in just outside of the town limits beneath a sparkling mural of stars.

Rising early the next morning, Antonio followed the road along the sea and through the ruins of the ancient Greek city of Pæstum which overlooked the sapphire Mediterranean. The picturesque scenery was indicative of the region as well as the terrain southward toward Calabria.

The journey was therapeutic, especially for his spirit, as it restored his faith in the beauty of life and the love of his homeland.

Two days later on the third day of his freedom, he descended the last of many mountains and drew his tired horse to a halt. He leaned forward and stood in the stirrups to get for a better look at his beloved town of Maida not far below. Anxious as Antonio, his horse pawed the ground impatiently with his right foreleg. It was a welcome interlude for both man and horse. Examining the landscape, Antonio noticed very little change since he had been there last. It brought back happy memories of his youth, of the many good times he shared with his Teresa and other friends as they rode through the mountains on their spirited colts during those carefree years.

He returned to the present and suddenly spurred his horse to a swift start. The surprised animal reared up and then bolted down the hillside toward town. He passed a few old familiar faces as he thundered across the amber plains. Without breaking his horse's stride, he continued until he caught the sight of his home, his first destination as it was first in line of travel.

He rode closer and was able to distinguish the figures of three men arriving in a wagon. Quickening his horse's pace, Antonio sped toward the men who were about to unload the wagon. The sound of pounding hooves first aroused the attention of the two younger men who were somewhat bewildered by the sight of a hurried rider. The older man looked up to see who the bold intruder might be. For a few seconds, he studied the oncoming stranger but then dropped his tools and ran toward him. "Grazie Dio!" Don Fortunato shouted when he recognized his son. "At last he has returned!" Still puzzled, the younger men followed close behind their father.

Antonio pulled his horse to an abrupt halt and rushed to his father. With tears streaming from his eyes, Don Fortunato embraced his son. The two happy men slapped each other on the back with joy. Antonio's two younger brothers, now full-grown men, joined their elated father as Antonio embraced them with his outstretched arms. Composure returned after a few moments as the four reunited men headed for the house.

Angelina parted the kitchen curtains and peered out to investigate the delay of her husband and sons to the supper table. She spied the figure of a large man with his arm about each of her sons and immediately realized his identity. She pressed her hands to her face in disbelief and darted out the door. Seeing his mother coming toward him, Antonio took a few quick strides and met the petite woman. With his hands clasped around her waist, he lifted her high into the air and hugged her ever so gently. Antonio looked behind her to see if Rosa was coming out of the house, but he was quickly informed that his younger sister was married and living in Nicastro.

The reunited family entered their home to eat and talk of the years gone by. Long after supper was eaten, everyone remained seated around the table as they caught up on events that spanned ten years. It was early morning; the kitchen lamp was still burning before they realized the hour and finally retired with reluctance.

It was almost noon when Antonio stirred restlessly in his too-soft bed which he was not accustomed to. Not yet fully awake, he was not completely aware of his newfound freedom. He thought of his Teresa and how surprised she would be to see him. He got dressed and crept downstairs to leave a note for his family letting them know he would be with Teresa at the Riccio home.

He saddled his horse quickly and galloped toward his in-laws' farm three miles east. Thoughts flashed through his mind how ten years might have changed Teresa. His image of her was that of her riding on horseback, sitting erect with her long, black tresses blowing behind her. He also wondered whether her feelings toward him had changed during his long absence from her side. No matter how much he tried not to think of this possibility, Antonio was deeply concerned. With a certain amount of apprehension, he rounded the last bend in the road.

The well-kept Riccio farm emerged in full view a quarter of a mile away, and he continued to gallop toward an uncertain reality.

He noticed a lack of activity when he pulled up in front of the house. Seeing signs of smoke coming from the kitchen chimney, Antonio got off his horse and walked to the rear of the house. He paused for a moment and peeked into the window to see his mother-in-law preparing food. He tapped on the window lightly and succeeded in arousing her attention. Signora Riccio wiped her hands on her apron and parted the half-drawn curtains to see what the disturbance might be. Startled, she jumped back when she saw the immense figure of a man. Antonio found her actions quite comical and broke into uncontrollable laughter. Signora Riccio summoned all of her courage and approached the window with caution for another look. This time she looked straight up into the face of the bearded intruder. There was something about the stranger that was familiar; it was his laughter. By now, Antonio had regained enough composure to address the woman. "Have I changed that much in ten years," he asked, "that you do not recognize your own son-in-law?" He smiled. Her expression of bewilderment immediately transformed into one of joy as she flung the door open.

Antonio rushed in, hugged her gently, and kissed her on the forehead. Signora Riccio apologized with tears in her eyes. "Please forgive me, my son, but it has been so long since I last saw you that my mind has become clouded."

"Do not worry, it is already forgotten, Mamma Riccio. I understand ten years is a long time, and I am not the young man who left here, but I am back now. Things will be better," he vowed. At that moment, he heard the light steps of someone descending the stairs to the kitchen. Antonio decided to press himself against the wall and hide himself beside the doorway. Within a second, the still lovely, albeit older Teresa passed by him with her long black hair pinned up.

"Mamma, did I hear you speaking to someone?" she asked, unaware of her husband's presence. Before her mother could answer, Antonio stepped forward.

"Yes, Cara Mia, she was speaking to me," Antonio said with a broad smile. With her back still turned and not believing her own ears, Teresa pivoted around. Her doubting eyes looked at Antonio's face, and dropping to her knees with her hands clutching her face, she began to cry.

"I don't believe it! You are really here! I thought you would never return. I was sure you would die on that God-forsaken island," she confessed, sobbing. Antonio knelt beside her and lifted her gently up from the floor.

"Cara Mia, don't cry. This is a time for joy," Antonio whispered. "We have a lot of living to make up for, so do not waste any of it mourning the past." Holding her ever so closely, he calmed his overwhelmed but thankful Teresa.

The news about Antonio's return to Maida soon spread throughout the area. There were many who were very glad to see the strong, straight-forward man, but there were some who belittled his return. One such antagonist was his enemy Baron Rota, whose animosity for him and the entire Lochetto family had not diminished over the course of decades. This land owner still resented the Lochettos, for unlike many others, they refused to pay homage and have a subservient attitude toward him. If one did not acquiesce to the baron's whims, severe consequences were known to follow. It was not unusual for a person to become a victim of his vengeance.

Luckily, not all of the local noblemen possessed the same nature; one such person was Baron Farrara. His kind and generous acts toward those fortunate to be in his employment were well-known. Contrary to many of his peers, Farrara treated the hard-working peasants with the same kind of respect that he demonstrated toward those of nobility. Because of his benevolent attitude, many of the other barons found his actions very distasteful and ridiculed him at every opportunity. To these men, he was a very dangerous opponent, for Baron Farrara's opinions were held in high regard by all. It was said that his influence reached as high as Victor Emmanuel, the King of Italy.

After a few weeks at the Riccio home, Antonio became very restless and was anxious to find work. His timing could not have been better; old Biaggio Petrillo had just retired as the town surveyor. The position was held in great esteem, for boundaries were settled on the surveyor's word alone. All of the local dignitaries, along with the wealthy landowners, vied with each other to get into the good graces of the surveyor.

Acquiring the position was based primarily on aptitude and knowledge, and Antonio outshone the other two applicants by far. His knowledge of trigonometry and geometry, thanks to the tutoring of Father Battone, contributed to his qualifications. In addition, he was supported by the good Baron Farrara which greatly enhanced his chances of being appointed.

The town officials met for two days, and it was unanimous in Antonio's favor when they reached a decision. The majority of the townspeople were glad to have the former cavalryman hold that position. Many recalled the amiable youth who was drafted into the Bourbon army. Conversely, there were those who were much against the appointment, namely a small group of wealthy nobleman who ruled their little kingdoms with an iron hand; among these was of course, the ringleader Baron Rota. He was outwardly and vehemently against Antonio filling that office. The baron's hatred still stemmed from the simple fact that Antonio's father and uncles refused to patronize him.

An incident had taken place a few years earlier which exposed the animosity harbored by the nobleman. One day, Don Fortunato had been in town for business. He had just left the local bank when Baron Rota stopped his horse and blocked Don Fortunato's path. The baron looked down with disdain and said, "Who do you think you Lochettos are? You are no better than the peasants who work in my fields."

"My dear baron, why do you hate me and my family so? We have never done anything to harm you. Is it solely because we do not want anything from you? Or is it because our existence does not depend upon you? You despise us and others, for you cannot control every part of our lives. Our only sin is refusing to kiss the ground you walk on!" Don Fortunato replied without restraint.

"My impudent oaf, if I desire, I could very easily make things very unhealthy for all of you," the nobleman warned. Hearing this, Don Fortunato did all he could to contain himself; he wanted to reach up and pull the bastard from his high horse.

"You pompous, arrogant ass," he said, "if you ever hurt anyone in my family, you will pay for it dearly."

"How can I, the elephant, ever be harmed by you, the mosquito?" he scoffed. With that, the nobleman spurred his horse and swiftly rode away and left Don Fortunato shaking his head in disbelief.

Regardless of the past friction, Antonio accepted his new vocation with all the zeal and energy of ten years' worth of frustration. He truly loved this type of work, for even as a child he had displayed a natural aptitude for mathematics. The reading of land maps and the calculation of their boundaries brought him much satisfaction. Antonio had finally found a niche which was undoubtedly his.

As the weeks passed, Antonio was called upon numerous times to settle disputed property lines. His amiable ways were an asset to the work. When he walked away, it often seemed that he had satisfied both parties, but in reality, he had not. His sincerity and genuine concern was such, that individuals involved accepted his decision without question.

He and Teresa were soon in the position to buy a small house not far from his parents at the edge of town. They had waited a long time to set up a home of their own. Things finally seemed to be going very well for the reunited couple as they looked to the future with optimism.

The following months were the happiest for both in many a year. Life was making some kind of restitution for all the years of separation.

However, an incident would take place that would again change the lives of Antonio and his family. Rooted in the past, an opportunity arose to avenge some old injustices. A boundary dispute between Baron Farrara and the despotic Baron Rota was placed into Antonio's lap.

Both landowners had been bickering over the ownership of a river that separated their vast lands. Each wanted, once and for all, to settle the argument about who actually had control of the waterway. The river was very important to whoever controlled it, for it was an invaluable means of transportation. Each baron owned thousands of acres that produced a variety of crops; the produce derived from the abundant fields was shipped west via the river to markets near the coast. Therefore, whichever baron was awarded the rights of the waterway could undoubtedly demand any fee from the others for its use.

Both barons supplied Antonio with ancient documents

that substantiated both claims. He examined and read them with care as each seemed to be authentic in origin. The decision would ultimately rest on Antonio's appraisal as to who would regulate the river. Things being equal, he arrived at a decision but did not reveal it to the public until noon on a Sunday afternoon.

When that day arrived, just after Mass had ended, the people of the town began to gather in front of the records building to wait for the appearance of Antonio and the two barons. The people milled about, anticipating a decision which could affect their own lives; many of them were employed as field laborers on both estates.

After a fifteen minute wait—Antonio and the noblemen—followed by a number of town officials—emerged from the records building. The new surveyor mounted his horse and held a long bannered staff and galloped toward the river. In Antonio's wake were both barons riding in ornate carriages drawn by matched pairs of horses. Far in the rear and on foot were townspeople walking at a brisk pace.

Antonio was the first to reach the disputed waterway and paused to wait for the others to arrive. Soon people lined the riverbank and waited with the two apprehensive barons. One of the town dignitaries finally stepped forward and asked, "Antonio Lochetto, as the official surveyor of Maida, have you reached a decision as to who will control the use of the waterway?" Antonio nodded, looking toward the official.

"I have, and I hope there will be no bitter feelings between the two landowners regarding my assessment," he replied, standing at the edge of the riverbank on Baron Farrara's land. Antonio nudged his horse forward into the slow-moving current; he held the reins with one hand and the staff in the other as he approached the middle of the river. He then paused and looked back at the puzzled barons. Many of the spectators whispered that Antonio could plant the staff in the middle of the river dividing its rights between both. Instead, Antonio continued to the opposite bank and placed the staff there.

Twisting in his saddle, Antonio faced the crowd and declared, "I, Antonio Lochetto, with the power vested in me by the people of Maida, proclaim that all the rights and revenues to this river belong to Baron Farrara, and he will be sole judge as to who will use it and will set whatever fees he thinks will be fair!" After hearing the decision, the majority of the crowd shouted their approval for the well-liked baron.

As Antonio re-crossed the river, he caught Baron Rota's piercing stare. Without a doubt, the nobleman was infuriated over the final outcome. Unable to contain himself any longer, the sinister baron addressed him, "You know that you have ruined me, don't you? You could not resist avenging a feud. I should have known better than to expect fair play from a Lochetto."

"What is this that I hear? Do you expect fairness from others when you've been grinding people into the ground all of your life? Time and circumstances seem to have reversed themselves, haven't they? Did you not say, 'how can the elephant ever be harmed by *the mosquito*?'" Antonio replied. With this, the irate landowner turned his carriage and rode off in haste, leaving Antonio savoring the moment.

XXI
DESPOT DEFUSED

It was a hot summer day in Maida; people were walking about and congregating around the piazza. The mood was pleasant as townspeople went from shop to shop. The calm was soon disturbed by the sound of hooves sharply striking the hard stone streets. Glancing over their shoulders, they saw an out of control rider bearing down upon them. Startled people darted out of the way of the wild horseman who was none other than the wealthy Baron Rota on his spirited black stallion. People swerved to avoid being trampled. He continued to advance with total indifference to anyone's safety. It evoked sharp stares and disgust from the dispersing crowd. Fortunately, no one was harmed this time.

This kind of behavior was not uncommon among the

nobility and was a form of low-grade tyranny that made everyone aware of who was in ultimate control.

One evening, as the daily pace slowed, an incident occurred which would reveal the reality of the situation. An hour or so after the evening meal, a local man having had too much wine was slowly maneuvering through the quiet town. Although intoxicated, he was a likable, hardworking young man. Out of nowhere, someone on horseback came trotting down the street. It was, as many times before, the well-known Baron Rota. He slowed his horse's pace as he came upon the swerving young man. When the nobleman came closer, he stopped to goad the inebriated youth. The baron had recognized him as Gregorio Sareao, cousin of the landowner's worst enemy—Antonio Lochetto. Rota challenged him without hesitation, saying, "Why are you staggering through the streets of my town? Don't you know that lowlife like you should be in your hole at this hour?" Gregorio squinted as he looked up at the baron.

"I did not know you owned the streets. You and your family are bullying swine who have never worked a day in your lives! All you do is harass the people who make you rich," he replied with agitation. The infuriated baron raised his riding crop to strike the impudent man, but before he could, Gregorio reached up and pulled him from his horse. He then mounted the baron's steed and added, "My good-for-nothing leach, I have more of a right to be up here than you."

He rode off and left the humiliated baron flaying his

arms in a rage. At the town's limits, the young Sareao dismounted and waved at the distant baron as his horse slowly returned to the half-crazed nobleman.

Of course, the incident would not pass by and be forgotten. The vengeful baron wanted the impudent culprit to be tried for horse stealing. The local authorities pleaded with him to not charge Gregorio with the crime because it was not the case, and at most, was only a civil disturbance and should be dealt as such. But the baron refused to drop the more serious charges and wanted the audacious ruffian to be shot for horse stealing.

When all of this got back to Antonio's ears, he vowed to put a stop to it. Fortunately, Antonio now had influence in town because of the association he had with Baron Farrara.

Antonio approached the town officials to talk over the strong accusations made by the so-called wronged baron. They were sympathetic with Antonio, but the nobleman insisted on the most severe punishment. It was now out of their hands as far as the seriousness of the charges; the only way was to have a trial to determine Gregorio's guilt. However, Antonio was quite aware that the baron would definitely sway the court's decision if it would go to trial, for most of the town officials were indebted to him, one way or another. Antonio realized he would have to come up with something quickly.

He thought of sending a messenger to the baron to see if he would consider reducing the charges. Antonio knew it was highly unlikely to happen. In the past, the nobleman had been very vengeful and unforgiving, a man who would certainly demand the most severe punishment when his pride was hurt. Antonio, knowing this, still believed there was a chance to have the charge altered. With little probability of this outcome, he nonetheless took the opportunity to contact the baron.

A neutral messenger was dispatched to Baron Rota's estate. The message beseeched the baron to lessen the charge and end the feud.

When the messenger arrived, he read the plea for leniency. The baron's response was predictable; he only laughed at the proposal. He immediately told the courier to inform everyone involved that he had no intentions of changing his mind.

Antonio was disappointed but not surprised when he was informed of the baron's refusal to drop any of the charges. He knew he had to devise another course of action to change the baron's mind.

Antonio had knowledge of Rota's daily routine and knew he was predictable and rarely deviated from his timely pattern of activities. Antonio knew that the pompous man always ate his evening meal around seven in the evening with few exceptions. Taking this in account, Antonio left Teresa one evening and said he had an important matter to take care of.

After a brief ride, he was on the grounds of Rota's estate. It was just getting dark when he halted and secured his horse. On foot, he positioned himself on top of a large knoll where he could see the baron's dining hall. Through the window, he could see Rota eating his meal alone. Under the light of the candled chandelier was the baron's small, pampered monkey. His owner would periodically give the animal a morsel of food, and the little creature would then swing from the chandelier as he waited for his next treat. Antonio thought if only the selfish baron could be as decent to his fellow man as he was to the monkey.

Antonio knew he could easily kill the overbearing and heartless nobleman. He had a perfect, unobstructed shot, but something made him hesitate and change his mind. He thought of his own family and what would happen if he went back to jail for killing this tyrant. It was a dilemma, but how was he going to allow his cousin to be made a victim of such injustice?

Within a moment, Antonio came up with the lesser of two evils. He could not let the opportunity go by without doing something. The son-of-a-bitch had to be taught a lesson without further delay. With that, Antonio asked God to forgive him as he aimed at the open window and took a shot. The small monkey, who had been hanging from the chandelier, fell dead in front of the shocked baron. The frightened baron dove under the table without hesitation. And so it was, Antonio had made his point.

By the end of the following day, someone informed Antonio that the baron had retracted his charge of horse stealing for a lesser one. As a result, Gregorio would serve only a few weeks in the town jail.

As far as the arrogant Baron Rota was concerned, he apparently realized that he could be eliminated if he continued to misuse his power, and from that time on, he tempered his disdain for the common people.

XXII
THE NORMAL YEARS

The following twelve months would be one of the happiest of times for Antonio and Teresa. This period of time had become an opportunity for each to get to know the other under more tranquil circumstances. It was an adjustment that drew both of them closer together. It was a well-deserved reprieve from a past that knew only deprivation and separation.

Antonio was now working at something he truly liked, and Teresa was more than content managing their home. The house was conveniently situated less than a mile from Antonio's parents' house and only a few miles further from the Riccio farm. In time of need, either set of parents could easily be called upon for assistance.

The happy couple enjoyed their home life and the security of Antonio's position. It was at that time they planned for a family as their future appeared to be very encouraging.

The months passed by pleasantly as an atmosphere of serenity returned to their lives. It was on an ordinary morning when Antonio was riding to work when he was overtaken by an impatient rider. The horseman proved to be a courier sent by Baron Farrara. He had instructed the man to find and inform Antonio that the baron wanted to see him at once. Obviously, it was very important, and Antonio chose to honor the request and turned his horse toward the Farrara estate.

In less than a half hour, Antonio was riding between the marble pillars that stood as sentinels beside the entrance-way of the wealthy baron's grounds. He continued another quarter of a mile before he finally arrived at the front of the Palazzo di Farrara. The thirteenth century turreted castle had been reconstructed and made into an elegant villa.

When Antonio dismounted, two servants hurried out; one led his horse to the stable, and the other escorted him to the baron. They walked past the western corner of the manor and approached the nobleman who was having breakfast on the veranda. The view was impressive with acres of grass and sculpted trees enhancing the expansive landscape.

Noticing his guest approaching, the baron put his daily journal aside and rose from the table. He beckoned Antonio to join him. The good-natured man greeted him with his outstretched hand and said, "I am very glad you found the time to pay me a visit. What you see before us continues to flourish as a direct result from you rewarding me the rights to the river. If Baron Rota had gotten control of such a prize, I assure you the other landowners would have paid exorbitant fees for its use. But enough of that, today I have asked you here for a business proposition. Because I have thousands of cultivated acres it is very difficult for me to be in all places at all times and still take care of my many other obligations. I am not as young as I used to be, and I've been thinking of hiring someone who is capable of dealing with men and above all, who can be trusted." The baron smiled. "You were the first to come to my mind, Antonio. I am convinced you can handle all situations that might arise. To be very candid, I am asking you if you would accept the position of overseer of my lands. You would be paid a full third share of all the profits, the same as I receive with the remaining third being distributed among the workers." He paused for a while and then asked, "Well, what do you think?" Antonio was silent for the moment, quite surprised at the generous offer. He finally regained his composure.

"You have made it very appealing. It is an offer any sane person would not refuse. But before I answer, I have to ask...do you truly believe I am the best person for such an important position? I realize that you feel indebted to me for granting the river rights to you. This should not influence your decision about who is most qualified."

"Not to sound too ungrateful," the baron answered,

"but my reasons for selecting you have nothing to do with you siding with me. I have seen and heard about your talent for settling disagreements, and the respect and trust the people have in you. Whether it is intentional or not, you have the locals eating out of your hand. It is because of your influence that I have chosen you for the job. You are the kind of man I need in this position as overseer."

"I am very flattered that you should think that highly of me. You make it very difficult for me to refuse such an offer. But do give me the opportunity to think it over for a day or two and discuss it with my wife."

"By all means, I insist you think it over, but please do not delay too long, for I am in dire need of a capable person to manage my affairs."

That night at the supper table, he discussed the baron's offer with Teresa. From the start, she was delighted with the prospect but left the decision entirely up to her husband. This was not difficult for him, for he had admired the fair-minded baron for many years. It did not take Antonio too long to reach a decision: he would accept the lucrative proposal.

To insure his intention, Antonio went straight to the Farrara estate early the following morning. He arrived at the manor and informed one of the servants to notify the baron that he had accepted the job offer. As Antonio turned his horse around to leave, a wooden shutter overhead flung open hastily. It was the baron still in his night clothes grinning with jubilance as he shouted down, "Bravo! This should work out to the benefit of both of us. We will talk more tomorrow about this. Take care!" Antonio waved and rode away.

The next day, Antonio finished his work by noon and immediately left for the baron's villa. When he arrived, the nobleman was on the terrace behind the manor in the midst of his midday meal. Antonio made his presence known. The gentle-mannered man wiped his mouth with a white linen napkin and rose from the table. "Molte bene, I am very glad you came. Please sit down and share some food with me."

"I do not wish to appear inhospitable, but I have already eaten, though I will have some wine," Antonio said with apology.

"As you wish, my friend, I am pleased you have accepted my offer. My land, consisting of vineyards, olive and lemon groves, and orchards of figs and nuts plus countless acres of other produce will now be in your capable hands. I think you have all the qualities and the intelligence to undertake such a task. This is why I have chosen you. Your ability to negotiate will also be a great asset in managing the workers. All things considered, you are the best man for the job."

"You flatter me once again, Baron. I hope I can live up to your expectations. I will use all of my resources in an effort to run an effective operation. Because you are a fair and good man, and that in itself is quite extraordinary among nobility, I will do my best to succeed," Antonio pledged sincerely.

The two men discussed the duties of the position for the remainder of the afternoon. Antonio would be responsible for tallying each of the harvested crops as well as coordinating the schedules of the laborers. A merit system was established whereby the more productive workers were paid a larger share of the profits. This incentive plan for more efficiency would hopefully prove to be successful. The marketing of the produce also rested upon the shoulders of the overseer. It was his responsibility that the harvested crops arrive at their destination at the exact time for which they had been contracted. It was obvious that this was a very vital and demanding aspect of the job, one that could not be handled by the average person. Antonio welcomed the challenge, regardless of its overwhelming demands.

Antonio gave his notice of termination as the town surveyor the very next day. He did agree to stay another week and train the new applicant who was to replace him.

The weeks passed very quickly, at the end of which, Antonio rode eastward to meet Baron Farrara for a guided tour of the estate's vast lands; due to the immensity of the territories, the journey would take a few days.

In the beginning, Antonio was awed by the mere thought of his new and tremendous responsibilities. The tour of the land included visiting various crop-producing sections followed by brief introductions to the laborers who worked the fields. The first few stops were the vineyards and then to an ancient portion of the land where olive trees bore fruit as they had for centuries.

The following day was spent examining the spacious fields where tomatoes, eggplants, peppers, and onions all grew in great abundance.

The last day of the tour brought Antonio and the baron to the fruit and nut-bearing region. Rows upon rows of trees were laden with fragrant peaches, citrus, and figs ripening in the heat. Not far from these groves were rolling umber hills studded with a variety of nut trees. Filbert, chestnut, and walnut faired very well in the area as did the pecan and almond.

Antonio had never dreamed that any one person could own such a monumental farming operation; he was impressed, to say the least. He was still secretly hesitant about taking on such obligations, but after the days of inspecting the land, he was a bit more confident and looked forward to the challenge. If Baron Farrara had placed trust in him, why could he not believe in his own capability? Here was an opportunity to play an important part of an organization as well as experience a degree of satisfaction he had never experienced before.

When Antonio arrived home, Teresa was waiting eagerly to hear of the events of his trip. As her husband related the facts of his new position, she detected his burning ambition and a level of fulfillment she had never witnessed during all the years of knowing him. Teresa was happy yet sad, for there would be many days and nights in the future she would be without him. She had thought about this and reached an understanding with herself that Antonio's long-earned happiness and the quality of their relationship was more important than the amount of time they spent together.

The first few weeks on the job were quite hectic, for there was much to learn. Because of Antonio's amiable nature, he was accepted quickly by almost everyone, from the peasants in the field to the foremen who managed them. All seemed to welcome the fair-minded new overseer.

His own desire to do well drove him to become very knowledgeable of each crop. His never-ending barrage of questions kept both workers and their bosses scurrying for answers. When they could not adequately satisfy his inquiries, Antonio resorted to finding them elsewhere, even in books. It was a habit he had not broken from all the years spent in prison.

Seeking further information, he rummaged through

Baron Farrara's private library. He would not cease until his curiosity was satisfied. He wanted to learn everything possible if he was going to be in charge of transportation and distribution of the crops; those who worked with him admired his dedication and were amazed at his quick, grasping mind.

Antonio, engrossed in his work, barely noticed the passing of months. This was an emotional period of adjustment for Teresa. At first, she resented her husband's absence but finally accepted the unavoidable conditions. One important reason for her resolution was the fact that Antonio was full of vitality when he was at home; she could not help but admire this. She had to compromise knowing that it is far better to have fifty percent of a lion than one hundred percent of a lamb.

Around this time, to their delight, Teresa became pregnant with their first child. Both would-be parents were elated, as were the grandparents.

Teresa was subjected to pampering from both sets of parents during the following months. It was with loving intention that these caring people did not permit her to raise even a pot lid. All the household chores were performed by doting family members as Teresa rested easier.

Teresa gave birth to a healthy baby girl at the end of the

last harvest, during the second week of October in 1875. The eight pound infant was named Carolina after a favorite aunt of Antonio's.

Well-wishing relatives representing both sides of the family traipsed through the small cottage with relentless enthusiasm. Gifts for both mother and newborn were brought in abundance. The entire week was spent in a whirlwind of joyous commotion.

The following days were less hectic as Teresa and Antonio recuperated from the excitement and adjusted to their new life as parents. It was a joyous time for them, and the time flew by too quickly. The family was healthy, and Antonio was doing exceptionally well at his job.

Before they knew it, little Carolina was almost six months old and crawling into everyone's way and into their hearts. Life was very good and in no way did it reflect the empty years of the past.

The winter months were quiet as Antonio's responsibilities were less, and he was home more often. This, of course, was in total agreement with Teresa's inner wishes. But as soon as the first signs of spring approached, preparations for an early growing season were launched.

The only bright spot during this busy time of the year was the opportunity for him and his family to relocate temporarily in the mountains to a stately summer house. The generous Baron Farrara offered the use of this mountain retreat for as long as Antonio desired to stay. There, the cooler air proved to be a great comfort during the broiling heat of the lower plains. Antonio would leave for work each morning and go to work at the farms below. July, August, and September passed pleasantly amidst the verdant mountains.

It was during the last days of September when an incident occurred which temporarily interrupted the peaceful pattern of their lives. Though Antonio had been readily accepted and liked by most of the working peasants, there was a malcontent who tried to disrupt this rapport. The individual was a twenty-five year old laborer named Marco.

Antonio became aware of the evasive tactics used by the young man to avoid working. On more than one occasion, his co-workers covered up for his laziness. It was apparent that it had been going on for some time. Those involved refused to say anything for fear of reprisals from the belligerent ruffian, but appeasement was not Antonio's way.

One day, he confronted the man who was yet again going through the motions of working. Antonio wasted little time in seizing the opportunity to expose and embarrass him among his peers. "You do not have to put on an act for me. I know this is not your style, Marco," Antonio said with accusation. "Why don't you let the others do your work for you as you normally do?"

"I don't have the slightest notion of what you are talking about," the red-faced Marco replied.

"I know for a fact that the others have been doing your share of the work for some time now."

"I do not know where you get your information, but it is

untrue," he refuted.

"Antonio, do not believe this liar," one of the laborers interjected, "It is true. We have been doing his work. He had threatened all of us with beatings if we told. I am an old man, and I have had my fill of his bullying tactics. I no longer care if he harms me. It is about time this loafer is exposed!"

"Don't worry about being hurt," Antonio assured the man, "This will be his last day here, and I will personally see to it that he does not bother anyone." The accused man immediately stopped what he was doing and walked away muttering under his breath that he would somehow have his revenge.

Early the next morning, the sound of horse's hooves woke Antonio from his sleep. A breathless rider called up to the bedroom window. Sensing urgency, Antonio flung the shutters open to see who it was. Gasparo, a trusted farm hand, wanted to warn him of what had just taken place in the fields. "Antonio, come quickly! Someone has ruined the olive oil in the underground storage urn," he explained.

"Figlio di puttana!" Antonio cursed, "Marco is dead if I ever get my hands on him! I will be down as soon I dress. I have to see this wanton act for myself."

In ten minutes, he and the messenger were racing southward toward the ancient olive groves. A quarter of an hour of hard riding brought the two horsemen to the edge of the grove.

As they made their way to the middle of the field, they saw half a dozen workers standing about and examining the underground vat of oil. Antonio dismounted in a hurry and walked over to the small group. They shook their heads in disbelief. Antonio knelt to the ground and peered through the urn's opening protruding above the ground. Its cover had already been removed by Gasparo when he went to check the depth of the oil. Antonio reeled back from the sickening odor when he lowered his head into the opening. He took a handkerchief from his pocket and placed it over his nose and mouth before he proceeded to have a second look.

There, a few feet beneath the opening, lay a large dead tomcat floating on the surface. Enraged, Antonio stood up and addressed the workers, "Do not tell me. I know who did this. I will find that good-for-nothing little Sicilian and make him pay for the thousand gallons of oil with his blood." Antonio turned and jumped onto his horse.

In an instant he was off in a full gallop; his plan was to return home, grab some provisions, and then ride south in attempt to intercept Marco who was presumably already fleeing back to Sicily.

The vandal's eight hour lead forced Antonio to ride the remainder of that day and well into the night before halting and then to only stop for water and to rest his horse. He took the coastal road south which by now was very familiar to him and arrived at Rosarno by daybreak. Without sleep and weary from constant riding, Antonio decided to rest for a while. This time is primary reason for stopping was to obtain information about the fleeing culprit.

He entered the local police headquarters and asked if anyone had reported seeing a stranger ride through town the day before on a gray horse with a black saddle. Antonio learned that someone had broken into a store around midnight and made off with an assortment of canned goods along with many rounds of ammunition. This careless act was obviously that of a desperate man which would fit Marco all too well. Even though he had departed from the town hours earlier, Antonio was optimistic that he could catch up with him.

Without further delay, Antonio continued southward. He guessed that Marco had stuck to the easier main road along the coast rather than take the more rugged direct route east.

Antonio became increasingly determined and continued his pursuit. Mile after mile of scenic road overlooking the sea passed by unnoticed, for Antonio's only objective was to overtake Marco. He became obsessed; his stops for water and rest became fewer and further apart.

Meanwhile, Marco started to feel an unwarranted sense of security and thought his escape was sure. Mistakenly depending upon the fact that had almost half a day's start, Marco journeyed south and stopped often; at the slightest provocation of thirst or fatigue, he halted for extended periods. By late afternoon, he arrived at the outskirts of Reggio. Feeling overly confident, he made his way along the busy streets and had timed his arrival almost perfectly; the ferry bound for Sicily would leave within the hour. Until then, he took advantage of the time and browsed through the many nearby shops.

Not many miles away, his pursuer was pushing his horse to his limits. Antonio refused to ease up even for a minute as he dashed southward to Reggio. He was well aware of the time and realized that the last ferry of the day soon would be embarking. With this thought in mind, Antonio continued the chase without pause.

Time ticked by, and the anchored ferry sounded its whistle signifying departure would be within five minutes. Marco had completely forgotten the time purchasing a cheap trinket in a curio shop. He barely heard the whistle and realized the ferry would be leaving momentarily. The thought of missing it evoked a gnawing, sick feeling, and he cast the trinket aside and ran out of the store.

He dodged past pedestrians, knocking aside more than one as he hurried toward the pier. He rounded a street corner widely then breathed a sigh of relief when he saw the ferry still moored to the dock. He slowed his pace and approached the gangway. At that moment, he became aware of the ever-increasing sound of horse's hooves coming from behind. Marco turned to look over his shoulder and couldn't believe his eyes. The sight of Antonio Lochetto bearing down upon him like an avenging angel was almost too much to bear. Marco frantically lengthened his stride and ran up the gangway, but it was already too late; Antonio and his horse pounded right up to his heels. Without hesitation, Antonio jumped from his horse and onto Marco's back, sending the fugitive sprawling across the deck. Spectators on board moved back out of harm's way. Marco struggled to his feet and managed to grab hold of a heavy oar and moved toward his attacker. He shouted, "Now my big overseer, I am going to cut you down to size!" He swung the oar with all his strength and it came crashing down on Antonio as he tried to block the force of the blow with his strong arms. But nonetheless, he was seriously shaken by the oar's impact. Stunned, he dropped to his knees and struggled to remain conscious. Taking advantage of the moment, the smirking vandal came in with a finishing swing. As Marco drew back to strike, Antonio gathered enough strength to lunge for his opponent's legs and grabbed hold of him. He upended the fugitive as the oar fell free and landed out of reach. The two men struggled to their feet. Once upright, Antonio quickly backhanded Marco on the side of the face and then went in for another blow and landed a hard right to Marco's jaw. Marco fell to the floor. Antonio moved in just as Marco was struggling to get up and grab a deck chair. But before Marco could make a move, he found himself being lifted into the air. With his strong arms extended overhead, Antonio had a tight hold on his dangling adversary and walked to the hand rail, stopping to say, "My good-for-nothing swine, I hope this teaches you to respect other people's property! Maybe a swim with the low life of the sea will do you some good!" He flung the squirming Marco into the gray water below.

After a minute or so, the saturated fool resurfaced and began cursing and muttering revenge. Antonio leaned over the rail and warned him, "Consider yourself lucky, for if you ever set foot in Calabria again, I will kill you. So my little crook, stay in Sicily if you value your life!" Scores of passengers who had witnessed the incident quickly removed themselves from Antonio's path and scurried away for fear of the same wrath, but Antonio wished only to return to his horse and be gone.

As Antonio rode away, he looked back over his shoulder to see a few seamen fishing the humiliated culprit from the murky water.

XXIII
OLD FRIENDS

One morning Baron Farrara summoned Antonio to his estate and asked him to travel to Catanzaro to fetch a horse he had purchased from a wealthy landowner who raised purebreds. The baron did not have faith in anyone else except Antonio whom he had come to trust with his life. Antonio was happy to do so, for he had not been there in many years.

He left a few hours later, after informing Teresa he might be gone for a few days. He took the road east out of Maida. The winding, twisting way was time consuming, but Antonio didn't mind; it was a pleasant, scenic route. He was eager to see any changes since his last trip, but to his surprise, he noticed only marginal differences in the landscape.

By late afternoon, Antonio arrived at the outskirts of Catanzaro. He met the stallion's congenial owner at a stable in the center of town and gave him a promissory note before he took possession of the fine, young horse. Antonio was taken by the animal's beautiful proportions and black sleekness.

He decided to stay the night and boarded both the new horse and his own at the same stable. He rented a room at the local hotel and treated himself to dinner at a fine restaurant.

The following morning, after having rested well, Antonio arrived early at the boarding stable. He saddled his horse, attached a lead line to the young stallion, and headed back to Maida, unaware that three seedy men outside the stable had watched his departure with unusual interest.

Antonio made his way westward, and after a few hours, decided to give the horses a rest. He found a stream near the road, and he and the horses paused to have a long drink of water. He leaned back against a tree and rested a while. He was rejuvenated in a short time and was about to mount his horse when he heard riders approaching. He thought nothing of it, for it was a well-traveled road. Three men pulled up and stopped. One of them commented, "You have a fine horse there, Signore. We think we will relieve you of him." They suddenly aimed their weapons in his direction. Taken completely off guard,

Antonio reached for his carbine, but it was too late. The man closest to him struck him with his rifle and sent him to the ground as another grabbed the stallion's lead line. They rode off in what seemed to be only an instant. Managing to get to his knees, the stunned Antonio tried to shake off his disorientation as blood seeped from his head. Within a few minutes he was only able to stand by leaning on his horse. He was oblivious to the sound of two other horsemen coming down the road. They were about to pass him by when one of them turned in Antonio's direction and shouted out, "Hey, Pisano! Are you all right?" The man moved closer and added, "There is only one man I know who has your large stature and red hair, and that is Antonio Lochetto." Antonio turned to look at the stranger calling his name. The small, lively man jumped off his horse and walked over to Antonio, questioning, "Do you not recognize me? Have I changed that much? It's Giacomo!" The injured and blurry-eyed Antonio squinted and then finally recognized his old friend.

"My God, it is my good friend," Antonio exclaimed despite much pain as the other man dismounted and came closer.

"And it's me, Francesco! I know, I know...I have some gray hair," he said with a broad smile as he ran to greet his old friend. Antonio embraced both of them.

"Forgive me, my friends, but a few miserable men just wacked me on the head and took off with a newly-purchased horse. My sight was still fuzzy when you both rode up."

"Well, we have to do something about that," Francesco interjected angrily, "We will teach them a lesson."

"He's right, "Giacomo agreed. "A good lesson in civility is definitely called for. Let's leave as soon as possible. I'm sure Francesco can pick up their trail." Antonio smiled.

"I'm positive that with the young stallion in tow, they cannot move as fast as they'd like. The horse thieves have about a half hour lead. I agree that if we want to catch them, we should leave immediately. But I am selfish. It's certain that you both had somewhere to go," Antonio said.

"Basta! Enough. You are our good friend, a brother. Do not insult us. What we have to do can wait," Giacomo replied. Antonio nodded in grateful approval.

"There are no words to express my thanks to both of you," Antonio responded. "And I am lucky they did not take my own horse. Let's go."

With the stolen horse following behind, it was not difficult for Francesco to track the thieves and stay on their trail. The prints indicated they were traveling north to higher ground. Unfortunately for the horse thieves, they were unknowingly headed to an area very familiar to Antonio and his friends due to the years of traversing the region when they had taken refuge in the mountains.

After some time, Antonio began to feel the effects of the blow he received to his head. Giacomo and Francesco slowed their pace to accommodate their injured friend's condition. They decided it would be wiser if Giacomo stayed with Antonio so he could get some rest while Francesco went on to see where the trail was heading. He told his friends to remain there until he returned. At first, Antonio objected but finally gave in when he realized he had little choice in the matter.

Giacomo made a small fire to make some hot tea for Antonio. A little reluctant to do so, Antonio fell into a deep sleep even before the tea was ready. Giacomo was worried but knew sleep would be the best thing for him.

Miles away, Francesco continued to follow the thieves. An hour or so passed as he gained ground. Rounding a curve in the road, he saw the culprits in the distance. Francesco stayed just out of sight as the thieves rode at a leisurely pace. It was obvious that the men assumed that injured Antonio would be in no condition to go after them.

Sometime later, the horse thieves stopped by the side of the road. Francesco watched them and concluded they felt safe enough to make camp for the night. He was betting and hoping he was right and decided to turn back to rejoin Antonio and Giacomo.

Hours later, Giacomo waited for Antonio to awaken. He knew it would be dark soon. As he gazed into the fire, he heard the sound of an approaching horse. He grabbed his carbine and was prepared for anything, but to his happy surprise, it was Francesco returning.

He told Giacomo what he had seen, but he was more concerned about Antonio's condition, especially after Giacomo informed him that Antonio had been sleeping for hours. The two anxious friends sat by the fire and tried to decide what to do next. As they talked, Antonio stirred and awakened within a few minutes. He instantly touched his head and groaned. "Did a horse kick me in the head?" he asked. His friends told him how long he had slept. "Even though my head is throbbing, I feel rested and not as weak as before," he responded, adding, "I think in an hour or so I will be feeling much better." They were relieved to see Antonio improving, and he was glad to hear that the horse thieves had stopped and made camp for the night.

Later, when Antonio felt well enough, the three friends postponed catching up about their lives and discussed the matter at hand which was their next move. Since they already knew the thieves' exact location, they agreed to leave as soon as possible. In the middle of the night, the former cavalrymen saddled their horses and left. Figuring the culprits would be retired for the night, they set a moderate pace.

They arrived later at a close distance from the camp. They would leave the horses there and walk the rest of the way. Francesco and Giacomo asked Antonio to remain on the fringe of any action because he was not fit enough to engage. Antonio reluctantly agreed as they approached the slumbering men. The campfire had been reduced to glowing embers, and the dim light was an advantage for them to not be detected. Giacomo and Francesco would attack from either side as Antonio stayed on the perimeter with his carbine for added support.

Giacomo and Francesco silently positioned themselves then pounced on the unsuspecting men. None were able to go for their weapons as they were completely caught off guard. The dumbfounded thieves offered no resistance and surrendered quickly. Their weapons were confiscated. However, the three former Bourbon friends decided to let them go, but before doing so, the thieves were stripped of every valuable article, even their stiletto knives and leather boots, and were graciously allowed to leave with only their horses. The man who had injured Antonio walked past Giacomo on the way to his horse, and Giacomo couldn't let go of the opportunity for reprisal. Unable to control his rage, he slammed the man across the back of the legs and watched him collapse to the ground. "Hey tough guy, how do you like being blindsided as you so cowardly did to my friend?" Giacomo questioned. The other two men helped their friend to his horse.

"You are lucky you have your lives and your horses!" Francesco yelled out as they left. "If it had been up to me, you would have never left here alive!" Ignoring the threat, the three defeated thieves never turned around and retreated into the night.

Antonio and his friends then took immediate advantage of the vacated camp and prepared to stay the night and utilize the food and drink the men left behind. Between Francesco and Giacomo, they managed to gather more firewood. Fortunately, the food was more than ample, and they made themselves reasonably comfortable.

They took the time to fill in the gaps of their long separation. Antonio told his old friends about the island prison, the other inmates and Father Battone's library. He also recalled how together, they had managed to create enough hope to endure. He went on to say that he was now a father to a healthy baby girl and was an overseer for a wealthy land owner.

Francesco and Giacomo then informed Antonio of the period of time after his capture. The two of them, along with Giovanni, returned to their high camp in the mountains and remained there for six months; after which conditions seemed to be safer, and they decided to return to their respective families. Giovanni chose to go further north to Salerno to live with his brother and his family, and neither Giacomo nor Francesco had seen him since.

Francesco had gone to Nicastro for a few years, and Giacomo had returned to his hometown of Pizzo. Antonio was happy to hear that Francesco had married and moved with his wife to Catanzaro; there he had worked for a shoemaker creating custom boots. After the owner of the business died, he took over the management and remained there. Apparently, a few years later, a familiar-looking man walked into his shop one day to order a new pair of boots. It turned out to be Giacomo. He liked Catanzaro so much that he decided to settle there. He soon married a woman from town and had a son. Giacomo had also become a proprietor, making furniture and cabinets.

Giacomo and Francesco had come upon Antonio on the road when they were heading west to meet up with another friend to hunt wild boar. Luckily for Antonio, the two of them had chosen to stop instead of passing him by.

The three kindred spirits spent the rest of the night laughing like no time had gone by, and as many years before, fell asleep under the stars by a dying fire.

The following morning, the men lingered at the camp as they continued remembering times past and the people they had encountered. It was late in the morning when they realized they all had to be on their way. Antonio was grateful for their life-saving help along with the recovery of the stolen stallion.

It was almost noon when the three good friends embraced and finally said their farewells. Francesco and Giacomo got on their horses and rode away northward. Antonio, on the other hand, took the road west with the frisky young horse following behind.

XXIV
LEGACY

In the span of fifteen years, life became more meaningful for Antonio and his family. During this time, another child was born, a son they named Fortunato in honor of Antonio's father. It was a period of contentment accompanied by the normal trials and tribulations of any family. Despite adversity, these sincere and simple people overcame much and ultimately endured.

Antonio continued on as overseer for Baron Farrara, and he was well rewarded for his loyalty and diligence and wanted for little. He was grateful for his many blessings. It was annually hectic between April and October, for it was the growing season. Though he maintained a busy schedule, Antonio managed to be with his young family, and every July the Lochettos would spend some time at the resort town of Pizzo. A summer house they rented was on the shores of the scenic Gulf of St. Eufemia and only steps from the blue-emerald sea. During the weekdays, Antonio was supervising the numerous farms that were under his management; on Friday nights, he would rejoin his family for the weekend. They would relax and enjoy good fishing, swimming, and the overall resort atmosphere of the town. He would return to his work come Monday morning.

When not at their summer cottage, they spent the rest their time with their close friends and relatives back home in Maida. The closeness of these amiable loved ones enriched their lives. There was always a celebration at the slightest provocation, whether it was in honor of a saint's day, someone's birthday, or a new infant's christening. It was a vibrant and nourishing relationship shared by individuals who were not afraid to display the depth of their emotions. Even when times were hard, this unity took them through the years with grace.

Antonio, now in his fifth decade, began to look back on his life with little regret; each road had led him to unforeseen blessings.

On a lazy Sunday morning, while he was catching up on a few extra hours of sleep, Antonio was awakened by a sharp, disturbing shriek. He quickly raised his head to peer out the window. He became disgruntled when he realized that the high-pitched sound came from his daughter Carolina. Apparently, her younger brother was chasing her with a large toad in his hand and was taking much delight in scaring his fifteen-year-old sister. Antonio leaned his head back on the pillow and grinned at their antics. It stirred up recollections of his own childhood pranks and consequential lectures by his father. Looking to his side, he realized Teresa had already risen and was most certainly in the kitchen preparing food. He swung his feet onto the floor and sat at the edge of the oak frame bed as he winced from pain in his back. He rubbed the troubled spot and was well aware of the passage of time. Indeed, the years were fleeting. He looked out the window again and saw Carolina running from her brother. She was already a young woman, and Fortunato would be thirteen the following month. Antonio was amazed that the year was 1890 and he had turned fifty-seven a few months earlier.

"My God," he muttered to himself, "the years have gone by much too swiftly." It had been twenty-nine years since he and his Bourbon companions had first retaliated against the rebel attacks on the garrison at Catanzaro. It was also more than fifteen years since he began working for Baron Farrara. "Life is much too precious to have it race by almost unnoticed," he declared, ignoring the pain in his back.

He dressed and descended the narrow stairs to the sun-filled kitchen where Teresa was kneading bread. She was unaware of her husband's presence behind her and was startled when he bent down and affectionately kissed her on the top of her head. She quickly turned and wrapped her arms around him in happy response. He hugged her and lifted her off her feet. Pursuing his mood, she questioned, "What is it, Antonio? Is something wrong?

"Why do I have to have a reason to embrace the person I love most in this world?" Antonio asked, smiling down at her. "But I must confess, Cara Mia, this morning I realized that much of my life has already gone by. I am suddenly aware of how much you and the children mean to me." Teresa did all she could to hold back tears as she pressed herself closer to him. Recovering from the brief moment of wistfulness, she then returned to the stove and continued baking. He reached over to lift the hot tea kettle and poured himself a cup. He pulled the chair out from the table and slumped into it.

"Would you like frittata?" Teresa asked. With his head bowed and obviously still in a pensive mood, he waved his hand and declined.

"No, Cara Mia, not this morning. I just don't have that much of an appetite. I'll probably make up for it at dinner."

"Don't you feel well?" Teresa asked with more concern than before, "This is not like you. I hope you are not coming down with an illness."

"Don't fret so, let me enjoy this cup of tea, for as soon as I do, I will be going out to the stable," he replied, a bit amused by his wife's worry. "I must clear away some unwanted worn harnesses and debris that have been accumulating for years. If I don't, the horse will have no room to move around." He finished his tea and quickly stood. He touched his wife's shoulder softly and then headed out the door.

He made his way to the stable, calling out for Fortunato

to assist him with his unenviable task.

Before he and the boy started to work, they led two of their three mares and one stallion out to graze. The last horse was left inside, for she had been ill. Without further delay, father and son attacked their work.

Their task progressed at a fast pace, and within an hour, the overall appearance of the stable was greatly improved. They had cleared much of the unwanted tackle and debris from the stalls. Once again there was ample room for the horses to move about. In another hour, the job was nearly completed, minus a few stalls that needed to be raked. At that point, Antonio informed his son it would be all right if he wanted to stop working and that he could handle the rest by himself. This delighted Fortunato, and he smiled widely as he raced outside.

Antonio continued to finish the unpleasant work of sweeping the stalls as his son returned to tell him that the midday meal soon would be on the table. Fortunato left the barn but failed to close the door behind him. Antonio, feeling much better and in higher spirits than earlier, continued his work as he hummed an aria from an opera by Verdi. He was finishing up the last stall that was occupied by the ailing mare, and she barely noticed his presence as she nibbled with contentment from the grain trough before her. At that moment, an unnoticed, uninvited squirrel scurried through the partly open door. The little creature darted straight toward the grain and dodged gingerly between the mare's heavy hooves. In a split second, the stout-hearted squirrel leaped up into the trough, landing directly under the feeding horse. Startled, the mare reared up and bolted past Antonio almost knocking him to the ground as she brushed by. The frightened animal then ran out through the open door and headed toward the other horses. The agitated mare ran at full speed within the fenced pasture and then darted out again. Antonio rushed to see where the horse had run off to. Looking over his shoulder, he saw the horse running at full gallop toward him and was relieved to see she had not escaped. Simultaneously, Fortunato had left the front porch and was walking toward his father. "Papa, hurry, Mamma wants us at the table. Food is getting cold," he said as the still-excited mare headed in his direction. Fortunato had no idea what was happening; his father, across the way, waved off his son. The boy waved back, but in an instant, the charging horse was almost upon him. Antonio frantically dashed toward his son. The oncoming mare did not break her stride. Fortunato looked up and realized he was about to be trampled. Opposite him, Antonio made a running leap just before the animal barreled down upon the boy. He managed to grab her head and mane and wrestled the kicking horse to the ground. Fortunato, stunned but not hurt, went to assist his father. When Antonio was sure his son had not been injured, he slowly released his hold on the bewildered animal. The mare struggled upright and slowly trotted back to the stable. Antonio raised himself on his knees but collapsed to the ground just as he was about to stand. When Fortunato went to help his father, he noticed blood trickling from a deep gash on his forehead.

Teresa, who had been inside, grabbed her shawl and went out to see what was taking so long. She opened the door and saw them both hunched over on the ground. She ran to them when she realized that something was very wrong. Fortunato cried as he held his father's head in his lap. Teresa pulled her hair with both hands at the sight of the bloody, unconscious Antonio. "Blessed Mother of God," she screamed, "Please don't let him be dead!" The half-hysterical woman pushed her son aside to get a better look at her husband. She calmed herself enough to inspect the wound and saw that is was deep, so much so, the bone was visible; his forehead had been fractured. Resting his head on her aproned lap, Teresa wept uncontrollably.

Somehow she managed to regain some composure and shouted to Fortunato to saddle up one of the horses and fetch help.

A half hour seemed like an eternity before Fortunato finally returned with the doctor. With his black bag in hand, the physician who was also a family friend, rushed to Antonio's side. He accessed the extent of the injury and asked that Antonio be moved to the house as soon as possible. It took the strained efforts of the doctor, Teresa, Fortunato, and Carolina to move the wounded man inside.

Making him as comfortable as possible was about all that could be done. The doctor cleaned and dressed the wound and then solemnly stood over the severely injured man with an expression of futility. All they could do was change the bandage periodically and wait for him to regain consciousness.

The days came and went, and Antonio remained in a coma; it seemed to be eternal. Teresa, to the doctor's dismay and that of the other family members, refused to leave her husband's bedside. She was determined to continue her vigil until he awakened.

With worn rosary beads pressed between her fingers, she relentlessly prayed for his recovery. The exhausted woman dozed in a chair beside her sick husband, and faint signs of movement finally occurred. The fingers of Antonio's right hand began to twitch and then the entire arm. All of a sudden, he turned over onto his left side. A few moments later, Teresa nodded as she desperately defied sleep and opened her eyes. She glanced down at Antonio and then closed her eyes once again. In a few seconds, she finally realized that Antonio had changed position. She sprang to her feet in disbelief, and with hope in her heart, ran to inform the others.

The doctor was summoned immediately. He examined the still-sleeping Antonio, and though encouraged by his recent movements, he informed the family that unless Antonio regained consciousness soon his chances for recovery were slim.

During the night, hours later, Antonio moved once again. He slowly raised his arm to his aching forehead. This time, Teresa was awake and detected his movements. She then heard him groan in pain. She rose from her chair and reached over to brighten the lamp. Antonio's eyes opened for the first time in days. Teresa wept for joy and leaned over him and softly called his name, "Antonio." He gently squeezed her hand and whispered her name in response. She tried to compose herself and asked, "How do you feel?"

"Cara Mia...my head throbs as if an iron anvil fell on it," he answered slowly. "What happened? I vaguely remember being in the stable and then...I can't recall."

"Antonio, do not waste your strength trying to speak. You were apparently kicked by the mare, perhaps something scared her. Rest. We will talk more in the morning. Thank God you are awake. It has been days since the accident. Please, you should rest now." Too weak to contest her wishes, Antonio closed his eyes.

The following morning, Antonio's parents and siblings were happily informed of his improvement and did not delay their visit. Though he was still in much pain, Antonio was thankful to be conscious once again. The tone of his voice was much weaker than usual, but at least he could communicate. He was very pleased to see his family standing around the bed. He smiled and looked up. "Papa, do you remember the mornings when we would pick up poor Uncle Vincenzo for work? And how he would run to overtake the wagon because I would never quite come to a complete stop? He looked so comical chasing after us. God rest his soul. Those were good days," he said and then closed his eyes. He was obviously tiring. "That old mare must have kicked me harder than I care to admit. I am so very weak. If I sleep, maybe my strength will return and my head will stop hurting." Antonio quickly dozed off and went into a deep sleep. As he did, his loved ones quietly and solemnly filed out of the room.

Antonio's sleep that night was ominous; Teresa was very distressed over his motionless slumber. When morning came she refused to wait any longer and decided to wake him. First she called to him, but there was no response. She gently shook him, but again, no sign of awakening. She became alarmed and shook him more forcefully. Still, there was no reaction. She frantically called Fortunato to get the doctor.

Arriving soon, the good doctor re-examined Antonio. He sadly informed her that comas are not uncommon in cases of severe head injuries. He further stated that this is the only method the brain has to repair itself. "Comas can last for days, weeks. But without nourishment or water, it's hopeless," he added. "But even more dangerous is the possibility of a blood clot which can happen at any time and be instantly fatal." The doctor shook his head, admitting that there was little that he or anyone else could do. Antonio's fate would be in the hands of the Almighty.

Teresa, broken-hearted, stood watch over her ailing husband. During this time, his children, parents, and siblings took turns standing vigil, and friends visited their injured comrade. An atmosphere of mourning shrouded the sad faces as they filed in and out.

That night, Teresa slept in the chair next to Antonio while Carolina slept across the bottom of his bed. Antonio moaned and stirred sometime before dawn and clutched his bandaged head. Teresa, hearing his agony, bolted upright and went to him. "Cara Mira, what is it?" she asked with fearful hesitance, "Can I help?" A few seconds had lapsed before he replied, "The pain is unbearable, Cara Mia. I do not know...how much longer...I can bear it," he responded, barely audible. "Please, come closer..." He reached for her hand and held her closely. When he realized Carolina was nearby, he reached out for her with his other hand. Antonio looked at both of them and pressed their hands to his chest and spoke, "God has blessed me twice, with two angels." Carolina could not hold back any longer and broke down in tears. "If I do not recover," his voice cracked under the strain, "always remember I love you and Fortunato very much. Cara Mia...please promise me...you will tell my father and mother that I consider myself very...fortunate to have had them as parents. And if...I had my life to live over again, my soul would again choose them." He turned to his daughter. "My dear Carolina, you must also promise that you and your brother will listen to your mother and always help her."

"Papa, of course, I will," she whispered as she knelt to the floor and rested her head on her father's chest and wept. He embraced her and advised, "You are a young woman now and you must have courage. God willing... someday we shall all be together once again. Remember I love you all forever." These last words were a whisper as Antonio weakened rapidly. He closed his eyes as he held their hands. His breath became shallow. He heaved what seemed a long sigh of relief, and his body became motionless. Mother and daughter, in despair, covered their faces and wept for their great loss.

Though, only fifty-seven years old, Antonio Lochetto had lived two lifetimes in one. His adventures became legendary and were spoken of through the years. Even to this day, if one walks through the streets of Maida it would not be too unusual to overhear some of the old timers sitting around the piazza still speaking of Antonio's sense of justice and valiant deeds.

JOS. C. DONATO

Joe Donato was born in Brooklyn, New York and was raised in Madison, New Jersey. Despite showing considerable talent in art and having aspirations to be a sculptor, Joe majored in finance with a minor in philosophy and received a degree from Seton Hall. He lives in beautiful rural New Jersey with his wife, the author Marlaina Donato, and their beloved canine companion, Noah. This is his first book.

To contact the author, please email
sabershonor@yahoo.com
or visit **Ekstasis Multimedia** at www.booksandbrushnet

www.ingramcontent.com/pod-product-compliance
Lightning Source LLC
LaVergne TN
LVHW091027080826
845145LV00002B/380